PRAISE FOR
THE GIRL SHE USED TO BE

"A compulsively readable, skillfully constructed first novel with well-drawn characters and a plot that twists and turns to what seems the best possible conclusion, marking Cristofano as a writer to watch."

—*Booklist*

"A vivid, bittersweet tale . . . will keep readers turning the page and guessing until the very end."

—*Sacramento Book Review*

"Alternately thought-provoking, poignant, and darkly funny . . . hooked me from the very first page."

—Lesley Kagen, *New York Times* bestselling author of *Whistling in the Dark* and *Land of a Hundred Wonders*

"A fascinating character study that places a totally unique limelight on the WPP."

—*Midwest Book Review*

"Everything I want a book to be . . . a humorous, poignant, and compelling page-turner that kept me guessing all the way to the end. I marveled at how utterly I was drawn into Melody's world and what a vivid picture Cristofano created."

—Patricia Wood, *New York Times* bestselling author of *Lottery*

more . . .

"Would make a terrific movie! Melody's character really gets the reader involved in this story . . . I absolutely loved this book. It's funny at times and also makes you do some thinking. This is David Cristofano's debut novel and he has done an excellent job."

—BestsellersWorld.com

"Eloquent, haunting, and totally enthralling . . . I absolutely fell in love with David Cristofano's writing, and couldn't wait to see Melody's mystery unfold. THE GIRL SHE USED TO BE is that rare novel you've been looking for when you wander the bookstore aisles, hoping to find something that will grab hold of you and not let go."

—Johanna Edwards, nationally bestselling
author of *How to Be Cool*

"The reader of THE GIRL SHE USED TO BE wants the unexpected and David Cristofano delivers. This mystery novel's concept is original, imaginative, and thought-provoking."

—TheMysterySite.com

"David Cristofano's debut novel captures the essence of the human spirit, and delivers a story that is simultaneously heartwarming and heartbreaking."

—Brad Listi, author of *Attention. Deficit. Disorder.*

"A fast-paced, sexually teasing story . . . with plenty of grit and emotional upheaval."

—TheRomanceReadersConnection.com

"A roller-coaster ride, both thriller and riveting psychological drama, and Cristofano is definitely a writer to watch."

—Elizabeth Joy Arnold, bestselling author of *Promise the Moon*

"Will keep you on the edge of your seat until the very last page."

—"Talk of the Town: The BookMan/BookWoman,"
WTVF (CBS affiliate)

"A brilliant debut by a magnificent new novelist."

—Will Clarke, author of *The Worthy* and *Lord Vishnu's Love Handles*

"A good plot and an interesting story . . . What really fascinated me was reading the thoughts Melody had about her life as a 'non-entity' . . . This story really makes me value my own life, and my own opportunities."

—ArmchairInterviews.com

"Fantastic book! An incredibly engaging, incredibly fast read. Melody's character was drawn perfectly, her thoughts, motivations, and conflicted emotions were realistic."

—DevourerOfBooks.com

more . . .

"A satisfying read. Snappy dialogue and scenes with unpredictable outcomes keep the novel going at a steady pace . . . Cristofano effectively sets up Melody's motivation to escape her life in the Witness Protection Program. Details about her life with her parents, her love of math, and her struggles growing up without any friends make Melody a compelling character."

—PopMatters.com

"I could not put this book down! . . . currently in the top five of the books I've read so far this year. This book was a merry-go-round of emotions and evoked feelings in me I didn't realize I had. David Cristofano is an author I will be eagerly watching."

—*Harrodsburg Herald* (KY)

the girl she used to be

david cristofano

GRAND CENTRAL
PUBLISHING

NEW YORK   BOSTON

Copyright © 2009 by David Cristofano
Reading Group Guide Copyright © 2010 by Hachette Book Group
"On Writing (About a Girl)" Copyright © 2010 by David Cristofano
"Overcoming the Identity Crisis" Copyright © 2010 by David Cristofano

Grand Central Publishing
Hachette Book Group
237 Park Avenue
New York, NY 10017

www.HachetteBookGroup.com

Printed in the United States of America

Originally published in hardcover by Grand Central Publishing.

First Trade Edition: March 2010
10 9 8 7 6 5 4 3 2 1

Grand Central Publishing is a division of Hachette Book Group, Inc.
The Grand Central Publishing name and logo is a trademark of Hachette Book Group, Inc.

The Library of Congress has cataloged the hardcover edition as follows:

Cristofano, David.
    The girl she used to be / David Cristofano.—1st ed.
      p. cm.
    Summary: "A woman who has lost her identity to the Witness Protection Program flirts with trusting her life to the Mafioso hired to kill her"—Provided by publisher.
    ISBN: 978-0-446-58222-3
    1. Witnesses—Protection—Fiction. 2. Mafia—Fiction. I. Title.
    PS3603.R578G57 2009
    813'.6—dc22   2008003280

    ISBN 978-0-446-58221-6 (pbk.)

Book design by Charles Sutherland

For Jana

Acknowledgments

Thanks first to my wife, Jana, who has unconditionally supported me throughout this journey, and who has endured and sacrificed in ways that I will never fully comprehend. No accomplishment on my part—including this book—would have occurred without her. She is my first reader and my first love.

Thanks to my editors at Grand Central, Michele Bidelspach and Melanie Murray, who caught the missteps and molded the story into the final polished product you're holding. It would not be nearly the same novel without their guidance and attention to detail. They are wonderful people to work with. And thanks to Tareth Mitch, Karen Thompson, and all the folks at Grand Central, especially Jamie Raab, for taking an early and active interest in the project.

I am eternally grateful to my agent, Pamela Harty, for her passion and commitment and professionalism, and for making the entire process fun and fulfilling. She is the kind of agent every writer hopes to have. Thanks, too, to Deidre Knight and all the pros at the Knight Agency for keeping the publishing machinery in motion.

Thanks also to Amelia Madison for getting the boulder to the edge of the cliff, and to Lauren Baratz-Logsted for being the impetus.

And to my parents, Francis and Helen Cristofano, for fostering a love of reading at an early age, and for providing a house always well stocked with books.

And thanks to God, for every page, every sentence, every word.

All farewells should be sudden, when forever.

—Lord Byron, from *Sardanapalus*

the girl she used to be

$$x = y^0, \ y \neq 0$$

Name me. gaze into my eyes, study my smile and my dimples and tell me who you see. I look like an Emma. I look like an Amy. I look like a Katherine. I look like a Kathryn. I look like your best friend's sister, your sister's best friend. Introduce me. Yell for me. Let me run away and call me back. Run your fingers through my hair and whisper my name.

Call me whatever you want; it's just a name, after all.

When I was born, my parents assembled a string of vowels and consonants so magical, so rhythmic and haunting, that the human form had yet to be married to such beauty.

When I was six, it was taken away.

And because of my ineptitude and innocent inability to keep a secret, they took it away again when I was eight.

And at nine. At eleven. Twice at thirteen.

Not to worry: the Federal Government was quick to replace the old with the new, to clean up the mess and move us along to the next bland, underpopulated town, to another dot on the map that serves as nothing more than a break from the interstate, a pit stop on the way to some greater place; you know them, but forget them. There has to be a Middletown in almost every state, and I've already lived in or near three of them.

But as temporary as it was, each instance was *home*, the place where Mom and Dad would be waiting at the end of the day, where the bills got paid, the lawn got mowed, and the mail was delivered. And it had to be. This was the consistent, perverted promise of the Federal Witness Protection Program.

Today is Tuesday, which means I'm sitting at the head of a classroom facing a semi-arc of high school juniors, all with their heads bowed, taking a geometry pop quiz. They are not the brightest bunch, having to take geometry as juniors and all, but they are sweet and genuine and seem to have more character than the Advanced Placement Calculus juniors I teach in the following period—especially since most kids do not elect to take math as a junior. I spend as much time teaching them proofs as I do the works of Euclid or Gauss or Pythagoras because it is the proofs that will serve them well in life; they're learning *logic*. Though I may be less effective than I hope; sadly, today is Tuesday and they are taking that pop quiz—the same day of the week, every week, that I give a pop quiz—and there are always a few who are surprised.

Life will be cruel to them.

But above all, I try to teach one central lesson in every class—and if they get this I will make sure they pass: Each and every equation brings an absolute certain conclusion. Well, that and *don't divide by zero*. You see, certainty brings security. Security brings trust. Trust brings love.

Pascal was quite the romantic, eh? And who knows what Edmund Landau was *really* thinking when he popularized Big O Notation, but I like to pretend.

These kids, America's future at its most average, are getting something from me that they're not getting from the loud, furry-nostriled political science teacher whose classroom backs to mine—that is, an understanding of life.

Under my wing, you'll learn that every problem has at least one solution, that logic may follow more than one path as long as it reaches the correct destination, that it's always best to break an equation down into its simplest parts before solving it. And then and only then will you reach a conclusion and find the warmth of certainty, a certainty you will need when you're grabbed from your bed in the middle of the night for the third time and whisked off to another town in another state, having left behind friends you will neither see nor communicate with ever again, where you will sit and listen to your parents cry themselves to sleep and keep secrets from you that you will only occasionally be privy to when their prayers turn into a discernible loud whisper, and you will need that certainty when your father looks at you at the breakfast table and tries to ask you to pass the Cheerios but pauses for three seconds—*three seconds*—to search for your name from the many pedestrian identities that have come and gone from your life, though not so long ago assigned to you by a federal employee.

So yes, Furry Nostrils can keep his histories of battles and conflicts gone by; we're fighting the real war right here in Geometry.

I reach behind my neck and grab my auburn hair and try to twist it into a ponytail, but it's a teacher's-salary haircut in the growing-out phase and the best I can do is leave myself looking like a svelte samurai. I put my arms above my head and stretch, and as I glance across the room I see one of my students, a boy named Benjamin, staring at my chest—likely a struggle at any distance, really, but his gaze is steady and undeterred. He, at sixteen, is only ten years my junior, but his interest in my body is just as much perverse as it is illegal. I drop my arms and sink in my chair and notice his gaze remains unchanged and it occurs to me he's not looking at me, he's looking *through* me. Suddenly he snaps his fingers and smiles, bows his head, and begins fervently writing on his quiz sheet.

I, you see, did not follow the path of logic and my punishment was arriving at the wrong conclusion. I, indeed, failed.

I glance at the clock and sigh. "Time's up," I say.

A few kids groan but the majority get up from their seats and deliver the quizzes to my desk, each giving me a saddened smile as though they were aware of my embarrassment. And with each passing student, I covet something, and not the tangible things I might logically want—less mousy hair, a wider smile, green eyes instead of hazel, a *4* on my dresses instead of an *8*, less clock and more hourglass—but the things I see *in* them:

A stable home, friendships, a heritage, a history, a legacy.

A future.

One of the worst parts of being in the Federal Witness Protection Program—or WITSEC, for the sake of verbosity—is that you will never be any of those things you dreamed about as a child, unless your dream was of cold anonymity. You will never be a famous ballet dancer or an all-star shortstop. You will never be an Oscar-winning actor or a world-class journalist. You will never be a congressman, a judge, a CEO, a rock star.

You will never *be*.

Your job as a pawn in the WITSEC game is to be quiet and deal with it. You'll make a great mail carrier, data-entry specialist, cosmetologist. And yes, you'll make an excellent teacher. Don't worry about not having a degree or the proper credentials and certifications—because you've got them *now*. Just be quiet, keep to yourself, and stay under the radar and the government will give you the best thing they have to offer: You get to live.

The price is an existence of tedium. You have just become irreparably average. You are not special. You are not unique.

You are not a prime number.

And as these kids walk past my desk, each with varying amounts of hope and potential, I can't help thinking that I am experiencing the slowest death known to mankind.

• • •

The geometricians shuffle out and the future MIT grads take their places on the warm wooden chairs. I assign them a problem on implicit differentiation that should take about fifteen minutes to solve, an attempt to buy myself some time to grade the geometry pop quizzes.

Okay, maybe *grade* is the wrong word.

Tim, for example, always manages to answer questions correctly when called upon, but actually shakes when a test is put before him, and he sweats right through however many layers of clothing he happens to be wearing that day. His quiz is a mess of scribbled-out mistakes. He gets a B.

Sharon, this wispy Jewish girl, comes to school three out of five days a week, and only after the bruises have started to heal. Even though she finished merely half of the questions, she gets an A.

Then we have Derek, a guy dumb enough to not understand the importance of birth control, yet smart enough to unconditionally love his girl while she drops out of school to have their baby—all while his best friends are out enjoying underage drinking and girlfriend swapping. A+, Derek.

About half of the class gets my subjective grading and the rest take it on their chins like typical juniors.

Sure, I'm credentialed by the state as a teacher, but I don't work like one. My interest—okay, *obsession*—with math is genuine, and has been since the first time I was ripped away from the life I loved. I buried myself in numbers and word problems where an answer was certain (or at least in the back of the book) and I knew I'd found something I could count on. But grading? My curriculum? The PTA? Who cares. The interest for that all sits in the part of my career that I spent no time earning: a bachelor's degree and the teaching certification that goes along with it.

One of my prior contacts at WITSEC suggested I not pursue a college degree for real, that I might have to *abandon* that persona at some point and start fresh, and who's to say I'd even stay in one place long enough to get a degree anyway. It's much easier to be handed one, with a snappy grade point average and all the bells and whistles. Just as it is easy to be handed an address, a credit history, a name.

I'm Sandra Clarke, by the way.

For now.

As Tuesday ends, I find my way to the Columbia Mall, located on Columbia Pike in Columbia, Maryland, a mere five minutes from my home. Columbia is one of the earliest master-planned communities, developed by some guy named Rouse, intended to be the suburban mecca that even Eisenhower himself could never have imagined. And of all the places I've been *relocated* to, this one breaks the scale of insipidity. It is a swirl of predictable shopping and cookie-cutter houses and architecturally vapid office buildings and family restaurants that specialize in salad bars and baby back ribs.

I hate it here.

But this place, this mall, has one thing in it I love, a thing present in every mall in every Middleton and Middletown and Middleburg and Centreville across this great land: a Hallmark store. At least once a week I visit this special place and slowly walk the aisles, for it is here that I get to witness the true essence of family, of love:

The man who clumsily pokes through the cards for a half hour until he finds the one that will touch his wife's heart, the one he *knows* will lift her spirit because he *knows* her, the one that brings a sigh of relief.

The daughter who sifts through the cards until she finds the one for her mother that makes her suppress a giggle, because mothers and daughters understand each other's idiosyncrasies— and frailties—and can laugh at each other that way.

The adolescent boy who sneaks into the card store, after telling his father he'd be hanging at GameStop, in order to find a card for his first girlfriend, because telling her how he feels is not only embarrassing, but elusive.

It is here I get to witness life, albeit the lives of others. I walk through the store and watch people select intimate items for their lovers, their friends, their family, and for the briefest of moments I get to pretend I am there for someone special too. I get to pretend that my parents are still alive and I am looking for the perfect anniversary card. I get to pretend that my mother did not miscarry my little brother from immense stress but instead brought a beautiful boy into this world who picked on me as a child but protected me as a teen, and I would search for an hour for the perfect card to explain my love for him. I get to pretend that my best friend is getting over another breakup from a guy who didn't deserve her in the first place and—*bam*—here's a card that brings it all to light.

This is my nameless family.

Tonight I stand close to a guy in his late thirties who looks like George Clooney—actually, like a regular guy who happens to possess all of George Clooney's flaws: exaggerated chin, droopy eyes, absent upper lip. But there is something about him, something real. He is here for a distinct reason, and because of that he has been selected.

I follow George around the store, a few steps behind, watching him fumble through the racks. After reading what had to have been a thirtieth card, he hangs his head and wipes the corner of his eye. I step a little closer. He muffles a whimper and I slowly reach out and gently—with the lightest touch I can muster—brush his shoulder, and as my fingers connect with the fabric of his coat, I inhale deeply.

He swallows and turns my way.

"Are you okay?" I ask.

He nods and looks back down, but something in my touch, or the interaction with another caring human, brings his tears to a pour and he wipes vigorously, as though it is sand, not water, filling his eyes. I wait and finally he returns the card to its holder, glances at me, and slowly lumbers from the store as he dries his eyes and nose with his sleeve.

I watch him leave, then find the card he just put back. It is a card asking for forgiveness, for one more chance.

I quickly reach into the back of the stack and grab the freshest card and rush to the front of the store and make a purchase—in cash, as usual.

As I exit the shop, I find George sitting on a bench five stores away, staring blindly into a babyGap. I don't bother to sit down—because, really, there is no point in getting to know George for real—and I hand him the bag with the card inside.

"She's waiting," I say, "to give you another chance. She just wants you to ask." I back up a few paces because I feel the need to ask George to get a drink, where it may turn into three, upon which I will carelessly spill the many beans of my lives and in the morning, with hangover in tow, the feds will have me on my way to another town, another job, another mall with another Hallmark store.

"Don't waste one more minute of your life," I say as I move in reverse. Then I smile and add, "And don't screw it up this time."

I drive home, through the suburban traffic that piles up on Columbia Pike with people who live in Baltimore but work in D.C., or the opposite. And today is Tuesday, which means it's the night I pay bills, after which I grade the remaining pop quizzes, the ones I always give on Tuesday, where there is at least one correct answer if you follow the path of logic. And I will eat one-third of a pizza from Carmine's, because it is Tuesday and they know to have it ready for me as they learned so many months ago. And then I will shower and watch one hour of television and then I will repeat my name to myself over and over until I lull myself to sleep. Because today is Tuesday.

$$\frac{x}{x/2}, \; x \neq 0$$

I'M GETTING THAT FEELING AGAIN—A SORT OF WANDERLUST fueled by the assumption that the grass has got to be greener somewhere. Anywhere. I've seen a lot of grass, mind you, having moved with the frequency of an army brat and having acquired all of the inevitable angst and rebellion. It is one thing to deal with the lousy decisions in your life and suffer from the relative regret and misery, to play the hand you've been dealt; it is quite another to be dealt hand after hand, with some federal employee leering over your shoulder, whispering, "*Fold.*"

Anyway, I'm getting that feeling again.

Randall Farquar, whose name I intentionally mispronounce toward the more phonetic, will not be happy when I call, but it's his job to talk to me, to protect me, to keep me safe and secure and toasty warm at night.

These are your tax dollars hard at work.

It is Farquar's job to pick up my pieces, no matter how many or how small, and glue them back together into a slightly different shape, feel, and sound. He takes what was once a Terry and converts her into a Shelly, carefully wipes clean the slates of bills, addresses, employers, credit histories, licenses, even my Social Security number—everything that makes me *me*. Or at least the government's version of me. For now I am whole.

I am complete.

I am a complete fabrication.

But it's only a matter of time. I may be whole now, but I've been living off Columbia Pike in Columbia, Maryland, for eighteen months and in some way I can imagine that little Farquar is waiting for his phone to ring, and he pinches his brow in anticipation, wondering how much longer I can remain whole.

Well, get ready; in approximately seven hours, Sandra Clarke is going to shatter.

I have no children, yet I can tell you without fail that the best baby monitor on the market today (and the most popular) is the Sony 27 Channel BabyCall Nursery Monitor, with The First Years Clear and Near 2.4 GHz Monitor a close second. I've got most of them—Fisher-Price, Safety 1st, RC2—but the Sony model will blow your mind. The sound is crystal clear and it has a range that is truly astounding.

Now, add to that piece of knowledge this: The two operating items in the baby-monitor system are the receiver—which the parent usually carries around so that he or she can hear the baby—and the transmitter, which is usually positioned near the child's crib or bed. Both have on/off switches but—and I can say this with certainty—the parents usually leave the transmitter plugged in and *on*.

I have lived in many different apartment buildings over the course of my adult life, and the first thing I do on the first night of my stay in my new residence is set up those monitors (no transmitter needed) one by one and fiddle with the channel combinations until the static disappears and the noise of a child begins. In a building with over twenty apartments, the odds are that one of those apartments has a youngster who needs a monitor and has parents who carelessly leave the transmitter on twenty-four hours a day.

While my neighbors are stealing connections to unsecured wireless networks, I'm stealing a family.

And here in Columbia, this is how I came to know little Jessica—a name I have always desired but WITSEC would never permit me to use—and her wonderful yet predictable suburban upbringing. I would fall asleep at night to her deep, rhythmic breathing and wake just before the sun to her gentle cooing. I weathered the long bout of pneumonia she had this past winter and called in sick for two days to make sure she was okay. I would laugh as her father read her the same story every night—*Where, Oh Where, Is Kipper's Bear?*—and how Jessica would giggle at the pop-ups and how her father would have to interrupt the story repeatedly to keep her from pulling the pages apart. And I would cry as Jessica's parents would whisper their loving approval of their daughter, their creation, each night as they put her down. *Isn't she beautiful? Isn't she perfect? Look at our baby girl.*

Jessica is the little sister I never had and the daughter I will never be able to have. They are a safe family, with a regular schedule and regular jobs and regular stresses. They live and love and experience what many would find boring but remains a dream to me. And of all the places I have lived, of all the families I have adopted, this one was the closest to home I might have ever known, though I never caught a glimpse of them or found out what floor they lived on or whether they were even in my building.

I will miss Jessica.

In my final hours in this place, I scan my apartment for anything I want to take with me. I won't have much room, so it needs to be small. I will be leaving with the clothes I'm wearing and not much more. I grab a garbage bag—because, *theoretically*, I'm in a hurry—and fill it with some undergarments, a robe, some personal hygiene items, a toothbrush. Everything that belongs to me, or this version of me, must stay. I can take no books, no pictures, no identification.

Nothing.

I am about to start over. Again.

I have a few hundred dollars on me, but they'll give me more—though not much more.

This is where I walk to the edge of the cliff, close my eyes, and take the dive. There is no turning back.

And all it takes is one simple lie.

I do not call the school and tell them I am not coming in—or *back*, for that matter.

I do not call my landlord and let him know he will have a new apartment for lease.

I *do* call the number that connects me—directly—to my federal contact.

"Farquar."

"It's Melody Grace McCartney," I say.

He sighs and I can hear him rub his beard through the phone. "Why aren't you using your proper name, *Sandra*?"

"They found me." I yawn.

"*Who*, Sandra? What are you talking about?"

"*Who*," I repeat, annoyed by his assumption that I'm making this up, as valid as that may be. "Is this a joke, Farquar? I answered my phone a few minutes ago and what I got was some guy with a New York accent, repeating, '*Sing me a song, Melody*.'"

He sighs again, but doesn't try to hide it this time. "I don't suppose you got this on tape."

"What? Of course not."

A pause, a third sigh, then he puts me on hold. It is important to note he is *U.S. Marshal* Farquar and not *Agent* Farquar. All of the dealings with Witness Protection are indeed struck out of negotiations with the U.S. Department of Justice, which sort of lends one to think that the FBI will be taking care of you down the road. But, in fact, it's a different branch of the Department of Justice that handles WITSEC: the United States Marshals Service.

Justice, *Integrity*, *Service*, or so the motto goes.

He comes back on, laughing, and hits me with "At least they didn't send you a dead fish. Because that really sends a message—"

"Listen, are you suggesting I should sit in my apartment and wait for something to happen? Would that make you feel better? That way you can repeat the excellent line of service you provided for my parents twenty years ago."

Guilt has managed to shut him down year after year and I had no reason to assume this time would be any different.

"Just sit tight," he mumbles. "Are you safe?"

"How should I know," I say, feigning a little anger.

"Well, you are now."

And with that, a squad car with three federal marshals pulls up to the front of my building. The marshals race up the steps, snatch me from my apartment, and whisk me into their noble chariot. These are my knights in shining armor.

One thing I am sure Farquar never liked about my most recent locale was the proximity to his office. He's based out of Baltimore, a mere twenty-minute ride from Columbia. And within thirty minutes of my call to him, here I am, seated in a cold, sterile conference room on the third floor of the Garmatz Federal Courthouse on West Lombard Street. I've seen the inside of so much government office space that it's come to feel more like home than any new address they've ever assigned to me. Phoenix, Little Rock, Raleigh, Louisville, Albuquerque—I've visited them all. I've had to sit on the same hard chairs and drink the same lousy coffee for two decades of my brief life. And here I am again, feeling like I'm under investigation, about to be given the cold, hard news about my future, with all the limited options of a heartless killer—except an attorney.

Three sips into my mud and Farquar comes strolling in. He looks thin and ill and about three or four years late for his retirement.

"McCartney," he says, tossing my file—now a solid two inches thick—down on the metal table. I let it resound for a few seconds before I respond.

"It's been awhile," is my meager response. I cannot look him in the eye.

He sits down and sighs through his nose, hard, like he's trying to make a point. All I notice is that he forced something out of his right nostril that has become lodged on the edge of his mustache.

"It's been less than two years," he says. "Do you know some of my cases I have not seen since we put them into the program?"

"You mean the dead ones?"

"This isn't a joke. We've tried to accommodate you every way we can. You wanted to live more urban, so we did that. You wanted to have a job involving math, so we got you one. And now here you are on our doorstep again. You think spending another hundred grand to relocate you—yet once more—is funny?"

I sit up. "Are we going to have this conversation again?" I lean toward him and give him a reminder of why I am here in the first place. "You want to talk about *cost*, Farquar? You wanna put a monetary value on my parents—both dead—so that the feds could spend millions on a trial they'd eventually lose anyway? You owe me, *big*—for the rest of my life."

He stands up, in a nonconfrontational manner, but I stand to match him anyway. He's about three inches taller than my five-foot-seven stature, but I can pretty much look him straight in the eye—though I can't help but stare at that thing on his mustache. I want to hammer him some more but I feel compelled to say something.

"Listen, uh, you got a—"

"I'm officially off your case." He looks down and puts his hands in his pockets.

As pathetic a protector as he was—even a pathetic government contact—he was *my* protector, my safety net. He was the only guy I knew in the system, in WITSEC. Ever.

"Wh—why?"

He makes eye contact again. "I'm leaving." He pauses for effect, it seems. "I'm done. I'm out. I can't handle it anymore."

I sit back down and slouch and all I can think of is how incredibly tired I am of *starting anew*.

"It's just time for me to go," he continues. "I'm sixty, and I've been here for almost thirty years and . . . I don't know, things have changed. The priorities have changed." He scratches his beard and the thing drifts from his upper lip into the dusty oblivion below. I'm thankful. "It's just time."

"When's your last day?"

"One week from today."

I bristle. The only person who ever understood me was Farquar—understood me in a sense that I met him when I was six, the day we entered the program, and has been the only recurring character in my weird drama. I consider saying something but I merely phase out, stare into the distance.

Farquar sits on the table in front of me and puts his hand on my head and strokes my hair gently, like I imagine my father might have at this moment. "You've got to make this the last time, okay? The last time. They won't allow this to continue." He bolts up from the table and walks to the door and I feel like, yet again, I am losing the only static person in my life. "Deputy Marshal Douglas will be taking over your case. He'll be in shortly."

I hold my breath and watch as he reaches the door.

He turns back and smiles and says, "Good-bye . . . *Michelle*."

And as the door closes behind him, I writhe; I don't want to be a Michelle.

I sip the last cold drops of coffee from my foam cup and begin to wonder what is taking Douglas so long. A few laughs at his new project with Farquar? Maybe making a few more Internet stock trades before having to spend the afternoon with the problem child in conference room number three? All I want is to go through the typical debriefing and document signing and be off and running with my new persona. I want my new moniker and my new address and my new hourly wage and my new apartment where I can set up my baby monitors and alphabetize my carryout menus. I want my new bed where I can dream of a person I can never be: myself.

The door eventually opens but the only thing I see is a meaty hand on the knob. I hear a voice and the end of a conversation with an unseen party, a laugh, and, finally, words in the form of a whisper, "No . . . unfortunately, I'm going to be in here the rest of the day."

And then U.S. Deputy Marshal Douglas welcomes himself into my life.

Time freezes for a moment as we size each other up. The first thing I notice—that anyone would notice—is his size. Easily standing six-foot-four, he has the build of a football-player-turned-coach. The guy was probably in great shape about five years ago; he doesn't show obvious signs of flab but he's definitely softening. The next thing I notice is his hair, which is short, but full and thick and black, in an Irish way, not Mediterranean. His eyes, too, blue like cobalt, speak of a northern influence and fade into not another color but a deeper hue of the same. Smooth skin, firm chin, pointed nose. I've forgotten Farquar already. Then he smiles and all I see are white beams and dimples and I feel like I'm looking at Matthew McConaughey and I wait for the matching goofy southern drawl to dribble out but instead he puts out his hand for a shake—oddly, his *left* hand—and instead of shaking it, I sink at the sight of a bright gold wedding band.

This is not my day.

"You'll earn a promotion for taking this case, you know." I half stand and reach out to shake. His hand is big and warm. But so is that freaking wedding band.

He holds my hand for an unusually long time and I sit back down while still in his grip. Finally, he lets go and stands back. He stares at me, gently, and all he says is, "Melody."

The fact that he chose to say my real name as the first word between us has already won my favor.

His stare acts as a reminder that he's sized me up too, that he's noticed I'm frazzled: no lipstick, smeared eyeliner, hair akimbo. I want to tell him *I really look better than this* but all I can deliver is, "Marshal Douglas." I better get used to saying those words; they will probably come out of my mouth again—in another eighteen months.

His smile fades, but he keeps those blues right on me and I'm starting to wonder if Farquar's vivacious nose chunk made its way to my face. I involuntarily brush my lip a few times.

"Before we start," he says, "is there anything you need?"

"I don't want to be a Michelle."

"I meant, like . . . food or a trip to the rest room."

"Oh." I shake my head and rub my temples.

He opens my file and starts perusing it for what seems like the very first time and I start getting a little fumed. Somehow I know this is Farquar's fault but I take it out on Douglas instead.

"You're a little young to be a marshal, aren't you?"

He looks up and smiles and suddenly I'm staring at McConaughey again.

"I'm thirty-three." He looks back down at the file, but continues, "I've been with the Marshals Service for about . . . eight years. With WITSEC for three. Before that I was with the Federal Bureau of Investigation."

"What?" I smirk. "Who leaves the FBI to come to the Marshals Service?"

He ignores me, but shifts his body enough to signal that I've touched a sore spot.

He closes the file and shoves it away, almost right off the table. "You can call me Sean." He stares at me again and smiles a little, puts his elbows on the table, clasps his hands and rests his chin between his knuckles.

I start to blush—and I'm really not in the mood. This is outside my realm of control. I point to the folder. "Don't, um . . . don't you want to familiarize yourself with my case?"

"That file is full of other people's opinions of you, of your history, of who you are. I'd rather hear it from you."

"We'll be here all week." I laugh a little, nervously. He stares into me and I quickly feel ineffectual.

"If that's what it takes." He says this like he's trying to win me over, in a professional but sublimely sensual way, that maybe, at some point in his life, he learned the only way he could garner the trust of a woman was by charming her, seducing her. He leans on the table, close to me, like he wants me to meet him halfway for a kiss, and I find myself reading his irises like a favorite novel. He closes the deal with, "I will do whatever it takes."

I swallow, hard enough that I'm sure he hears the gulp.

Regardless of how convenient it would be to have a marshal

as a lover, I break myself away and remember where I am and why I am here—or, rather, why I put myself here—and that there is nothing charming or sexy about the Federal Witness Protection Program, their generic suburban addresses, and their boring names.

"Well, *Sean* . . . I guess I can start with how this is all my fault. How I managed to kill my parents."

He slowly sits back in his chair, rests his hands on his stomach, and begins to twist his wedding band around his finger, as though it's his only weapon against me.

"I'm not a psychotherapist, so if you want to go down that path you can become Michelle Smith or some other faceless digit and we'll send you on your way to rural Wisconsin." He inhales deeply. "Or . . . you can help me understand what makes you tick. And we'll get you a better life."

"You guys have done such a great job so far in—"

"I'm not Farquar."

We stare at each other for a moment and with the patience of a dog I am determined to stare him down. He looks like he's trying to read me—like he actually *is* a psychotherapist, or studied the discipline at some point—and as I feel my eyes yearning to look away, to blink, I slowly raise my arms above my head and put my hair into a ponytail to see if he'll let his eyes stray to my chest.

Alas, his eyes do make the journey away from mine, but not to my breasts. Instead he glances up at my hair and raises a curious, slightly disapproving eyebrow.

Call me *samurai*.

I look down and slowly pull the band from my hair as I say, "No, you see . . . I did cause my parents' death—I mean, indirectly." I purse my lips. "You familiar with the Bovaro family?"

"You're kidding, right? I work for the Justice Department."

"I know, Sean, but since you were probably fourteen when this happened, I figured it might not be *fresh*." I begin tapping my empty coffee cup, staring at the black residue lining the bottom. "You know what led to the arrest of Tony Bovaro?"

"Your parents?"

"No," I say with a sigh, "eggs, actually."

"Eggs."

"Eggs Romana, to be exact."

He frowns.

"It's got, like, celery and parsley and Parmesan in it, and you finish it with a little red pe—"

"About Tony Bovaro," he says, inhaling and holding a breath as though this afternoon will be even longer than he'd imagined.

"Right. At the time, we were living in the Caldwells, and genuine Italian food was in short supply in our particular corner of New Jersey. My dad used to take my mother and me to Little Italy for our birthdays so we could really savor the experience, you know? Not just the food, but the people, the culture, the gentle flow of the Italian language." I stare at the cup and focus; eye contact at this point is impossible.

"I was the only child so far, with one in my mom's belly—a younger brother in the making—so I pretty much got whatever I wanted out of unconditional parental love." I grimace. "And for whatever reason, I woke early on this especially bleak Sunday morning in late March and asked in my most sincere, sweet six-year-old voice if we could hop in the car and go to my favorite place in Little Italy, this dump called Vincent's, that made the most extraordinary eggs Romana."

I stop and eventually look up at Sean. He is paying close attention.

"The older guy who seemed to run the place—I never knew if he was Vincent or not—he used to bring me my order. Just mine. He would, uh . . . he'd put my breakfast on the table and speak to me in Italian and pinch my cheeks and hold my chin in his hand and reel off the most beautiful words I had ever heard. *Dolce, bella, angelo, perfetto.* I'd smile and giggle and savor the tastiest eggs I've ever eaten in my life."

Sean passes a smile my way. "That's sweet."

My vision blurs as I recall the memory. "No, the sweet part is coming. My mother explained to me that this man, the owner, had something called Alzheimer's disease and that he had no idea who I was each time I came in." My eyes are slow to refocus. "You see, he thought I was this perfect, pretty angel every time, and every time was the *first* time." I pause. "Do you know how beautiful that made me feel?"

He doesn't answer. Good for him.

"Anyway, this particular morning, I really wanted to go to Vincent's. My folks reluctantly agreed, so we piled into the Oldsmobile and headed to New York. When we got there, however, the place was closed." I begin to sober, the images coming faster. "My dad was determined to please his little girl so, after checking out the sign in the window, which clearly stated they should be open at seven in the morning, he suggested we find another place. Well, I didn't relent. I wanted eggs Romana and the nice man who spoke Italian flatteries."

"So they opened for you?"

I shake my head. "Not exactly. My mother and father pleaded with me to let them find another place, but I was six and didn't really care or understand that the sign didn't match the reality of the moment. So my dad walked down the alley to the side door, saw a light on, and tried to open the door—which opened with ease." I exhale slowly. "He waved for us to come over and meet him, and my mother and I did."

I stop.

Sean opens his eyes wide. "And?"

"And after we walked in through the side entrance to the kitchen, we stood motionless as we watched a stocky, relentlessly hairy man—whom we later came to know as Tony Bovaro—plunge a knife into the belly of another man and pull upward, like he was trying to open a sack of rice." I lean toward Sean. "But that wasn't the truly terrifying part. Tony leaned over the body, reached inside the man, and pulled out some organs and spread them over the now lifeless body." I sit back. "I was much older when I realized he was exemplifying the expression *spilling your guts*."

Silence.

Sean—U.S. Deputy Marshal Sean Douglas—swallows hard, and this time it's my turn to hear *him*. Eight years on the job has not hardened him yet.

"Um," he says as he clears his throat, "who'd he kill?"

"Who knows. Probably some guy who wasn't paying his ten percent or whatever the Mafia gets, but based on the gutting, I'm guessing he was a snitch. The point is that three average citizens had just witnessed Tony murder someone—three people with no criminal records, with no need for plea bargains or attorneys or anything else."

"So then what?"

Everyone, at this point in the story, expects my response to be *"We ran!"* Sean needs the truth, though. And I doubt the truth is in my two-inch file. "Well, let's see. I threw up and had pee running down both my legs. My mother screamed and collapsed. My father, after breaking out of his initial shock, tried to pull my mother up off the floor but kept slipping in all of the blood and urine. Is this what you wanted to know, Sean?"

He slowly nods. "It is."

He earns one point.

"Bovaro just stared at us, like we were this big collective fly in his ointment, arm at his side, blood dripping off the knife. And my father, bless his strong heart, pulled my mother to her feet, picked me up with his other arm, and tossed me over his shoulder, and we skated out of there."

"Tony never came after you?"

I chuckle. "He didn't. And I can't help but wonder to this day if he *let* us go, if he realized that we had nothing to do with his business and that we had no interest in getting involved—because his assumption would have been right on the money."

"But you went to the feds."

"Get real, Sean. The feds came to us."

He squints, gives me a look of disbelief. "How's that possible?"

I sit back and cross my legs in an angrily superior way. "I never thought to ask. What difference does it make?"

Sean grabs my file and begins flipping through it in a slightly more attentive manner than he had moments ago. "It's just odd," he says as he turns the pages. "How many people were there when this happened?"

"What, are you joking? How many restaurants do you think were open in Little Italy at seven in the morning on a Sunday? There were no other witnesses."

Sean stops and looks at me. He leans back and puts his hands behind his head and his shirt pulls tight against his chest and my eyes drift right to his pecs with none of the restraint he'd shown to me when the same opportunity arose.

As much as I want to prove I am in control, that I am one tough lady who can handle being tossed about in their ocean of anonymity, I feel myself shrink a little, even crumble, and suddenly I am a little girl again and all I want is for this guy to look at me and smile and whisper *bella, principessa*.

"Okay," he says, "somehow the feds found you and your family. What compelled your folks to testify?"

"Are you asking if my parents were engaged in some illegal activity that the FBI or the Department of Justice used as leverage? Hardly. My parents didn't even cheat on their taxes."

"So what made them agree to testify?"

"Well, I was young at the time and not really made a participant in those conversations and decisions, but I later came to understand that the FBI put the fear of God into my folks, first by making them retell the story over and over, making sure it was as vivid as can be, then by suggesting the same thing would happen to them—a visceral ending—and that it was only a matter of time." I set my jaw. "Then, of course, they hit us with those four magical words, and those four words turned the tide for me and my family forever."

He gives me a sideways glance, like he's thinking.

"Surely, Sean, you know what I'm talking about. You must learn this phrase your first day in training." My sarcasm increases. "What are those four words?"

He shrugs. *"We're here to help?"*

One demerit.

"We. Can. Protect. You." I stand and take my coffee cup and chuck it across the room and into the garbage can. "Not even close."

I walk out and find the ladies' room, where I sit in a stall and bury my face in my hands and try to get myself together; a normal person would have dashed out the front door, but where exactly would I be going? I sit for the longest time. Women come and go, but many seem to stay in the stalls beside me, completely quiet or softly sighing but doing nothing more, appearing to rally their own selves for some unknown pending process, and I can't help but wonder if this is a normal occurrence here on the third floor of the Garmatz Federal Courthouse on West Lombard Street in Baltimore, Maryland.

I return to the conference room a good thirty minutes later and Sean is a changed man. He is professional and solemn. My file is spread across the table in chunks, with fresh Post-it notes sticking out from various sections. When Sean looks at me, his eyes seem more intent, sort of probing.

Marshal Sean Douglas has decided to take me seriously.

He plays with his hands nervously and says, "Do, um . . . do you still like Italian? I can get some rookie to go out to Little Italy and grab us some food. Um, Chiapparelli's has a killer Caesar and they—"

"That's fine, Sean." I sit and smile. "Whatever you suggest."

He nods and watches me for a moment and then leaves the room.

I immediately start flipping to the pages he has place-marked to find he's put a Post-it at the beginning of each of my new identities, and seeing the names is like recalling an old lover or a near-death experience—all with three syllables.

May Adams.

Karen Smith.

Anne Johnson.

Jane Watkins.

Terry Mills.

Shelly Jones.

Linda Simms.

Sandra Clarke.

I came to think the folks in WITSEC were rather daft with their naming conventions, though I later assumed it was a subtle form of punishment. "The name needs to be forgettable," they would tell me. What I wouldn't give to be an Emmanuelle or a Carina or an Alexis. Geez, even a Tiffany or a Heather. And to have surrendered Melody Grace . . . well, it makes it hard to wake up as Michelle.

Though undoubtedly I shall.

A few bites into my Caesar and my concern isn't sustenance but what might be jammed between my incisors: lettuce, black pepper, Parmesan; I'd rather that none of these add to my already diffused personality. Worse, I realize my interest in my protector is more than it should be. After four mouthfuls, I tire of licking my teeth clean and slide the salad out of reach.

Sean waits to swallow before asking, "You didn't like it?"

I look at him and grin. "It's delicious, just as you'd said it would be."

The phone in the conference room rings and Sean answers it quickly. He grabs a pen and begins tapping it on the lid for his rigatoni amatriciana and it occurs to me that, since he ordered a dish with pancetta, sautéed onions, and garlic, his interest and concern for me will not lead to infidelity.

He doesn't talk but appears to be listening attentively. He grabs a pad of paper from under my file and starts writing fast, in scribble surely discernible only to him. He writes and writes and writes and ends the call without saying good-bye, without saying a single word at all, and after the phone is back on the cradle, he writes some more. Then he points to my salad with his pen and says, "You should really eat up. We've got a long night in front of us."

This is, of course, not the first time I've heard this. The last time was eight years ago, a mere nine hours after my parents were shot dead on their way home from the A&P. What he really means is *We're going on the road.*

$$\ln (x^2 - 1) - \ln (x - 1) = \ln (4)$$

I'M SITTING ALONE IN THE BACK OF A BLACK, LATE-MODEL FORD Explorer and though it is nighttime, I can tell the windows are tinted—far darker than your usual tint. I gently tap the glass and the lack of resonance suggests bulletproof protection.

I am simply not this important.

And now the guilt sets in over my lie, how I have set into motion the lives of countless people because I tired of my surroundings, because I allowed the subtle weight of ennui to overwhelm, and I pulled an escape cord that virtually no one else in this country can reach. And they believed me (for the most part) because they promised to.

A deputy marshal sits in the driver's seat with the engine running, a man I will likely never see again after this journey; I do not make idle chat. Through the hazy glass I can see Sean speaking with two other deputy marshals and it becomes apparent that Sean is the one in charge. I've seen this scene before. *Get her to the motel and we'll regroup from there. Call me if there are any problems. She's been through a lot, so take it easy on her.*

I put my head to the headrest and stare out the window, and I drift into a shallow sleep.

•   •   •

I wake to the car shimmying over broken pavement and before I can bring my eyes into focus, I try to brush off a dream that is actually my reality. I am being taken to some unknown location by two men I do not know. I do not know my name, my Social Security number, my address. I do not know where I work or what my trade is. And though this has happened to me so many times before, I shake a little and my stomach turns. I utter something about feeling sick and I reach forward and tightly grip the shoulder of the driver and he knows to pull over so I can retch.

And I do.

Someone hands me a bottle of Aquafina and I rinse my mouth and take a few swigs. I get back in the car, turn to say thanks, and realize that Sean is in the backseat with me.

"Let me guess," he says, "bad salad?"

I clear my throat and take another drink. "I didn't know you were coming." I'm happy; I've known the guy for a few hours but he's now the most stable thing in my life.

He nods a few times in my direction, then turns to look out his window; we are in motion again. "I, uh . . . wanted to make sure you were okay, that you got to your new location safely."

I sit up and our knees touch. He doesn't move his away and neither do I. Sitting next to him, I finally get an idea of his actual size and he's just as bulky as I'd imagined. You could fit me inside him, literally, with a few inches to spare all the way around. I sink down in my seat and feel warm and cozy—but safe is what I'm really after.

"I'll take what I can get," I say. I catch a glimpse of myself in the rearview mirror and realize this is the end of a long day. My hair has deflated and my blouse is wrinkled and my jeans are stained from God knows what.

Sean plays with his wedding band again, spinning it around

his finger, and I now realize it's an activity derived from anxiety, not aggression. He cocks his body in my direction, looks at me and asks, "Do you ever get to that point? You know, where you actually feel safe?"

I brush the bangs from my eyes in order to read his expression better. "For real?"

He nods.

I think about it for a few seconds, but my answer is predetermined. "I haven't felt safe since the night before we went to breakfast at Vincent's. I was six. That was twenty years ago."

"So, *we* don't make you feel safe?"

I shake my head a little. "Let me give you an illustration. After you guys managed to manipulate my folks into testifying against Tony Bo—"

"*We* didn't do that, Michelle."

I hang my head. "Okay, the *feds* manipulated my folks into testifying. And would you please call me Melody while we're safely secured here?"

Sean shakes his head, then nods toward the driver. I roll my eyes.

"Anyway, once we entered WITSEC and were relocated to a lovely little town in Arkansas," I say, then pause to let the sarcasm get across, "I began attending school in a neighboring rural town. On my fifth day in class, the teacher asked each of us in turn to spell our name for the other students." I move a little in my seat so I can face Sean more directly. "It sure would've been easier to spell *May Adams,* but wouldn't you know, without even giving it a second thought, there I was, unveiling myself to my teacher, her aide, and seventeen other first-graders."

M-E-L-O-D-Y G-R-A-C-E M-C-C-A-R-T-N-E-Y.

Sean groans under his breath; he knows what's coming next.

"A few minutes later the aide disappeared. Ninety minutes after that, I was grabbed off the playground and tossed into the back of a Chevy van, flanked by three of your finest along with my ghost-white parents."

Sean winces. "I can't imagine what that must have been like for you. How long had you lived in Arkansas?"

"About five weeks. We lived in a motel outside Texarkana while waiting for you guys to set up our new identities for a longer period of time—almost two months."

I turn to look out the window and groan under my breath. Man, I hated that place. Not Arkansas, mind you—the motel. I always despised the motel phase. I remember being so bored, so lonely. There was nothing to do, no kids to play with, no toys. I would just sit around and watch television and pray that my parents would have a few free minutes to talk to me or read to me or play with me. But they were busy, always busy, with what they gently termed *big guy stuff*.

I turn back to Sean. "I felt bad, though—even then. I sort of knew what I'd done, even though it was unintentional. My dad had just gotten a new job—as a warehouse foreman, a significant departure from his career as a senior chemist for Pfizer—and we were just on the verge of getting settled . . . and I accidentally threw it all away."

"I'm sure your parents didn't blame you."

"No, they didn't, as a matter of fact." I look down and whisper under my breath. "At least, not at first."

"What do you mean?"

Ignoring Sean's follow-up, I glance out the window and see a road sign that reads POCOMOKE CITY and it occurs to me that I know neither what road we're on nor where we're heading—and worse, I don't even care.

I undo my seat belt and twist in my seat and prop my leg up; Sean and I are distorted mirror images of one another.

I try to think of something to continue a lighter conversation, to enjoy this tenuous form of company, but the weight of the day rushes in and sleep is again forcing itself upon me. Just on the verge of dozing, I accidentally tip over, drop my head to Sean's shoulder, fall into his embrace like a lover. He gently places his hands on me, one on my head and one on my neck, and pulls me down to his chest where I rest—awake—for a long time, long enough for the other deputy to have brought us to the fringe of the Commonwealth of Virginia. I have not enjoyed the smell and feel of a strong man enveloping me since my father passed away, and I decide I will not leave this position until I am asked to.

The car comes to a stop and the engine is turned off; we have either reached our destination or someone needs to get a drink or relieve himself. I open my eyes and see the red sheen of a Sheetz convenience store sign beam into the car and, though thankful we are still on the road, I realize I must lift my head.

Sean casually strokes my hair—fixing it, really—as he stiffens his back, stretching.

"You need anything?" he asks.

I shake my head. "We almost there?"

"Another hour."

The deputy gets back in the Explorer and the air that rushes in is warm and moist and the smell of the sea remains long after the door has closed. My command of typically useless rudimentary math finally comes in handy: 4.5 hours, heading south, at an average forty-five miles per hour, with two five-minute breaks. Then I factor in the smell.

"Virginia Beach?"

Sean laughs. "Close." The other deputy tosses him a pack of Hostess CupCakes. "We're not crossing the Chesapeake. We'll be staying at the end of the Delmarva Peninsula, in a town called Cape Charles."

Never heard of it, and I'm not surprised. I do know this much, though: The town will consist of a smattering of fast-food joints, a couple of gas stations, maybe a bank; the motel in town, the *only* motel, will be a dump; the rooms will have old, noisy radiators and the walls will be thin and I will be able to hear the conversations in the neighboring rooms, including the phone calls of the marshal who is protecting me, who is complaining of me, who is wishing he was home, because he has a home, and there is no place like home.

Sean wrestles with the wrapper and I catch the waft of synthetic cream-filled cake. "Do they have the orange ones in there?" The two guys look at each other. I smile and say, "Sorry." Out goes the driver.

Your tax dollars hard at work. Again.

Sean shoves half a cupcake into his mouth and stares inside the Sheetz. After a mighty gulp, he says, "You really want to know why I left the FBI?" In goes the rest of the cupcake.

In all my years on the run, this is the first time a marshal has ever offered one shred of personal info; I seize. "Sure."

Sean responds with a laugh, as though preparing me for a naive notion. "I joined the Bureau because I wanted to help people—*protect* people. Kids, mostly. Take down child abusers and child pornographers."

"Certainly noble." I catch his eye. "Were you successful?"

He shrugs a little and wipes his lips. "Somewhat. We nailed some bad guys, closed some rings. We were gaining some momentum."

"*Were*? What happened?"

"Nine-eleven happened. Suddenly, the only thing anyone cared about was terrorism."

"They cut your team?"

"That was only part of it. All the prestige and excitement had shifted to working on the terrorism cases. I'd get guys on my team who were annoyed to be there. Heaven forbid you got detailed on the Ashcroft porn cases, where you were going after illegal pornography. Most of those agents were whining all the time, calling themselves the porn police. You know, the *why are we worried about porn when our country is in danger* sort of thing." He turns and looks into the Sheetz again. "Once you've seen the crap I've seen, you quickly realize our country has been in danger long before the towers came down. Just because it's not biological or chemical doesn't mean it's not a poison."

Sean ends his rant and I watch our driver jog back to the car. The deputy hops in the front seat and tosses the cupcakes in my general direction and they fall to the floor. I pick them up and ask for a napkin but he ignores me and pulls onto the road. Sean hands me a half-empty pack of tissues.

Though I know in my gut the reason Sean joined WITSEC was to continue to protect people, I ask, "So your solution was to leave the FBI and abandon the effort of ridding the world of abusers and pornographers altogether?" I unwrap my beauteous imitation-orange-flavored treat and wait for him to answer.

He snickers, like I could never understand his plight, and raises his cupcake for me to clink as if we are toasting. "Here's to running."

I smile and bump his cupcake with mine and a little orange gets on his and a little chocolate gets on mine, and that's as close as we're going to get to *becoming one* tonight.

The deputy driving is getting either bored or annoyed, as his speed is topping the posted limit by at least fifteen miles per hour. Sean and I are getting too chummy for his taste, I would imagine.

"I read in your file that you never asked for a specific job type until we moved you to Columbia. Why'd you want to teach math?"

"If you're asking why I wanted to teach, it's pretty simple. Summers off, steady union pay scales with mandatory increases, spring break, Christmas break, blah, blah, blah. You guys gave me five inauthentic years of teaching experience, which landed me forty-five grand a year. Not bad for ten months of work. But if what you're really asking is why I wanted to teach *math*, well . . . that's a different story."

"I am."

I lick the sticky, orangey residue from my fingers and think of how to answer, wondering how to explain that I might be in love with the discipline as much as I could ever be with any man. I inhale and breathe out my answer. "It's rigid. It's firm and unyielding. It never lies."

Sean smiles, and for the first time it seems he has realized there is some depth to me that he does not understand but wants to make the journey there.

I continue, "It is always right, and all you have to do is take the most logical path to find an answer. It brings reality and truth to every scene on earth. Every business that has fudged its numbers gets flamed out in the end. Every woman who riskily toys with her menstrual cycle increases the odds of yielding human life. If you have six chambers and two bullets, the worst you will do is pull that trigger five times. Everything comes back to math. Build a bridge, cut out paper snowflakes with your kid, balance the federal budget—everything gets answered, built, and destroyed with math. It always tells the truth."

"Like, the whole is always equal to the sum of its parts?"

"No, more like . . . no matter how many times you cut a number in half it never reaches zero." I giggle suggestively. "You're not going to seduce me with your amateurish Euclidean axiom."

"You're right," he says. "I'm not going to seduce you."

Lousy chocolate-cupcake-eating, wedding-band-twirling, garlic-and-onion-breathing scumbag.

Oh, what do I care; he's a nice guy and a good-looking guy, but the most alluring part of this young marshal is his compulsory interest in my well-being.

Sean drinks half a bottle of water and I can't help but imagine he used to do the same with Gatorade on the sidelines of some game. He nods at me, like he's waiting for more.

I deliver. "I became obsessed with math after my parents were murdered. I spent all my free time going through puzzle books, but they became too easy. I started working through high school math textbooks, then moved on to college textbooks." I shove in another bite of cupcake and say through a full mouth, "I pretty much mastered everything through differential equations and linear algebra."

"Sounds like a blast."

"Yeah? I've got a super book on stochastic processes I could lend y—oh, that's right, I left it back at my apartment in Columbia."

"Now, that's a shame."

"You know what's most valuable, though? The math that every person on this planet should be forced to master?"

"I'm trembling with anticipation."

"Probability. You'll use it every day of your life."

"I'm not much of a gambler."

"You think probability is just for Vegas? Here, let me save you some time: The odds are in favor of the house. Now go save some money."

"Thanks for the tip."

"But if you really want to put this to some use . . ." Sean suddenly looks bored. I need to bring him back around; the fact that I'm going to make my point is incidental. "What are the odds you'll get hit by a car crossing the street?"

Sean shrugs.

"About one in eight thousand. How about this: What are the odds you'll die from food poisoning—not from terrorism, mind you, just your everyday case of salmonella?"

He shakes his head.

"About one in twelve thousand. But what do you say we get

more practical." I lean in toward Sean, close enough for him to smell the orange cream on my lips. "What are the odds I'm going to live a full, normal life?" He swallows. "There is a number, Sean, and I want to know what it is. As my protector, I want you to apply the math and bring me the honest, perfect truth."

He licks his teeth, though it seems it's more of a nervous reaction than a need to clear his molars of chocolate cake. "I don't know."

"Let's work the numbers. How many victims and witnesses have entered WITSEC since its inception?"

He takes a deep breath. "About seventy-five hundred witnesses. If you include the family members and loved ones, it's closer to seventeen thousand."

"And how many have been murdered while active in WITSEC?"

Sean thinks, but it seems like he's pondering whether to tell the truth. He lowers his voice, I assume to keep the other marshal from hearing, and says, "Forty-seven." He scratches his head and adds, "So, roughly one in four hundred."

"Not so fast, Slick. How many of the forty-seven were from Mafia cases?"

"I would guess all of them."

"How many witnesses and family members are tied directly to Mafia cases as opposed to drug- and gang-related cases and so on?"

He clears his throat. "About five thousand, give or take."

I move a little closer. "And how many of the thirty-seven deaths were tied to the Bovaro family?"

He stares into my eyes, and it seems that for the first time he's noticed their color. "At least . . . at least twenty-five."

I move closer still, so he can feel my breath. "And how many witnesses and family members were being protected because of the Bovaro family?"

He swallows. "No more than two hundred fifty."

I fall back into my seat. I grab the other orange cupcake, break it apart, and shove a piece in my mouth. "That's one in ten, Sean. The odds of my survival are one in ten. Not too good, huh?" I gobble the rest and wipe my fingers on my jeans.

I can feel him staring at me, stuck.

Eventually, I say, "You asked me if I ever get to the point where I feel safe. The answer is *no*."

He reaches over and touches my leg in a way that is not romantic. "C'mon, no one is going to hurt you. We're going to keep you safe."

I wash down the remainder of the orange cake and savor the flavor, as though it may be the last one I ever eat. "Like I said, Sean . . . math never lies."

Cape Charles is just as I imagined: another freaking pit stop. In this case, it's your last chance to take a potty break before crossing the arduous Chesapeake Bay Bridge-Tunnel, a twenty-mile-long combination of bridge spans and tunnel pieces that must be the nightmare of every gephyrophobe and claustrophobe on the planet. If you're going to take a break, this is a good place to take one. Though a bed-and-breakfast or two and a few antique shops give this town character, it still holds no more promise for me than any other two-month layover.

And sure enough, we make our way to the motel with the paper-thin walls and the old radiators. The managers know we are coming and, like always, they are not happy. We walk around the side of the motel and it seems the only thing going for this place is its location right on the bay, with a hundred yards of grainy beach that points toward the bridge spans and the Chesapeake.

The other marshal hands Sean the car keys and gets in the passenger side of another Explorer with a marshal who was waiting for us at the motel. Sean and I watch the vehicle speed away. We are now alone.

As we head toward our rooms, Sean scopes the place, looking around every corner, behind every tree, up every stairwell.

I cannot take my eyes off the water and the stream of cars flowing over the bay, all with a destination, with intent. I'm equally jealous and depressed.

It is mid-May and it seems summer has arrived early in this part of Virginia. A breeze pushes us along to our rooms and it's warmer and more inviting than anyone who works at this dump.

"Listen," Sean says, "are you curious about your last name at all?"

I laugh at him. "Government issue. What is it?"

"Howard."

"Geez, Michelle Howard. You threw me an extra syllable. How lavish."

We reach the door and he hands me my garbage-bag-suitcase, then gives me an additional plastic bag. "You'll need this, too."

"Let me guess. Scissors and hair dye."

"And some other things, but the scissors and dye are the items you'll need to use tonight."

I reach in the bag and pull out the box that has L'Oréal on the label. "Creamy Caramel?"

"It'll match your eyes."

"Probably not better than my natural color."

"Which is what?"

I play with the doorknob to my room. "When I was six, it was sort of blond. It's been dyed ever since. Based on the other hair on my body, I'm guessing it's still blond. Or gray."

He reaches for his doorknob too. "Well, no matter what, I'm sure it will be stunning."

"And stiff."

He smiles and suddenly Matthew McConaughey returns. "I'll

be right over here. You need anything, just tap on the door or poke a hole through the wall or something."

I walk up quickly, stand on my toes, and kiss his cheek. "Thank you, Deputy Marshal Sean Douglas."

He blushes and loses his smile. "Sleep well, M. You're safe with me."

$log_3 (81)$

I INDEED FEEL QUITE SAFE WITH SEAN NEXT DOOR. HIS MERE SIZE— and commitment to acting as a valid protector—are enough to warm the cockles. I drop my head to my pillow and feel a rush of warmth that suggests slumber is a moment away. Even with being in a strange town and a strange bed and my hair now short and stinking of chemicals, I feel safe. Very safe.

But now that there's a knife pressed against my neck? Not so much.

This is the moment I have imagined a hundred times over, the nightmare that has caused me to wet my bed regularly since I was six years old. And the fact that I have lost control of my bladder once again is a reminder that this is not a joke. This is not an exercise.

This is not a dream sequence.

I reach for my neck as anyone in my situation would and suppress my scream just as I've practiced for when this day might come. I cry under my breath, "*Ow.*"

The response I get is odd and unexpected: "Oh, sorry."

The assailant weakens his grip and I touch my neck and feel no blood.

He leans over the bed and whispers in my ear, "I'm gonna let you go. *Do not scream*, do you understand?"

I nod, fast, repeatedly grabbing my neckline in an attempt to find that crimson wetness.

He slowly releases me and steps back. He stays there for an uncomfortably long time and it runs through my mind that this guy may have rape on his mind instead of murder—and, if so, will not be happy when he realizes who's staked out in the next room.

I gingerly slide out of bed and we stand a few feet apart, the only sound a few droplets of bodily fluid running off the edge of my pajama bottoms onto the cold tile floor. Panic subsides. A little.

We are both waiting for something.

"Um," I whisper, "now what?"

I can tell he's trying to look around the room. "Is there a light anywhere?"

I squint, even though it's dark. "A light?"

"Hold on," he says, then fishes through his jacket—very loud leather—and pulls out a tiny flashlight, turns it on, and starts whipping a minuscule beam of light around my scummy motel room. He finds the switch and turns on the lamp.

I stand still—frozen—as he slowly walks in my direction.

"You know who I am?" he asks, no longer whispering. His voice is rich and deep and soulful, and it reminds me of a young Morgan Freeman or a forgotten Baldwin brother. Or a smoker. He steps a little closer and his youth—still older than me, though—becomes immediately apparent. I am hoping his age equates to inexperience.

Then he says, "I'm John Bovaro."

And with those words, I start to shake. My chin wrinkles, my face loses its blood, the room spins. And I am pathetic; the best I can do in my quivering posture is half whisper my guardian's name.

"Sean . . . Sean!"

John smirks and casually points to the bed for me to sit, as though nothing physical—sexual or violent—is on his mind. "If Sean is that clown in the next room, he won't be here too soon. Have a seat."

I gasp and bring my hands to my chest. "*You killed him?*" My knees buckle. No matter how many times you imagine nearing death, you simply cannot prepare.

He laughs and reaches in his pocket for what I imagine is the knife he had to my neck or a loaded gun, but he pulls out a pack of cigarettes, puts one to his mouth, and lights it. "Killed him? No, he's out on the beach, walking the shoreline." He takes a long drag, then turns his head to avoid exhaling in my direction. "He's got his dress pants rolled up like he's going digging for clams. I gotta tell you, that guy's a useless fu—" He glances at me. "Fellow."

I feel like I'm going to fall to the ground and I quickly take him up on his offer to sit on the bed.

He puts the cigarette to his lips and the end glows red. I can actually hear the paper and tobacco burn. "You know what that guy makes a year? About forty thousand. Seriously, what kind of protection is forty thousand gonna get you?"

After a few seconds of sitting, I notice how cold and wet my clothes are, and it appears that all of the nightmares I had as a child were simply dress rehearsals for this final moment.

I garner the strength to look at him but I cannot speak, nor can I stop shaking.

He takes a double drag and holds it and extinguishes the butt on the floor. "I like your hair this way." He exhales from the side of his mouth and a cloud fills the corner of the room.

I look beyond him, at the mirror, and it seems the caramel isn't looking too creamy at the moment. I look like a boy.

He stares at me, as if it's my turn to say something.

All I can offer is the predictable canned line from a million lousy movies: "*What do you want from me?*"

He throws his hands up. "Geez, I don't know. Fifty bucks?" He reaches back into his jacket for his cigarettes and holds them out to me. "How rude of me. Cigarette?"

I swallow. My nervousness fades enough for me to say, "My parents always told me cigarettes would kill me."

He laughs. "The death I can handle. It's the bad breath and yellow teeth I find troublesome."

"Why not try the nicotine gum?" I'm stalling, hoping Sean will hear this conversation and burst through my door—though now I, too, am starting to think he's useless. And should I survive, Sean will receive a long diatribe about what it means to be someone's protector.

"Yeah, I've considered Nicorette, but you can't intimidate someone by snuffing out a chewed piece of gum on his forearm." He chuckles.

This guy is way too cavalier, almost goofy. I rub my eyes and analyze him on the off chance that I may need to remember him for a lineup or a sketch artist. The stupid ones always talk too much.

So I start recording data: deep, raspy voice; wild, green bloodshot eyes; olive skin—as expected; thick black hair—this time Mediterranean instead of Irish—in a short progressive cut; medium nose—no hook; clean-shaven—no, *fresh*-shaven; strong chin; wry smile; full red lips. It hits me that, if you take away the deadly weapon, he's kind of attractive. But here's the odd part, the piece that doesn't match the name Bovaro: black, small-rimmed glasses.

He leans against the dresser before I have a chance to gauge his height but I'm thinking maybe six feet tall, and bulky on top but average from the buckle down. This is the best I can do.

I look away. "John Bovaro," I say, loud enough that if Sean has returned to his room he could hear me. I get not so much as a stir out of the marshal's room. I'm getting pissed off at everybody. "But let me guess, I should call you Johnny? Or is it Little John?"

He adjusts his glasses and says, "Actually, if you really want to know, I prefer Jonathan."

I cannot suppress a giggle. "You've *got* to be kidding."

"I shi—er, kid—you not."

He smiles but it annoys me; with the hair and the glasses and the *Jonathan*, I feel like I'm being threatened by an investment banker.

He scratches his cheek and thinks. Then he reaches over to the chair next to the window and tosses me my robe. "Here. Why don't you slip into something dry." I pause before taking it. "I'm sorry if I scared you."

I stand, put the robe on, turn my back to him and take off my panties and pajama bottoms, close the robe, and pull it tight enough to cut off my circulation.

As I spin back around and sit on the bed, he says, "Can I ask a question?"

"You *may* ask a question."

"I'm gonna cut you a break on the attitude because you're a teacher—*sort of*." He sighs. "How did you know I was on to you back in Maryland?"

I lick my lips and shake my head. "I had no idea who you were until two minutes ago."

He looks down, concerned. "You mean, someone else from my family threatened you?"

"No."

"Then why are you being relocated?"

I hesitate, but I really don't care anymore. "I . . . decided I was bored and needed a change."

He smiles brightly. "You mean . . . you made up a threat to get the government to relocate you and get you a new identity."

I think and nod. "Yeah, pretty much."

"Because you were bored."

I smile a little. "Yeah."

"Stickin' it to the man!" He throws his hand up for a high-five. I slap it, mostly because I have no idea what's going on here. "You're all right, girl. . . . You're all right."

I cross my legs and wiggle my foot a little. "You're not going to kill me, are you."

"*Please*," he says. "If I'd come here to kill you, you'd be fighting rigor mortis and I'd be halfway back to Brooklyn. That fed they got protecting you—what, was he gonna step in and save the day?" He reaches in his pocket and pulls out his Marlboros, stares at them, then puts them back.

"Sean's a good guy," I say, like I'm defending my spouse.

Jonathan looks at me, stern, like he might have changed his mind about slitting my throat. He takes a few steps toward me. "Do you feel safe right now?"

I can't look at him, so I bite my tongue and stare at the floor as I slowly shake my head. "No."

All of a sudden, he flips his wrist over and checks his watch. "Well, I'm afraid we're out of time."

I frown. "Meaning what?"

"Just get a good night's rest. I'll be back for you tomorrow. I just wanted to let you know I was here—and that you'll be leaving with me." He walks to the window, peeks outside, and reaches for the doorknob.

"Wait! What do you mean?"

"What confused you, Melody?"

Hearing my birth name from someone other than a deputy marshal throws me off. He is a real human being in the real world who actually knows who I am, the first person in twenty years to discern the genuine and uninvented me, a superhero recognized without her mask; I feel a subtle pull inside, the rise of a new and inconvenient emotion. "Where, uh . . . where are we going?"

"A road trip." He turns and faces me. "Melody, listen—I promise I am not going to hurt you. But you have to come with me. And we have to move very quickly."

I'm totally muddled, and instead of asking what his intentions are, I say, "What about Sean? What will I tell him?"

"Nothing. Just have breakfast with him and tell him everything is okay."

"But he'll find out about you. He's—"

Jonathan sighs, then waves me over. "Come here." He pushes up one blade of the blinds and points to the water. "Are you telling me that guy is gonna be your hero?"

I stare out the window and watch as Sean sits in the sand, picks up a handful of shells, and gently tosses them into the water.

"He probably just misses his wife," I say. "Marshals need chill time too, you know."

"Sure, but that guy isn't married."

"Yes, he is."

"No, he's not."

"*Yes*, he is."

"*No*, he's *not*, Melody. What, you think only the feds can do research or check someone out before getting involved?"

As I stare at Sean sitting on the shoreline, Jonathan manages to slip out—and he must be good because I never heard a step and I never heard the door close, and if I wasn't confused before, I sure am now.

After stripping the wet sheets and replacing them with a few abrasive blankets, I curl up in bed and play with the straw that has become my hair. I cannot fall asleep. I mean, who's ever heard of a wise guy who wears trendy glasses or makes sure he's not blowing smoke in your direction or genuinely tries to refrain from using profanity in your presence? I couldn't even detect a New York accent.

And at first I imagined that the term *road trip* meant it would be easier to bury me in a field somewhere rather than at the toll plaza for the Bay Bridge-Tunnel, but now I think he might actually be planning to take me somewhere. I just don't know why.

I dissect my situation and though my sensibility suggests that I should knock on the wall and tell Sean about my visitor and be whisked away yet once more, my heart suggests that I have been running for as long as I can remember and that, in some way, I have been waiting all my life for this moment.

For it all to end.

And for some reason I feel free, that I have been in touch with both sides, with the light and the dark of my existence, and that I have somehow managed to find peace. Whether there is validity to this notion is irrelevant; right now, it *feels* valid. I'm not going to destroy it by overanalyzing.

I hop out of bed, undress completely, wash myself clean, and turn up the heat. The old steam radiators burble to life. I pile on the remaining blankets from the closet and slip into bed naked.

This is not a metaphorical womb, but it sure is warm.

I close my eyes and I can feel sleep coming fast. I let go, and the wave lifts me and carries me far, far away.

$$3x = 15$$

SEAN KNOCKS ON MY DOOR AND THOUGH I TRY TO OPEN MY EYES, they ache—apparently the only part of my body lacking moisture; my room is a poor man's sauna and I wake to find myself sprawled nude, lying diagonally across the damp bed, a thin layer of sweat covering me from head to toe, and in all the years of coloring my hair I have never seen it bleed onto the sheets like this. I begin to think I really was murdered last night.

"Hold on," I say, pretty much to myself. I walk to the door and open it textile free; the thought of throwing anything over my body is revolting. I hide the important parts behind the door.

"You okay?" Sean peeks in and the heat rushes out to meet him. "Holy—what, is your heat broken?"

I rub my eyes, hoping to squeeze out a little fluid. "No, it was intentional. Let me turn it off." I close the door—or at least I think I do. I get to the heater and turn the knob and as I look back toward the door, I notice it didn't latch. Sean casts a curious eye. It is either that I met my captor last night and he seemed convincingly nonthreatening or that the heat is making me woozy, but I am slow to cover myself. I smile at Sean and grab my robe on my way back to the door.

"Your wife know you're a peeping Tom?"

"What?"

"You just saw my naked body. Don't pretend you didn't."

"I don't have to—because I did *not* see your naked body. I was looking beyond you at the stain on your sheets." And he's right. The stain was directly behind where I was standing and in the time it took to turn off my heater it would have been impossible for him to scan me and analyze the mess on my sheets.

Miserable seashell-tossing, assassin-ignoring dirtbag.

I quickly throw on the robe and swing open the door, mostly to let the heat out. "That's not blood on the bed. It's your government-grade, over-the-counter hair color."

I turn around and walk into the room and Sean follows me. I look in the mirror and stare in horror at the reflection. My creamy caramel looks like someone left it on a dashboard on a sunny summer day. Sean looks over my shoulder and grimaces a little.

"Interesting," he says.

I bite my tongue.

"Have you ever had your life stripped out from beneath you?" I ask. "Ever been forced to change your clothes, your name, your address—and your hair color and style—all at the behest of some clod who claims to be your guardian?"

Sean stares at me, or rather my hair, clearly with no intention of answering. His silence vexes me.

I think for a second, then try to provoke him with my insider info. "I guess I can't expect you to understand that kind of thing on forty grand a year."

Sean's eyes move about in confusion. "I have no idea what relationship income has to comprehension, but I make a little over fifty-three thousand."

Never trust your captor.

"So," he adds, looking around my room in a surveillance-oriented way, "you sleep well last night?"

I turn to him and smile widely. "Like a baby."

He nods, continues his inspection. "Well, that's what we're trained to do: bring security."

"Sean, I can tell you that you managed to bring a whole new level to my idea of security and safety last night. You're really in command of this situation." His eyes cease wandering and land on my face. "I need to shower."

Sean nods and inspects the bathroom, comes back out and says, "I'll wait right here," and flops down on the sofa next to the bed.

I walk toward the bathroom and check, from the corner of my eye, to see if he is watching me. My robe is short enough that its magnetic pull might have the required strength to drag his eyes my way, but I get nothing. I slow my pace. More nothing. I sigh and drop my head, for just once I would love to be pursued for something other than being murdered or the prevention thereof.

I close the bathroom door and run the shower. The head sputters a few times, then red-brown droplets begin to fall from the multi-decade–old shower massage. I'm certain the Chinese could never have contrived a water torture this slow and painful and overly chlorinated.

I drop my robe and look at my sighing body in the mirror. It seems I am starting to sag all over, which I want to blame on getting closer to thirty, but it might just as well be from sadness or lack of use. The last time a man had his hands on it was three name changes ago, when I shed my common sense and consumed a third gin and tonic—one too many, as it turned out. In a local bar outside Lawrenceburg, Kentucky, I managed to convince this man—a man whose name I never acquired, by the way—that I was sexy and dangerous and ready to ignite.

He believed my lie.

All I'd wanted was a kiss. I wanted to feel the way my parents did when I was young. I cannot recall a moment, before that fateful day at Vincent's, when my parents would see each other that they did not embrace and kiss, whether it was after a business trip or having just come back from the kitchen. Whenever they slept, they would be entwined in a manner suggesting they wanted to be part of each other for every moment of their lives, awake and otherwise. With all of the discussions I've had with federal marshals about being secure, I cannot convey to them the veritable security my parents brought to me through their ardent love. But they were emotionally long gone by that point, their immediate affection slowly destroyed by that unexpected encounter with Tony Bovaro. They managed to get through the tough times—the initial move and the few others after that—but eventually I watched their love turn a dull gray. The constant failure—*my* constant failure and inability to be true to our fiction—destroyed my parents. They became distant. They became untwined. Their bodies were eventually separate on the bed, equidistant even in their movements, like two human wipers on a satin windshield.

Their broken hearts eventually broke mine.

I managed to categorize all their lessons of love and harbor them deep inside, ready to recall them whenever in need. My mother told me you end up making love long before you think, that the act should be reserved for your one true love, but that so should the first kiss, because the first time you kiss is the first time you open your body up to someone else, the unprecedented moment when someone else is inside you. And after watching my parents all those countless times, watching as they would take each other by the hand and smile while gazing into each other's eyes, pulling each other closer, and—then the real magic—the closing of the eyes, and finally, as if by command or celestial force, their lips would slowly, softly meet and they would push against one another until the act had produced the sufficient and expected ecstasy.

All I'd wanted from Nameless Guy was a kiss.

I'd wanted a chance to feel love, no matter how temporary or imaginary.

The gin was talking. Screaming.

We managed to make it back to his place and we weren't in the door two minutes before I could read his libidinous mind. I wanted that slow-motion attack, the gazing, the eye fade, the lips, the pressing.

This guy quick-stepped it over to me and instead of a brief embrace or a longing look, he grabbed my left breast and started swirling his finger around searching for my nipple, as though my boob was actually his sixth martini. I nudged his hand out of the way and hugged him, mostly to give him an opportunity to start again.

He backed off and made a little progress by kissing my neck lightly, running his fingers through my hair. Then he whispered my name—or what my name was at the time. "*Shelly* . . ."

I let him do it a few times, hoping it might work for me, but having paired my bogus name with his traversing my chest, along with the dreaded effects of the alcohol, I said this: "Call me . . . *Melody*."

Somehow, this made me naughty.

Nameless Guy pulled back, smiled at me, and moaned softly. Then, suddenly returning to his impassioned search for one of my nipples, he muttered, "Yeah, babe . . . call me . . . Steeeeve."

Now I still consider him nameless because of the *way* he said *Steve*, like it was this highly forbidden thing. And the truth is, what bothered me most wasn't that he was creepy, asking me to whisper some different name, but that he somehow found the name *Steve* to be lurid. It was throwing me off. I kept thinking, "Steve?" I mean, who was he fantasizing he was? Steve Carell? Steve Austin? *Steve* Buscemi? Each possibility was worse than the last.

My interest was quickly retreating and, though sobering, I had just enough alcohol in me to say something totally moronic. "No, I want you to call me Melody because it's my real name."

He smiled and moaned again and said, "Yeah, baby, I'll call you Melody if you want."

I pushed him off but his hand remained superglued to my chest. You'd think he was searching for a wire or a wad of twenties.

"My name is Melody."

He shook his head. "You told me your name was Shelly." He laughed a little. "C'mon, no one names their kid Melody."

I took a deep breath and straightened out my clothes. "My parents did."

His tone changed as the mood of romance decidedly vanished. "Get real."

Then I walked up to him, grabbed his chest in an effort to twist *his* nipple, but it turns out those things are actually pretty hard to find. I poked him a couple times instead.

"I *am* real," I said. "My name is Melody, as in Melody Grace McCartney, you jerk."

I grabbed my purse and bolted for the door and just as I was about to slam it behind me I heard Nameless Guy say, "Oh, man. . . . You were the little girl from the Bovaro murder trial."

I froze. Even in my alcoholic haze I knew what I'd done.

Nameless Guy fumbled around for a minute, then came lunging at the door with a disposable camera. "Can I take one picture, please? Just for me, to show the guys at work?"

I ran from Nameless Guy's apartment—and, in fact, ran for two days straight, flanked by two federal marshals and a pile of paperwork and promises for a better life. And within a month of my drunken flirtation, Farmington, New Mexico, became my new home.

But I am here now, looking at how my body is fading in the now steamy mirror in my crappy motel room in Cape Charles,

Virginia, wanting so desperately to be loved and touched, to find that man to take my hands, draw me to him, close his eyes, press his lips to mine, and lose himself—and pull me with him—in that sensual oblivion. I want to be unconditionally loved for who I am and to feel him find his way inside me because I am open to him, and I want to feel us push and pull and push and pull and get lost in each other in a way that, through all of my twenty-six years of living, I have yet to experience.

So, yes, I want to be loved for who I am.

And I wonder if I will ever know who I am—or what it means just to *be myself*.

And I wonder if I can ever surrender myself when I am not sure who I am surrendering.

I take a long shower, not because I need the time or enjoy the sensation, but because the droplets are coming down in decreasing speed, like whatever is causing the clog in the showerhead is the water itself. I dry myself and play with my hair and all I smell is chlorine and minerals. I have no perfume, no scented soaps, no body lotion—nothing to reaffirm my femininity except the Mitchum invisible stick I tossed into my garbage bag.

Try as I might to look like a woman, the best I can manufacture is a middle-schooler. My fingernails and toenails are chipped of their polish and a third of my fingernails are broken. My hair is short and spiky no matter what I do to it, and there is no conditioner in my government-issue bag of goodies. No eyeliner, no mascara, no blush. Why didn't I pack these items that are so crucial to the existence of a woman? Because when you are on the run—for real—you would not make time to pack them, or much else, for that matter; anything beyond clothing might seem suspect to the Marshals Service.

So I look like a boy. Again.

I slip on a fresh pair of jeans—one of the few items I did bring with me (the only pair that has fit me this well in the last five years)—and a tight blue cotton T-shirt that is more functional than suggestive.

I walk out of the bathroom and Sean is missing. A slight tingling runs through me at the thought that Jonathan forced his way into my room and was caught off guard at the presence of the marshal—a notion that in retrospect seems unlikely—and that he dragged Sean's bloody, limp body to the Chesapeake.

So I am not surprised when I find Jonathan next to the side of the bed, out of view of the bathroom.

He covers his eyes and asks, "Are you decent?"

I move over to the bed and stick my hands in the pockets of my jeans, annoyed by the constant switching of men in my room. "You're very polite for a captor, you know that?"

He peeks out of the corner of his eye. "We have to leave *now*."

Nervous perspiration begins to pool on my body; I'm miffed since I just showered. "Today is the last day of the rest of my life."

He sighs and steps closer to me. "I promised I wouldn't hurt you, didn't I?"

"Yes, but you're a liar. I've known you for just a few minutes and you've already lied to me."

"What did I lie about?"

"You told me Sean makes forty thousand a year. He makes fifty-three."

He frowns and reaches for his cigarettes. "Perhaps you missed my point, Melody. You feel any safer with him knowing he makes an extra thirteen K a year?"

Fair enough.

He lights one up and adds, "Pay a guy a half mil a year and you'll get real protection."

"Is that what you guys charge for protection?"

"Bite me."

"The President of the United States is guarded by guys that make the same amount as Sean, you know."

"The President is guarded by *ten* guys that make what your deputy makes. So we're right back at a half mil." He glances at me. "I find it entertaining that you call your little clam-digging friend Sean, instead of marshal or deputy."

"We have a . . . sort of . . . connection."

He laughs and tries to muffle his voice, as though Sean might be around the corner. "Yeah, well, expect to get disconnected very soon."

I roll my eyes. "Are you going to tell me what's going on? And where is Sean?"

"Sean is . . . delayed. He's having a bit of, um, tummy trouble."

I inhale a lungful of side-stream smoke. It feels good, actually. "Is that some inane metaphor for having sliced his stomach to pieces?"

He slouches in my direction, like he's disappointed in me. "Now, does that seem like my style?"

"What do I know? It was definitely your dad's style."

He quickly looks away. "Yeah, well, that's sort of why I'm here."

"Your daddy send you on an errand?"

He stares at his cigarette and extinguishes it instead of taking another drag. Eventually, he looks up at me and his eyes sag and it seems I've genuinely hurt his feelings. I'm guessing poor Jonathan might have some issues with his father. I can only imagine.

He stops looking me in the eye.

"Meet me out front in five minutes," he says, staring at the floor, his voice weakened. "And be alone." He heads for the door.

"Wait! Should I bring my stuff?"

Jonathan scoffs. "*What* stuff?"

He grabs the door and pulls it behind him and though I expect a slam, he closes it so gently that I never hear the click of the latch.

If you ever find yourself getting ready to go on the run—or in WITSEC, even—the best advice I can give you is to go to the bathroom first. Between nerves and unplanned fluid consumption, you'll wish you had taken the requisite thirty seconds to do your business.

This leaves me four and a half minutes.

I have nothing to take. Again. No photos or memorabilia. No clothes, except the pee-stained and sweat-soaked clothes from yesterday, which will not be making the journey. So this is everything about who I am: a T-shirt, a pair of jeans, a bra, a pair of panties, and a pair of abused sandals.

Nothing but the Clothes on My Back: A Memoir.

I have three minutes and for some reason I'm playing with my hair—and not from nervousness; who knows why, but I'm trying to make it look good.

I am officially losing my mind.

I have two minutes and out of some real fear and last-second panic, I bolt from my room and start banging on Sean's door. I get no answer but I can hear him coughing and retching somewhere deeper inside.

I have thirty seconds left and Sean, apparently, will not be saving the day. And here's the kicker: I don't try any harder to give him the opportunity. I know that behind this motel door resides the same answer, the same solution, the same level of commitment and concern for my welfare that I've been using as a feckless crutch for almost my entire life.

I stop knocking.

I loosen my fist and drop my hand to my side and lumber up to the front of the motel, where I find Jonathan sitting in the driver's seat of a cherry red, late-model Audi S4 convertible. With the top down.

I slow my pace.

He smiles, and though he's wearing sunglasses, I'm pretty sure he just winked at me.

I stare at him and say, "Why not just paint a target on the back?"

He waves me over to the car. "Meaning what?"

"Meaning I cannot think of a more conspicuous way for you to get me out of here."

"What do I care? I've committed no crime, at least none that would concern the pukemeister back there. And besides, I'm not holding a gun to your head or a knife to your throat. You're coming willingly."

"Wh—are you kidding? The gun or knife is implied, Jonathan."

"I specifically told you I would not hurt you."

"And I specifically told you I perceive you to be a liar." I take a few steps closer and touch the car. It is hot from the sun and the smell of the warm leather keeps me still. "Besides you *did* have a knife to my throat not too long ago, remember?"

He laughs. "You mean this?" He reaches in his jacket and pulls out a Montblanc pen. "Hop in."

I bite my lip and gaze over my shoulder, back toward the motel, looking for a sign from Sean, for a reason to stay, for any notion that this time, this relocation, this persona, will be different.

I get nothing more than a cool, salty breeze.

I gulp as I open the car door and slowly ease my way down on the seat. It fits like a glove.

"I'm not really dressed for riding with the top down," I say. "I mean, you've got a jacket and sweater on and I—"

"Wait." He reaches behind his seat and grabs a mangled shopping bag and hands it to me. "I crossed over that monstrous bridge-tunnel thing last night and picked up some clothes for you. I figured you weren't going to have much." He turns away and swallows. "I hope these are your style. I was guessing you were about a six?"

I almost correct him. "You . . . bought me clothes?"

"Yeah, Norfolk's not even an hour from here. I did a little power-shopping last night."

I reach into the bag and remove a dark green cotton sweater; the texture and quality are something I have never been able to afford or enjoy while working low-income jobs. The color is something I would not have picked for myself, but suddenly it is the most beautiful thing I have ever seen.

Jonathan watches me bring the sweater to my face and rub the cotton against my cheek and breathe in the smell of the fabric. I can feel him staring.

"It matches your eyes," he says.

I do not return his gaze, but slowly pull my face from the cloth. "You've seen me for just a few minutes of my life and you know my dress size and the color of my eyes?"

Never in all my relocations had a marshal ever taken such notice. And the best I can do with Sean is get some cheap hair color, a travel-sized bottle of shampoo, and a bar of Lever 2000.

He clears his throat and looks at his watch. "I got you a bunch more stuff in the trunk, but we need to get going."

The sun shines hard and the black leather is holding the heat. I sink down a little and drape the sweater over my chest, like a blanket. Part of me wants to turn around and see if Sean is behind us—mostly to make sure we're out of reach—but I just close my eyes and Jonathan accelerates and my body presses against the back of the seat and gravel flies from under all four wheels and the air rushes all around us, harder and harder, and as we blend with the traffic I feel oddly whole.

For the first time in twenty years I am not running. Because I am captured.

I have never felt freer than I do right now.

The wind whips over my face and for a moment my hair feels long and beautiful and I imagine it is flowing behind me like a silk scarf.

Jonathan weaves in and out of the cars well above the speed limit, showing absolutely no concern for police attention. His strange confidence warms me.

He keeps one hand on the wheel and one on the stick and it seems both are in constant motion. For whatever reason, I cannot take my eyes off of him.

He catches me and smiles, then reaches under his seat and pulls out a small case full of CDs and hands it to me. "Pick anything you can listen to at top volume."

I smile and begin to unzip the pouch. "What do we have here? Bach? Mozart?"

"Sinatra. Bennett."

I laugh, but believe him. He lied to me again. I flip through the collection and am once more surprised—and confused. Beth Orton, Coldplay, Aimee Mann, Guster, Frou Frou, Keane, Finn Brothers, Glen Phillips, Jack Johnson.

"You're a pretty mellow guy," I say.

He shrugs a little. "I have my moments."

I turn to the last slot in the case and remove *Hot Fuss* by the Killers and wave it in front of him.

"Funny," he says, snatching it from my hands and pushing it in the player.

And for the next hour the car is screaming up the conifer-lined highway and so is the music and the wind is tugging my hair and the sun is making me melt and Jonathan keeps steering and shifting and passing and zipping side to side and all I know is that we are driving north and I have no idea where we are heading but I hope and pray this road will never end.

●   ●   ●

I stir from a deep sleep at the same time a sign that reads BAL-TIMORE 14 comes into focus; I've been asleep for hours. I rub my eyes and clear my throat. The music is gone.

I yell above the din of the wheels, "Are you taking me back to Columbia?" It seems like something that should have come up by now.

Jonathan merely shakes his head. "We're going home—to *my* home."

I sit up a little. I'm not sure I understood what he just told me. "What do you mean?"

He looks at me, then back to the road. "Home. My home."

I'm dumbfounded. "Please tell me you live in Pennsylvania."

He smiles, then laughs, then takes his hands from the steering wheel and waves them in the air. "New York City, baby. The Big Apple!"

My life flashes before my eyes.

My lives flash before my eyes.

I yank up on the parking brake and grab the steering wheel and suddenly we're slipping and spiraling about the highway and as the car comes to a stop on the shoulder, still on all four wheels, it occurs to me that the Germans produce some fine engineers.

Cars skid around us and the inevitable sounds of screeching tires and car horns reach our ears.

Jonathan catches his breath, then screams, "Are you out of your *mind*?"

I turn off the car and pull the key from the ignition. "Why are you taking me to New York?" Jonathan stares at me like there's something he needs to say but is not quite ready. "What's the matter, can't handle the wet work yourself? Need a big brother or an uncle to do the—" I inhale sharply and narrow my eyes at him.

"That *is* it, isn't it?" I laugh to myself. "Oh, you were so clever with your '*I'm* not going to hurt you. I promise *I* won't hurt you.'"

He looks down, still breathing heavily. "You've got me all wrong, Melody."

The Bovaros have destroyed my life, killed my parents, sucked every ounce of hope out of me. I want to hate Jonathan—I want to *destroy* him—but I can't. Despite the fact that he's some vague threat to my life, he's also the only person who has any authentic interest in me, in who I am.

And he calls me Melody; hearing my birth name acts like a tenderizer.

People slowly drive by and stare.

Jonathan lowers himself in the driver's seat, still panting, and it seems he has never been this close to death before, which I find odd. He slowly raises a hand and says, "Hear me out, okay?"

I glare at him a few seconds longer, to sort of make a point, then I look away and pull the sweater to my face again. It is the first gift I have received in ten years. I decide to cut him a little slack.

"I'm listening."

He wipes his face free of perspiration and says, "You want to grab a bite? Let's get a table and talk." Some guy blows his horn and gives us the finger. "There's a great restaurant not too far from here."

"You know this area?"

"It's a great place to bury people, well distanced from New York. The dirt is loose and moist, so it's easy to dig."

He doesn't laugh.

"My nerves are shot . . . but I guess I should try to eat something."

He puts out his hand and I reluctantly hand him the keys. He grabs the keys and my hand at the same time. "You're safe with me, Melody. Okay? As long as I am with you, you are safe."

I nod a little and stare at the road ahead. "This great restaurant have any wine? I need something to help me relax."

He starts the car and pulls onto the highway. "A restaurant can't be considered great if it does not have wine."

There was a part of me that was hoping Jonathan would blow my mind once again and take me to a Thai restaurant, but for the first time in the brief period of our acquaintance, he was true to the cliché.

We're sitting in an Italian restaurant somewhere deep inside the city of Baltimore but not in the neighborhood referred to as Little Italy. The background music is a boring mélange of crooners. And though the place is a messy hole-in-the-wall, there is something that makes it feel like we've been welcomed into the home of a large family.

We are the first customers for lunch.

After being seated in a far corner of the restaurant, significantly distanced from the kitchen, the waiter offers us menus, but Jonathan pushes them to the side. "Allow me to order for you, Melody."

I make a face.

"I don't mean to offend," he adds, "but I believe I know what you'd like."

I turn to the waiter and say, "We've been dating now for about two hours." I cross my fingers. "We're tight!"

Jonathan apparently takes this as a green light. "She will have the rabbit, very rare, in red wine. Three orders again, honey?"

I roll my eyes.

He starts over. "Okay, she will have . . ." He stares at me until I stare back, then he puts his elbows on the table and leans in my direction. "She will have the carpaccio of beef with watercress and garlic aioli and eggplant croquettes and I will have the veal chops with lemon sage sauce and the risotto with arugula and goat's cheese."

I can't suppress a smile. "Beef was a risk, Jonathan. So was eggplant. Especially for lunch."

"Did I fail?"

I study him for a moment and I wish we were anywhere but the wrong place at the wrong time. "Not yet."

He smiles back, then turns to the waiter and adds, "You have Medici Ermete Concerto Reggiano Lambrusco?" The waiter nods. "A bottle."

I laugh.

"What," he says, flipping his hands out.

"Lambrusco. Highly predictable, not to mention cheesy."

"Not *this* Lambrusco. You didn't hear me order Riunite, did you? This bottle is much drier. Besides, this is wine for drinking with food, you know. It should be a little sugary, a little sweet, a little fizzy maybe, and not only bring the flavor of the food to life, but help wash it down. I love fine wine—and if you ever want to go head-to-head on the subject, prepare for defeat—but I prefer to drink it when my palate is going to stay clean and sharp. With food, especially Italian? Different story."

Jonathan grins and it seems he starts to blush, then he looks down and clears his throat. He picks up his knife and tilts it back and forth between his fingers, very gently, and I cannot imagine him ever taking one and plunging it into someone's chest. But no matter what, it is impossible for me to forget who he is. Or where he is from. Or why he is now in my life.

I take a deep breath and sit up. "You wanted to talk."

Jonathan puts his knife down and sits back and it appears he is going to tell me how it is. I've been waiting my whole life.

"Do you wonder," he says, "how it is that I knew what was on this menu without even taking a glance?"

I shrug. "Photographic memory?"

He leans forward again and speaks in a hushed tone. "We are the only customers in this restaurant because they are not open yet, and will not open for another hour. We were given the best table in the restaurant because they would not give me anything less. We will sit and eat a delicious meal, the finest they will prepare today, and we will drink a bottle of wine, and when we are done with our dessert and cannot finish another bite, we will get up and walk out of the restaurant without paying a penny."

I shake my head in disgust. "Should I be impressed?"

"You should be *concerned*, Melody." He leans forward even farther and progresses to a slightly angered voice. "I'm trying to show you the depth of my family's influence, okay? People think you can run away to Tennessee or Ohio, but the truth is we have a presence in those places too. I mean, do you really think there are all of these Italian families vying for the same chunk of business in Manhattan and Brooklyn? Get real. Forget the Mafia, what about the damn Russians or the Chinese or the Dominicans? The fu—*lousy* street gangs are tapping into what used to be our exclusive interests. It's like a cold war." He thinks for a second. "Kind of."

"So you move to the suburbs like everyone else, bringing all your crime and misery with you."

He takes off his glasses and rubs his eyes. "You're missing the central issue here. You can't hide, Melody. The deputy marshals they assign to you cannot move you far enough away. We could have snatched you long ago."

The waiter drops a basket of warm bread on the table and shows the bottle of wine to my Italian friend. Jonathan nods, puts his glasses back on, and says, "I'll pour, thank you," and the waiter leaves as though it's the response he was expecting.

Jonathan takes my glass and slowly allows the wine to leave the bottle and gently splash down, somehow preventing any air from gulping back in.

He explains his actions as if he were reading my mind. "This keeps the sediment in the bottle," he says. "I don't want you to have any excuse for denying the greatness of this vino."

I am about to comment when I recall his previous statement. "What did you mean when you said you could have snatched me long ago?"

He looks up and sighs, continues pouring. "I've been keeping an eye on you for years." He pulls the bottle from the rim of my glass, turns it slightly to avoid a drip, and lifts. He tosses this information to me casually, and though it seems innocent, I know he realized the gravity of the comment—and he does not flinch.

My chin quivers and my breathing becomes erratic. "What . . . what do you mean?"

He stares at me for a second, takes his glass and fills it with wine in three seconds, then downs two huge mouthfuls. He whispers, "Jane Watkins. Shelly Jones. Linda Simms. Sandra Clarke." My teeth are clattering like I'm naked in the snow. He takes another drink. "You want me to tell you the kinds of jobs you've had? The places you used to get coffee in the morning? Your favorite restaurants?"

The only thing worse than living a lie is living a lie for no reason whatsoever.

"That's how you knew my size . . . and my eye color, and the kinds of food I like, and what you meant that first night you came into my motel room and said, 'I like your hair this way.' You knew me. You've known me all along."

I stare Jonathan down; he tries to wait me out but he can't, and the steel that he exemplified a moment ago is starting to break back down into iron and carbon. He spins the wine in his glass, but I think it's an act of nervousness or embarrassment rather than a way to aerate his wine.

There is a new truth in my life: No matter how incredibly slight I may have found my security over the years, not a single notion

was true. I've been at risk all along, and all the moving and changing and fear and carefulness was for nothing.

Nothing.

The food arrives, so I pull myself together, snapping out of
the chilly daze I've been in for the last five minutes. The scents of
our dishes collide, and it trips my senses. I realize I'm hungry and
without hesitation I reach for my fork. If this is going to be my last
meal, I can't complain.

Jonathan stares at me while moving his fork in and out of his
risotto. "Aren't you curious as to why I was watching you all these
years?"

I ignore him, as I have been since he unfolded this new truth in
my life, and start going to town on the beef. I skewer a nice forkful
and bring it to my mouth. I am amazed—I will probably throw it
up soon, but I am still amazed. I scoop up a few croquettes, chew
them and swallow them, and I feel I might die before any Bovaro
gets the chance to do the deed.

Jonathan answers his own question. "I was there."

My chewing slows. "Where?"

"At Vincent's."

My chewing stops.

"You should try the risotto," he says, pushing his plate to my
side of the table.

I push it back. "*When* were you there?" I ask through a mouth-
ful of watercress.

He looks down and sighs. "That Sunday morning when my
dad was gutting Jimmy 'the Rat' Fratello."

I'm speechless.

Jonathan laughs a little and adds, "Turns out Jimmy really was
a rat. Which is why he got, uh . . . you know."

I keep my eyes locked on Jonathan's, but I manage to fill my glass with more wine. I do not care about sediment.

"You're about to tell me some tragic news," I say.

Jonathan sits up, puts his fork down, and takes a long, loud drink from his water glass. "I was there with my dad." He nods a little. "The kids in the family were always kind of around. I mean, where could we go, really." He takes a jerky, nervous breath. "I was supposed to stay upstairs and play with my cousins in a big billiards room on the third floor of Vincent's place. You know, normally us little guys weren't allowed to touch the pool tables for fear we'd rip the felt or something, so it was supposed to be this big deal for us to hang upstairs while my father and Jimmy did a little business.

"Well, I thought my dad was the greatest, you know? Like any kid, I guess. So I wanted to see what he did for a living. I figured he was in the restaurant business. I mean, we were always eating in the best places and we could always pick whatever table we wanted and order whatever food we wanted and we never had to pay and stuff . . ." He wipes his forehead of sweat. "Well . . . I snuck down when no one was looking and tried to catch a glimpse of his high-business dealings."

He pauses and I am about to leap across the table and beat the rest out of him. I try to finish his thought. "You saw him slicing up Jimmy Fratello?"

Jonathan throws me for a loop by grabbing his fork, piling up a huge mound of risotto, and taking a bite. "No . . . actually, I saw my dad and Jimmy just talking. It was pretty boring, really. I watched for a while but lost interest, so I walked down the hallway and went outside." He pokes at his veal as though he might begin slicing, then tosses his utensils on the table. "I remember that day: it was cold and dark outside. I stood in the alley next to Vincent's and just stared at the gray sky." He looks at me and purses his lips.

"Until I stopped to watch this guy try to parallel-park his Oldsmobile." He chuckles. "I swear it had to be his first time."

I hold my breath for a second. "My dad," I say. "He couldn't parallel-park to save his life." I wish I hadn't put it that way. I start nodding. "You saw my dad."

"And your mom and . . . *you.*" He smiles at me. "You had the cutest blond curls." He takes another bite. "I think that's the last time I ever saw you with blond hair. Anyway, a few seconds later you all come screaming down the sidewalk, hop in your car, and zoom off."

I have completely lost my appetite. I slide my dishes and the wine bottle to the side so there is little between Jonathan and me. I lean on the table and Jonathan does too.

"Sean told me," I say, "that the police got there long after the crime, and that he had no idea how the feds found my parents—or how they even knew there were witnesses at all." I squint and point a weak finger in his direction. "It was *you.*"

Jonathan sighs. "What can I say? I wanted to be a grown-up and big and important like my father. I had no idea it was my dad that killed Jimmy. I didn't even really know what killing *was* yet." He looks at me but it seems like a struggle. "When the cops were asking everyone on the street if anyone saw anything, I stepped up to bat, told the cops I saw a family run out of the restaurant."

"And you magically knew our address?"

"No. But I did notice your license plates were from Jersey and I remembered two numbers and a letter. And that the car was an Olds." He shrugs. "Apparently, it was enough."

The beef and eggplant feel like they are on the rise.

"So," I say, festering, "*you* are the one who brought all of this pain and misery and destruction into my life. *You* are the one who is responsible for my parents' deaths!" I stand a little. "The most I would have had to deal with was post-traumatic stress disorder and some minor therapy. I still would've had parents and proms and friends and birthday parties and a heritage and something to look forward to!"

"Melody, I was ten years old—just a few years older than you." He's looking at me and pleading with his eyes and for a second he seems like he's still ten years old. "Do you have any idea what this did to *my* family?"

"*I do not care.*"

"I turned my own father in—not intentionally, of course—but I did it!"

"Your father is a sick bastard! Who wants a dad who eviscerates people?" I flop back down in my seat.

"My dad wasn't Jeffrey Dahmer. It wasn't *all* weird." Jonathan lowers his voice. "I mean, he was still my dad, the guy who took me to Yankee games and taught me how to throw a football. He taught me about food and wine and how to live a good life. He wasn't the typical dago, with his Friday-night wife and his Saturday-night girlfriend. We attended a Catholic church and he cried when I made my first communion. He cheered me on when I hit a homer in Little League and consoled me when I blew a critical double play. He was a *real* dad. To me, at least."

"You don't get it, Jonathan. I didn't have a chance to play Little League or dance ballet or anything else. We were always trying to stay hidden and out of sight. My dad might have taught me how to toss a ball if he hadn't been so worried about one of us getting plucked off on the way back from the mailbox!"

"Look, Melody, I am not comparing my parents to yours. My point is that my family—and this business we're in—makes people do bad things. But the bottom line is *it's business.*"

"My family never did anything to the Bovaro clan."

"Your parents testified."

"And if they hadn't?"

Jonathan snatches his fork and starts eating. That is his answer.

I watch him for a moment and as his chewing comes to a regular pace, I realize he is in for the long haul. I start eating again too.

The food is truly noteworthy and I do not deny that, as Jonathan suggested, the kitchen staff nervously prepared this meal with the greatest of care, and it is a decided plus to be eating here on this day with a notable Bovaro. This leads me to a thought.

"Where do you rank in your family?"

Keeping his eyes on his food, Jonathan chews and inhales at the same time. "Not high."

"Why?"

He licks his teeth a little and looks up. "The fact that I indirectly turned my father in to the cops embarrassed my family greatly."

I frown. "How sad."

"You can make fun, but the truth is, the only way I could earn back the trust of my family, of my peers, was to correct the . . . mistake."

I squint and play with my wineglass. "Correct it how?"

"In order for me to regain my honor, I needed to kill you and your parents." We stare at each other. "Most kids are worried about getting their driver's license at sixteen; I was worried about rubbing out three people."

My hand finds my utensils and suddenly I'm thankful Jonathan ordered me beef. A sharper knife, you see. I am going to thrust it into the side of his neck. "*You* killed my parents?"

"No . . . but I tried." He drops his head and wipes his face. He looks back at me and says, "I was supposed to do the killings, but I didn't have the stones. I had your folks in my sight and I pointed the gun but I couldn't pull the trigger. I tried and I tried but I couldn't make it happen."

I use all the energy I can gather to stay in control. "So who did?"

"My older cousin, who was with me for backup—and sort of a witness, to tell the guys back home. He just . . . pushed me out of the way and snapped off a round of bullets. Then he took me back to the car and beat the crap out of me."

"Why'd he do that?"

"Because I failed. I failed my family once again. It was like there was no way to honor them."

I give him time to complete his thought, but I can no longer take the gap in silence. "Except . . . by killing *me*."

He looks at me and after a long period of silence, he nods. "I kept going to wherever you'd moved and . . . waited." He leans in my direction. "I could never do it, Melody. Never. I mean, sure, I used to rough guys up at home once in a while. It's the way things are handled in our business, but please believe me: I could never—*will* never—hurt you."

I calm, finally, at the notion that I might really have nothing to fear with this guy. "What did you tell your family every time you came back empty-handed?"

"That I couldn't find you."

"But . . . what made you keep coming back? Why didn't you just say you had no idea where I was in the first place unless you really had some intention of killing me?"

Jonathan leans forward and softly takes my hand. The fact that this man's bloodline is directly linked to the death of my parents and the miserable life I've led should make me cringe—but for some inexplicable reason, I don't. I close my eyes and curl my fingers around his as though he has gained control of my nervous system.

"To make sure you were okay, Melody."

"I was never okay, Jonathan."

He squeezes my hand tighter and says, "You are now."

And with that simple statement, his urgency and his presence in my life begin to unfold.

"But now you're here. No longer hiding." I say this very slowly: "Why?"

He watches me closely, tries to read my reaction. His grip on my hand becomes firm, a clear transition from affection to something else, though not restraint. "Because they finally found you."

I look down and ingest the information. "Your family?"

"Someone in our organization; I don't know who."

I look at my hand in his, how small my fingers are in his fist. I'm not sure why, but I do not consider trying to run. Even if I did, Jonathan offers me a reason to stay.

"You're safer with me than the feds, Melody." He slowly releases his grip and sits back. "My family didn't have to try hard to find you. The information was given to them."

"What do you mean? By who?"

"I'm not entirely sure, but the information they had was completely accurate." He sighs. "And if you believe it's possible for a good guy to be in the Mafia, you must also believe that it's possible for a bad guy to be in the Justice Department, so the converse is true."

I am so effete from being disarmed, I'm numb. I stare into the distance. "Actually, it's not a converse, or an inverse, or a contrapositive, or any other geometric derivative. Your statement was just a mess of attempted logic. But I get the point." He laughs a little and returns to his risotto. I watch him eat. "Why am I safer with you?"

He swallows and thinks before answering, "My family will kill you if they find you alone. My family will *not* kill you if they find you with me. And if you're with a fed or anyone else?" He shrugs.

"But why? Why do they want me dead? You know how many times I sat in my bedroom and imagined that all of my running was for nothing, that you guys had forgotten who I even was? I mean, what damage could I possibly do to your family? The government lost all the cases that involved my parents' testimony."

He licks his lips and takes a swig of wine. "I don't mean this to sound casual, but they don't want any loose ends. You never know when the feds will try to build some other case where your testimony may be useful—or even critical. It's just easier if you're gone."

I close my eyes and drop my head. "Just like that, huh?"

Jonathan puts down his fork and takes my hand, as gently as he had a moment ago, though this time my fingers are lifeless. Jonathan whispers, "I will protect you, Melody. *Trust me.*"

I open my eyes and realize there is no way to turn this around. Before, there was one good guy and one bad guy; now I'm lost in a world of distrust and corruption and the odds of my survival have slipped to about one in a thousand. The only person left I can trust is myself—and I have no idea who I am.

Eventually, I stop playing with my fork and begin using it. My stomach is a knot of stress but the quality and flavor of the food ensures that it will be consumed. In silence, we finish our meals and slurp down espresso, both without room for even the smallest cannoli. My stomach has not been this full and my palate this content in, well, ever.

And, as Jonathan predicted, the waiter never brings the check.

I allowed myself the luxury of this fine food, but as it's clear it's time to leave, I return to my original dilemma.

"What are you planning to do with me once we get to New York?"

Jonathan starts playing with the spring-operated ignition key for the Audi. "I, uh . . . I want to take you back to my family and introduce you to them."

I fall back in my seat. "You've *got* to be kidding. This is your plan?"

"Hear me out, okay?"

"I might as well jam this knife in my gut right now."

"Hear me out."

"Spare me some misery and just tie me to the bumper of your car."

"Melody, just wa—"

"Talk about a death sentence!"

"Melody!" He waves his arms wildly, as though he's trying to get my attention from across a crowded room. "Nobody is killing anybody, okay? If you are with *me*, you are safe."

"That's the same thing the feds say."

"Yeah, well, you just made my point."

I shake my head in half-disgust / half-amazement and give him the floor. "Let's hear your brilliant scheme."

He clears his throat. "I'm going to show my family what a nice woman you are, how you are no threat to them, and—how you are a *person*. Not some file of incriminating evidence they're trying to erase or a rat spilling his guts to the cops, but a real human being with feelings and emotions and something worth—"

"Are you stupid?"

"What? No, I—"

"You take drugs?"

"Of course not."

"Do you suffer from any mental disease or deficiency?"

He pauses. "Uh . . . no?"

"Then I cannot figure out what could possibly make you think I stand a chance of living if you bring me to your home. It's like bringing a deer to the front door of a hunting lodge."

He looks at me and sighs, stands and motions for me to do the same. He offers his hand to help me out of my seat and I take it.

We plod to the door, walk outside, and stand in the bright sunshine.

"I'll tell you what," he says. "I left my keys on the table in the restaurant. I'm gonna go back in and get them. If you think you'll be safer with the feds than with me, feel free to leave. If you think you'll be safer with me—and I hope you will—then be here when I come back out."

Jonathan looks at me for a minute, like I might give him an answer on the spot, but I merely nod.

He walks inside the restaurant and as the door closes, I do not ponder his offer but instead get stuck on the fact that he left his keys on the table. For a guy who has been so deft at repeatedly finding me and remaining in control of these various situations, it's an odd slip. Frankly, it seems more like something Sean would have done.

I move close to the door and nudge it open a little to peek inside, and sure enough Jonathan's lied to me again. He is swinging his keys around his middle finger as he walks back to our table. When he gets to it, he looks over his shoulder and waves the waiter to the table, says a few words to him, and the waiter smiles. The waiter walks away and Jonathan looks around—seemingly to make sure no one is watching—then pulls a wad of bills from his pocket and drops them on the table.

I smile and close the door.

And when he comes outside he gets his answer; I am waiting for him.

He looks relieved. "Thank you," he says.

Jonathan gently puts his hand on the small of my back and I shiver. He guides me around the side of the restaurant to where the Audi is parked and we find two kids hovering over the car with their backs to us. They are both laughing quietly.

Jonathan stops, assesses the situation, takes his hand from my back, and whispers to me, "Stay here."

"Do it again," I hear one of the kids say.

Jonathan moves closer and from my distance it appears these two kids, both young teenagers, are spitting on the seats of his car.

That's sort of what he gets for leaving the top down in the middle of Baltimore. I do not voice my opinion.

Jonathan pulls up his sleeves as he sneaks up behind the kids and says, "What do you fu"—he looks back at me and winces—"funny guys think you're doing?"

The kids try to run but he snags one around the neck with his arm, as with a cane in a burlesque show. Jonathan grabs him by the hair, and just as he is about to slam the kid's head down on the side of the car, he looks at me—but I cannot look at him. I turn away, because all of the good he just did at the restaurant is about to be unraveled.

The other kid comes back, I guess out of loyalty to his friend, and bobs nervously from foot to foot.

No one says a word, and when I finally look at Jonathan, he swallows.

I shrug and say, "It's just saliva."

Jonathan withers a little and he and I both realize that his lifestyle and family heritage is more a part of him than either of us would like to admit. He loosens his grip on the kid and pushes him to the ground. "Go home and hug your mother," he says to him. "And say a prayer of thanks tonight, kid." He glances at me. "An angel was looking out for you today."

"Yes, sir," the kid says, stumbling to his feet.

Both boys stand and look at Jonathan like soldiers waiting for instructions from a commanding officer.

Jonathan frowns at them. "Run! Run, you little sh—shysters."

And they do.

I walk up to Jonathan and watch the kids quickly fade from view. They actually left a cloud of dust.

He gazes at the gobs of spit on his leather upholstery and grunts. "Let me go back in the restaurant and get a paper towel or something."

I nod. I grab my new green sweater, ensure that it is free of spit, and slip it on. As Jonathan walks away, I stand in the light breeze with my eyes closed. The warmth of the sun tranquilizes me and nearly brings me to my knees. Something is changing inside of me; though I have never been certain of who I am, I feel I am changing anyway.

I am replete.

I am sanguine.

I am being shoved into the back of a large SUV with seats composed of stiff vinyl.

The vehicle shakes and, after fumbling around for a few seconds, I garner the strength to look out the window and I see we have created a dust cloud of our own.

"Keep your head down," Sean says. He pulls onto the road and the SUV is swaying in every direction, fishtailing from one lane to another, and the wheels are squealing like they're begging for mercy.

The Germans had nothing to do with this vehicle whatsoever.

I pop my head up to say something and Sean smashes it back down like he's playing Whac-A-Mole. "I said stay down!"

I'm not sure what bothers me more: that Jonathan, for better or for worse, is going to get the wrong impression about why I am not there when he returns to the Audi, or that I'm lying on the dirty floor of a Ford Explorer with my head resting on a pillow of empty Big Gulp containers.

After a few minutes—and once the Explorer has stabilized—I pull myself up from the floor and sprawl across the backseat.

"Are you okay?" Sean asks. He does not bother to look at me in the rearview mirror.

"This is getting pretty freaking old."

"Look, I'm sorry for what happened back at the motel, but we've been following your trail since you left. The motel manager saw you get into a car with someone who was not me. We had people looking for a red convertible Audi in multiple states and we got a tip when your car spun out on I-95. Another marshal, Deputy Cooper, is two cars behind us and we're going to take you to—"

"Are you married?"

Now he looks in the rearview. "What?"

"Are you married, Sean?" If Jonathan lied to me again, *he'll* be the one who needs a guardian angel.

He looks down, then back at the road. He says, weakly, "I . . . was married."

I yawn. "Divorce?"

"No. My wife, she . . . she died of breast cancer at a very young age."

Don't I feel like a jerk.

I try to change the subject. Sort of. "But you're wearing a wedding band."

"Well, I'm still married to her." He catches my eye in the rearview for a few seconds. "There will only ever be one Mrs. Douglas, if you know what I mean. My heart is hers, will always be hers, and I wear the ring to . . . well, partly to remember her and partly to send the message to other women that I'm not available."

I raise an eyebrow. I'm not sure whether to be moved by his sentimentality or annoyed at his arrogance.

I go with the arrogance. "Need to beat 'em off with a club, Seanster?"

"We're going to rendezvous up here in a few minutes with the other deputy."

Sean is all business, but I'll tell you I do not feel like an appreciated customer. Fifteen minutes earlier I was finishing four-star Italian food, drinking good wine and fresh-ground espresso. Now that I'm back in the government's care, I am relegated to a plastic backseat and taking orders from a guy making fifty-three grand per annum.

Thanks to Jonathan, salary has now become a hot-button issue for me.

"I need to know everything that happened," he says.

"He had veal chops and I had the beef carpaccio."

Sean does not laugh.

"You and *who*?"

Now I'm confused. "What do you mean? You don't know who I was with?"

Sean mutters under his breath about cars in his way, drives like we're leaving the scene of our own crime. "The car is registered to an Anthony J. Bovaro, which tells me plenty. What I want to know is who was driving and where they were taking you. Are you hurt?"

Sean swerves around a U-Haul and skates back into the fast lane. "Not yet." I sit up. Even though Sean thinks there's a threat, I know the reality. "And there was no *they*. It was just one guy driving."

"Did he tell you his name?"

I catch a glimpse of myself in the rearview, and if I didn't know better I'd think someone had supplanted the real me with an abused, punked-out, and less-seductive Keira Knightley. "His name, uh . . . I don't think he told me his name. I mean, if he did, I don't remember."

"How did he apprehend you? Did he have a weapon?"

I smile a little but do not let Sean see. I rub my hand over my sweater and realize how surprisingly powerful textiles can be. "No, he didn't have a weapon."

"Did you know he was part of the Bovaro family?"

"Um, sort of."

"Did he try to hurt you?"

"No."

"Did he threaten you in any way?"

I start to daydream and my answers are less responsive. "No, he didn't."

Sean stares at me in the mirror for a few seconds and the car suddenly tugs backward; Sean moved his foot off the gas.

"Wait a minute," he says, "did you go *willingly*?"

I blink a few times and let his question hang in the air. His tone is understood; the feds are not going to allow me to stay in the program if I'm screwing around with security. I'm probably already on some watch list for scamming them, for letting my underlying fears and daily languor push me over the edge and in search of a new locale and a new persona.

But if I start to dabble with the folks from whom the feds are protecting me? Things will not be pretty.

I tug at my sweater, hoping it will fall apart and give me a living metaphor to use as a basis for decision, but just like the man who purchased it, the weave is die-hard.

The choice might seem obvious, but the vague truth quickly surfaces: Jonathan is one single man—one single man who wants to deliver me to the door of his murderous family—and Sean is a law enforcement officer with the physical backing—and budget—of the Justice Department. No matter how I feel in Jonathan's presence, no matter how strong and intense his mysterious pull is, he could never outweigh the power of the feds.

I take a deep breath and whisper my lie: "I don't know, I just . . . I'm very confused right now. I'm very tired." The *tired* thing almost always shuts them down.

Sean guns it again. Deputy Cooper pulls up next to us as we move into the right lane in order to exit. I watch him for a moment. He puts a cheeseburger to his mouth and, as he bites, a big glob of ketchup and mustard falls to his chest. He doesn't notice.

I'm not sure what bothers me more: that it took them this long to catch up or that Deputy Cooper managed to find time to hit the Golden Arches before heading into pursuit.

I pinch the bridge of my nose and repeat, "I'm very tired."

"I understand," Sean says. "Well, just relax. You're safe now."

That's what they all say.

3!

WE PULL INTO THE PARKING LOT OF THE MARYLAND STATE POLICE
Barracks on the northeast side of Baltimore. I can tell we're on the
northeast side by the smell. I once drove through this area, the
little twist of land connecting the Back River to the Middle River,
and I was never able to rid my clothes of the smog-tinged pun-
gency. Sean and Deputy Cooper park side by side, then they both
get out, leaving me in the back like a little kid in a car seat.

They talk for a moment, hands in motion as they speak, then
they lean on their vehicles and start laughing.

I'm not sure I see the humor.

They both return to their respective SUVs and start the
engines. It appears they had no intention of getting the state police
involved; I guess they figured no criminal would knowingly enter
a police station parking lot. Aren't they clever.

Sean pulls out and Deputy Cooper goes in a different direction.

"It's just going to be you and me?" I ask.

"For now."

"Isn't that against policy? Shouldn't there always be two depu-
ties transporting me?"

"Afraid I'm going to take advantage of you?"

I smirk. "Not as long as that inch-width wedding band is on your finger."

He points down the road. "We're going to head west and get you out in the country."

"Ingenious." I'm already bored.

The wheels spin and the signs and trees fly by, and now that we're on I-70, the subdivisions are spaced farther and farther apart, and then—*nothing*. Nothing but farmland and cows and old brick or clapboard farmhouses.

I take off my sweater and carefully fold it. I try to open my window but, as usual, it's locked. "Can I get a little fresh air, Sean?" He glances at me in the rearview. "It's a warm afternoon. I just want to take in some of this great country atmosphere."

Sean checks all around the car and reluctantly unlocks the windows. I press the button and balmy, clean air swirls about the cabin. I close my eyes and breathe it in, but it's not enough. I slide over in the seat and rest my head on the edge of the door and let the wind rush through my short hair. I pretend I am still with Jonathan and the top is down and he is taking me somewhere safe.

As much as I want the daydream to last the evening, the sound of Sean's beeping phone and whatever else is making noise on the dashboard reminds me that I am not safe and not about to experience pleasure of any sort. Hours earlier I'd felt like I was living—no matter how close to dying I actually was—for the first time. Jonathan gave me a glimpse of the sweetness of being free and I realize now that I may need to harbor that memory for the rest of my life.

Though I have been on this earth for twenty-six years, the last twenty have been one long string of boredom knotted by a few moments of unimaginable terror. I have never traveled overseas. I have never stayed up late partying with my friends. I have never

been able to study at a university because of the risk that I would
be whisked off at a moment's notice and lose all the years of education I'd worked so diligently to achieve. I have not worked my way
up the corporate ladder just to have it pulled from beneath me on
my way to another small town where a job as a shop clerk was
waiting for me. I have never, for one moment, understood what it
was like to create or design or build something long lasting.

But today I got to eat fine food with a good-looking, strong
man, and for the first time the boredom and fear made way for a
new emotion, *delight*, to enter the picture. As much as I want to
experience it again, I know I can't.

I open my eyes and glance out the window and I see a sign that
reads MIDDLETOWN EXIT ONLY.

I don't know where we're going next, but I already hate it
there.

Before I realize it, we're in the parking lot of yet another
convenience store, some local-yokel variety with half the sign's
lights burned out so the name is a jumble of consonants; the
quality of quick-mart seems to be paralleling my life. Sean spins
his head around and asks me if I need to hit the rest room. I
don't, but I know I should try because I've learned from my
past mistakes.

Sean escorts me to the bathroom, makes sure it is empty and
safe and window free. He waits outside as I force myself to pee. I
wish I could count on one hand how many deputy marshals have
stood by a rest room door and listened to me urinate, but I'm sad
to say it's in the dozens.

"You want anything?" Sean mumbles through the door. I hear
him picking up cellophane-wrapped objects.

I stare at myself in the mirror and I look like a middle-aged
woman. My skin is pale and worn, and my hair is frizzy from the

chemicals of color. I wash my hands and take handfuls of water and run it through my hair, an exercise in futility.

"Nothing for me, thanks."

I exit the bathroom and go to Sean's side, not because I need or want his protection but because he won't let me go anywhere without him anyway. He puts his hand on the small of my back, in the same spot Jonathan had—but not in the same way. I stand next to him as we wait in line as if I were his daughter. I stare at the floor the entire time.

When we return to the Explorer, I get in the back and slump down. To my surprise, Sean gets in the back with me. I wonder if he really is considering taking advantage of me or if he just enjoys our little backseat visits. He smiles at me and chucks a pack of Hostess Orange CupCakes into my lap. It's sort of chivalrous, I suppose, his remembering my affinity for this particular junk food, but his offering, having come just a few minutes after I said I didn't want anything, has him shifting slightly from arrogant to bumptious. As for his intentions? I do some simple math. Add the cupcakes to my hideous reflection in the rest room and the answer, obviously, is that Sean simply likes our backseat visits.

He offers me a bottle of Aquafina. I've known Sean for less than two days and he's already become predictable and dull. There are only so many times you can win a girl with trans fatty acids and distilled water.

I daydream, for a moment, of cannolis.

Sean opens up a bag of Nacho Cheese Doritos, grabs a massive handful, and shoves them in his mouth. He crunches so loudly it actually hurts my ears.

I say, "You know those things are loaded full of MSG?" He shrugs. "Or do you eat them to fend off the ladies? Because believe me, after a bag of those, your breath will be a far greater defense than your wedding ba—"

"Tell me the truth," he interrupts, "have you been duping

WITSEC into relocating you because you're bored or scared?" He pauses, then adds, "Or because you want to live off the subsistence checks?"

I play with the wrapper of my cupcakes. "You can't be serious." My response is so lackluster I don't even convince myself.

"Because I've got to tell you, Michelle, you—"

"Oh, geez, we're sticking with the Michelle thing?"

He waves a chip at me like a switchblade. "I'm not using your real name outside of a federal facility. It's against regulations." Another handful of Doritos goes in.

"Then call me by some other name. Give me a nickname."

He looks at my hair, slows his chewing, and says, "Okay . . . Spike." He licks his molars. "C'mon, it's the subsistence checks, isn't it?"

"Look, over the years I've talked to enough people involved in the program to know it's possible to rip off the government left and right, but I'm not about that."

He studies me for a moment, then nods, apparently believing me. I'm pretty sure I was telling the truth.

Sean takes a big drink. "I had this one guy who'd actually been relocated more than you. Guy was a real piece of work, a lazy slob, wouldn't pick his nose if the government didn't do it for him. Well, he got, just as you have, three months of subsistence checks while securing a new job in his new location. And every time he got near the eleventh week, he'd receive some mysterious call or letter—nothing we could ever verify—that sent him into a panic and we'd end up moving the guy again."

I swallow. "Huh. What a loser."

"One time he got a bunch of credit cards under his new ID, most of which were furnished by banks working with WITSEC, and he maxed all of them out at strip clubs and dive bars."

"Let me guess. He ran out of credit and suddenly asked to be relocated."

"You got it. The government made him disappear along with all of his debt. He started over from scratch."

I smirk. "I'm on the flip side of that coin. The government *took* from my parents and me."

"How?" he asks, looking deeper into his bag of chips.

"Well, for starters, the house my folks had in New Jersey was worth quite a bit. Not to mention the savings and investments my parents had. All gone."

"It's true that you can't keep profit from the sale of a home if you're in the program." He says this like it was an idea he came up with on his own.

There are so many things you assume you should accept, or are *told* to accept, in the program—and surrendering your assets is one of them. I never understood it, merely allowed it to be a de facto experience in my wayfaring from alias to alias. I learned the value in not accumulating emotional investments, so the monetary type acquired the same fate. As a robot built by the government, I was not programmed to ask the obvious question:

"Why?"

Sean mulls it over. "It's complicated. But to begin with, the person in WITSEC is no longer the person who owned the house. I mean, names don't match, Social Security numbers don't match. It's a real legal mess. And even if it can be worked out—as it has in a very few rare cases—it might no—"

"*Very few* and *rare* mean the same thing."

He speaks louder. "Even if it can be worked out, there is now a tie between your former life and current life. People can trace checks and legal documents. Even if you have the money turned over to a friend or family member, all you're really doing is potentially putting those people in danger."

Sean has officially become a government dweeb in my mind. He seems to have no grasp on what is at stake—or no longer at stake—when one enters the program. He has been drained of empathy and filled with indifference. Where is the man who supposedly cared so heartily for abused and mistreated kids?

I toss my cupcakes aside, open my water, and take a drink. I turn and watch a young man buckle his little girl into her car seat and give her a kiss. She smiles back and kicks her legs. I am tired of living a vicarious family life through the brief shopping events of mini-mart patrons.

I so long for the simplicity of those moments everyone takes for granted; how I would cherish a smile from a child of my own. What do I get? Sean giving me textbook examples of criminals past, dishing out another way-it-is rendition of *Welcome to WIT-SEC*, points delivered as static and sterile as a course in criminal procedure. All this takes a toll on what remains of the threshold of my composure. I try to refrain, to shelter my frustration—and to shelter Sean, really. But the cab of this car is awfully freaking small.

So everything harbored begins to leak and slowly pour out, the first droplets of magma down the volcano's side.

"The money isn't even the real issue, Sean; it's the predetermined hopelessness. I mean, what's the point in ever wanting to establish roots, to buy a home and build a family, when it could all be eradicated one afternoon on the walk back from the Dairy Queen? Who wants that?"

He looks at me for a second and shrugs.

His vague apathy begs me to give him some more, but now my tenor has progressed and my voice is a little stronger—the inevitable eruption, you see. "It's ridiculous. These people, especially the *innocent* people, risk their lives for the feds. They give up their careers, their families, their *dreams*—all so the feds can *try* and make a case. Meanwhile, if Justice comes up short on evidence or something gets thrown out of court on a technicality, the criminals are free, if they're not out on parole anyway, while the people in

Witness Protection are running for the rest of their lives. Seriously, who's really being sentenced here?"

Sean stops looking at me and his chewing is accelerating and he starts tapping his foot.

I nudge his knee to get his attention. "What kind of deal is this?"

"It's better than death."

Boom.

I smack the bag out of his hands and chips fly all the way to the dashboard. "You callous dick! The Department of Justice did not give my folks all the information. My parents would never have done this if they knew how things really worked. You played us and threw us into the wind!"

"Don't yell at *me*. I had nothing to do with your parents!"

"Who did, Sean? *Who* is responsible? No one wants to take responsibility!"

Sean turns his body to me, faces me square, and unleashes. "You want to know, huh? You want to know who is responsible?"

"Damn straight!"

"*You* are! You caused all the misery you've had these past years! You think we don't know what happened back when you were in high school? It's all in your file, every bit of it. You had a bitter argument with your parents about a boy you wanted to date. Your folks thought it was a bad idea and they kept you from seeing him, didn't they?"

I sit back. Tears fill my eyes and all I can do is watch as the pendulum slowly swings back in my direction.

"And what did you do, huh?" he asks.

I wipe my eyes. "Don't do this."

"You figured you'd get even, didn't you."

"Stop."

"You were going to fix your parents' wagon once and for all.

You were so smart. Who were they to tell you what you could do with your life?"

I look up at him and a few tears drop from my eyes to my lap. "Please, stop."

"You figured you'd teach them a lesson they'd never forget, yeah?"

"Sean . . ." I start to sob.

"Well, you succeeded. Storming out of your house and calling the local paper and telling them how there was a family of Bovaro witnesses living in a neighboring community? Sheer brilliance."

Reliving this moment—an action I rarely allow myself to conduct—along with Sean's jarring critique of my decisions, sends an upward heat through my head and chest. Like driving through a bad neighborhood, I want to speed through it, hit all the green lights, arrive safely in a reposeful future. But the outcome is inevitable: I'm destined to break down on the bleakest, most dangerous block.

"I bet your folks were willing to let you date whomever you wanted after that, right?" He pauses and scratches his chin. "Hmmm, wait. I guess you never got the chance to find out. Refresh my memory. How long after the paper ran that story were your parents murdered?"

My face is covered in saliva and mucus and tears. I look up at Sean, but he is a blur—a cruel, indomitable blur. "I have no doubt . . . that you are a tough marshal, Sean. If that's what you're trying to pro—"

"How long?"

I shrivel. Everything about who I am, whoever I am, is fading to black, and Sean is delivering the darkness. I answer, "Twenty-nine hours."

Sean finally gets around to brushing the crumbs from his clothes and he seems to be taking his time. I am staring at the floor but I can see in my peripheral vision that he keeps grabbing short glances of me. He hands me a handkerchief, which I accept, and I can't help wondering how many weepy women and children have dried their faces with this cloth. It must be part of the U.S. Deputy Marshal's official uniform.

I wipe my face, my eyes, my nose—and the thing is saturated. I do not hand it back.

After catching my breath I say, "You . . . are a bastard."

"I'm sorry," he says immediately. "I was out of line."

"Well," I say after a moment, "it was all true. I might as well have pulled the trigger myself." I play with the stitching on the handkerchief. "My folks were at the A&P buying a few things for our imminent trip to yet another town." I sigh. "We almost made it." I gaze out the window and focus on nothing. "Worst of all, my parents are buried in a town far from their family, with some names no one would ever recognize on their gravestones. They weren't buried on the plot reserved for them by generations of McCartneys dating back to the Civil War. I would have to fly hours to put flowers on my parents' grave—and we both know I won't be flying anywhere anyway."

"It's a bad story. Sorry I brought it up."

And so it ends. If divorce could possess a specific sound, its fading resonance would be lingering in the cab of our vehicle. This unrecoverable moment is like the first bullet added to a magazine, waiting for that future argument when no other thing can be said to trump or wound a loved one, and the gun is drawn and the bullet is fired and resentment and anger and distrust emerge as the only available emotions, and they stick in the air like sulfur, with everyone gasping.

We stare ahead, entranced by the backs of the headrests, listening to each other swallow. And as the minutes pass, the margin of whatever acceptable silence remained has vanished.

I finally look at him and he tries to smile a little, but the effort is obvious. "You know," I say, "you really need to work on your bedside manner. Don't they have classes for that?"

He sighs with relief. "It's, uh . . . harder than you think. The Marshals Service is a rare group of individuals. I mean, the motto is *Justice, Integrity, Service*. They didn't even think to put *protect* in there. You've got to understand that most of us are folks sent out to bring in criminals who have escaped from prison or jumped bail, so we already despise the people we're pursuing. Then, if you become a WITSEC inspector, well . . . then the odds are you're protecting some dirtbag terrorist or mafioso, which doesn't exactly instill compassion among folks in the Service, you know what I mean?"

I nod, though this is hardly my problem.

"These criminals," he adds, "they're just horrible. And such a bunch of whiners, always complaining. But we have to keep them happy, and that rubs the marshals the wrong way."

"No one ever kept me happy."

"According to your file, we tried. Kept moving you to places we thought you'd like, got you jobs we thought you'd thrive in."

I sniffle a little. "What were the mob guys getting?"

"You don't want to know."

He looks at me and can tell I'm serious. What he probably doesn't know is that I'm going to use all of this for future negotiations.

"Uh," he says, looking around the vehicle.

"What, you think I'm with Internal Affairs? For the love of Pete."

He lowers his voice anyway. "For starters, they get a lot of money. I mean, we draw the line, but we'll give them lump sums for setting up businesses or . . . even just spending cash."

I open my eyes a bit. "How big?"

"Like, five or six figures big."

"You can't be serious."

"We've done worse. We actually put one guy's wife *and* his girl-friend into the program—and his wife had no idea what was going on." My response is a slack jaw. "You can see why the marshals have no room for compassion."

I shake off my shock and pick up where I left off. "That's my point, really. I am not a terrorist or mafioso. I'm just an innocent girl."

Sean shrugs.

"That's all you have to say?"

He reaches for the door handle. "It's not up to me, Spike." He gets out, walks around the car, opens the driver's door, and brushes the Doritos off the seat. "My job is to get you from point A to point B in one piece." He sits down but turns around to face me. "The Justice Department really isn't supposed to support you your whole life, you know. WITSEC is here to get you started, get you situated in a new town with a new job. After that, you're supposed to be on your own—unless there's trouble."

I've heard this before. He's *definitely* taken the class on tripe.

"Yes," I say, rubbing my sore eyes, "but there's nobody in those new places to bring security and reassurance all those times I hear a noise in the middle of the night, or to help me explain my past to questioning neighbors, or to help calm my fears when I'm reluctant to turn the ignition of my car."

"It's an imperfect system, but it's all there is."

I look out the window as a car pulls in next to us and a young couple gets out, holds hands, and walks into the convenience store.

The worst part, the piece the feds can never correct, is the unbelievable loneliness. I consider asking Sean if he was ever ignored when he attended elementary school, but I can tell by his swagger that the bastard probably had a hundred friends his entire life, king of his freaking fraternity and whatnot.

My elementary school days were lousy even *before* WITSEC. I remember sitting at lunch in first grade and no one would sit with me, like everyone already had friends and there wasn't any room for one more. Not that anyone really picked on me; they just acted as though I wasn't there. My mom would put little notes in my lunch, like, "I'm thinking of you, kiddo" or "I have a surprise for you when you get home" and stuff like that. Those notes were the only thing that kept me from crying every day while I ate my bologna sandwich off in a corner of the cafeteria. And the impossible thing to convey to the people assigning me a new life is that *that's* what it's like for me every day. It never changes. I just move on to the next place where I will once again not know anybody and not feel accepted. I am still six years old, having never really learned how to make and keep friends or how to negotiate in a relationship or even how to open up—because I'm *not allowed* to open up.

Two months ago, while I was showering, I slipped my hand under my breast and I was certain I felt a lump. I panicked. I got out of the shower still covered in soap and reached for the phone. I needed a mother, a sister, a friend. Who was I supposed to call, Farquar? There was no one. *No one.* I just stared at the phone and wept.

Sean can tell he's lost me, takes in a breath like he's going to ask another question or provide some great insight, but, alas, it becomes a great exhale of nothingness.

"You know," I say, watching as the young couple hops back into their car and speeds away, "I don't even care anymore. Just take me somewhere and dump me. No matter what place you take me to, I've been there before."

Sean tries to get me to look at him, like all of a sudden he's testing out a little compassion. I got news for him: He should attend the class first.

I drift down in the seat, close my eyes, and feel the early pangs of a headache. "Point B, Sean. Just take me to point B."

Night falls as we drive directly west. The sun and stars have no meaning when I'm on the road—that is, en route to my new locale—because you can sit in the back of a car and eat junk food and do nothing equally over a twenty-four-hour period. Time only matters once you have your hotel room and the television becomes your best friend.

It turns out point B is a small town in West Virginia, and though it feels like this is punishment for arguing with my protector, I know Sean had nothing to do with the logistics of the operation.

Sean parks the car in the nearly abandoned parking lot of a skanky motel. He opens my door as I begin to collect my thoughts and my belonging (that's right, not *belongings*—all I have is that green sweater from Jonathan; for now, it's enough). As I reach over the seat, I notice two Sudoku puzzle books on top of my sweater. I slowly pick them up since I'm not sure they're for me.

"Oh," Sean says, "I bought those for you awhile back. Thought you might like some math puzzles to work on in your, uh, free time."

I smile as I get out. "That's sweet." That, of course, is all it is; Sudoku is as much about math as crossword puzzles are about literature.

This time, as Sean walks me to my room, we do not speak. He opens the door to my contrarily luxurious suite, hands me the key, mumbles something about seeing me in the morning. I close the door before he is finished.

If you blindfolded me, I could not tell you if I was sitting on the bed in a motel room in Arkansas or Kentucky or New Mexico or West Virginia. The smell of the radiators, the squeaks of the mattresses, the sound of the couple arguing in the room to the left and the sound of the snoring marshal in the room to the right, the feel of the worn blanket that has likely been the canvas of a thousand sexual trysts and never washed, the frayed carpet under my bare feet, and the undeniable scent of mildew tucked away in the far corners of the room—all the same.

I am tired of crying and I am tired of blaming and I am tired of

Sean and what will end up being his cookie-cutter replacement. I am tired of being force-fed my life.

I am tired of living, but what keeps me from dragging a blade across my wrist or diving off one of the crippled bridges that cross the polluted rivers my motel rooms predictably border is the *idea* of life—that somehow, someday, I will figure a way to experience what it is like to live in unfettered happiness, to bask in the freedom of security, and finally to understand the person I am supposed to be.

I am tired of . . . dreaming about it.

The digital clock on the nightstand reads 10:38 P.M. and I can't help but think the night is young. Somewhere.

I open the door to my motel room and walk away.

$$2b^2 + 5b + 3 = 136$$

I MEANDER TO THE ROAD THAT LED US TO THIS FORGOTTEN TOWN and walk as far to the side as possible. I walk for hours in one direction and I can feel the dirt building on my feet as the road dust collects on my sandals. Miles later, signs of life emerge with each step closer to West Virginia University. My journey ends at the fringe of the Monongahela River, where I climb up on a bridge and stare at dozens of college students milling about the campus and the city of Morgantown. I wonder what has all these kids so lively in these very early morning hours and I remember the season: final exams. If I hadn't decided to take this journey to another neverland, I'd be preparing my students for exactly the same.

A breeze washes over me and tugs at my hair and clothes; Jonathan's gift prevents me from shivering.

Something lures me toward the campus. It is a hopeful place, an entity bearing the happy sentiments of kids getting educations and starting careers and hanging degrees on their walls that bear their birth names. Instead of treading the collegiate sidewalks, I opt to move toward a bar on the edge of the campus. I reach into my pocket and remove everything in it: two unused tissues, a crumpled Post-it note reminding me to bring home the paperwork for the parent-teacher conferences that will be occurring tomorrow, and the change from my last trip to Starbucks: sixteen dollars and twenty-one cents.

I gaze through the window of the bar and it seems the place is winding down. A few young couples are standing and reaching for coats while the rest shoot pool and watch reruns of the day's sports highlights on a handful of outdated televisions.

I walk in and glide to a stool at the bar, where I make myself comfortable under a bright Rolling Rock sign. The green light on my pallid skin makes me look like I belong in a morgue.

The young girl behind the bar comes over and asks what she can get me, but her tone speaks of displeasure at having to start another tab so near to closing. I assure her I will not be here long. She returns with a Budweiser draft, ordered because it's cheap—and can be easily nursed, if needed.

I scan the room curiously and it appears every element of the town is here: the college jocks; the good-looking-yet-slightly-effeminate frat boys with their competing Greek letters; the townies—that is, the folks who probably once ruled this bar and refuse to relinquish to the students; and the stragglers, the lonely people, like me, sitting idle and waiting for someone to tell them to go be idle somewhere else.

What I don't see is any sign of a hit man, but how can I not imagine that danger lurks most gravely for me no matter my locale, that the Bovaros may already be aware of where I am, in this state, this town, this bar.

I turn back to my glass of beer and sip. As the brew delivers internal warmth, I realize why people become alcoholics; booze is a true and responsive friend. I play with the condensation on the side of my glass as my stomach rumbles, and as I begin to feel the slightest effect of the alcohol, my thoughts turn to Jonathan. I must be exhausted because I think puzzling and inappropriate things, like the way his confidence is more substantial and intrinsic than any marshal I've known, the way his body fills out his clothes, and what it might be like to kiss him. It isn't long before these ideas evolve to issues of concern for him. It occurs to me that, since he's going to be returning home empty-handed, his life may be in danger.

Three college guys in their early twenties glance my way and smile. Then they whisper, then they smile, then they nod, then they whisper, then they smile. Nothing good will come of this.

I return to thinking of Jonathan and the alcohol breaks my anxiety and fear and really allows me to open. I figure it's not only that Jonathan may be physically harmed by his tyrannical family, but that his feelings will be destroyed as well.

The college guys get a little louder and I assume that it's a loss of inhibitions that brings one of them in my direction. He keeps looking back at his friends and, based on how horrible I look and feel, and how dirty my hair and body are, there is a wager involved.

Where's a bag of Nacho Cheese Doritos when you need one?

He stands next to the bar for a few seconds, then slowly moves toward me. The way he keeps looking back at his friends—and their reactive laughter—would certainly bring any girl to her knees.

Up until the very last seconds, I am preoccupied with thoughts of Jonathan, and I think I might need a second beer to sort it all out. The bartender glances at me and I nod, and she quickly replaces my glass with another dollar draft. I drink, hard.

The college doofus—a real Tobey Maguire wanna-be, all short and small featured—stands right by my side and does not sit on the available stool, which tells me he is ready for quick flight. This will not have a happy ending.

He offers me a napkin and a pen and says, "C-Can I have your autograph?"

I roll my eyes in his direction. "Sorry?"

"I was just wondering if I could get your autograph. I love your early work, especially 'Rebel Yell' and 'Eyes Without a Face.'"

His buddies laugh and somewhere deep inside I understand Jonathan's proclivity for reactionary violence.

I consider a retaliatory remark but I really just want him to go away. Alas, no one knows more than I that the shortest distance between two points is a straight line.

"Billy Idol," I say, patting him gently on the shoulder. "It's sort of funny, but since Billy is retro-cool, the humor attached to your punch line is diminished, so it's probably not something I would suggest you use again should you ever come across a woman who weakly resembles the British rock star simply because she has short, stiff hair.

"Now, on to more important things. You have a serious character flaw, and I can say this with certainty based on the surety of one or both of the following conclusions: One, you are viewed among your group as the weakest member, which is why you were targeted and so easily cajoled into coming over here and harassing some person you do not know and will never see again; or, two, you have a serious problem with insecurity and feel the need to prove yourself as a man to your buddies when you know deep down that you will never reach the bar they've set—or that society has set—for how to act as a real man in this demanding world. You may have some difficulty deciding which item it is, but I'm leaning toward both, with heavy emphasis on item two. You may be unsure of my comments right now, but they will be hammered home one day soon when you are with your girlfriend or wife and you are trying desperately to fulfill your sexual promise to your beloved—but your body will sputter and smoke and be unable to deliver the goods. You will, indeed, be amazed that you cannot produce the simple biological reaction that pretty much every other living, breathing man on this planet can produce within a few seconds of seeing his lover's naked body. No, you, my dear friend, will stand there or sit there or lie there as limp as a horse's tail, and I am sorry to say that you will remember my face and you will remember this conversation, and the truth, the essence of your very life, will come into focus and blind you in a permanent way as five simple words echo throughout your brain for the rest of your life: *I am not a man.*"

My college friend stands with his mouth open and hands at his sides. It seems he's about twenty or so words behind. When he finally catches up, he glances at his buddies, who are no longer laughing. He turns back to me and asks, "Are you a philosophy professor?"

I chug a third of my beer, burp under my breath, and answer, "Worse. I teach math, which means I'm all about *certainty*, Noodle-boy."

I drop five bucks on the bar, walk toward the door, and wink at the other two college guys while whistling the tune to "White Wedding." As I walk down the street, I glance back through the window and see the kid still standing at the bar, head down, hands in his pockets. His friends do not rise from their seats.

My point has already been proven.

The unexpected clarifying effect of the alcohol along with the fresh air brings everything to the edge of my mind and I try to seize the moment. I have no idea where I'm heading, but I'm in no shape to continue walking. I am ready to burn out. I have just over ten bucks on me and I am in desperate need of a shower and my feet and body are aching and I have nowhere to go and I think, "This is how you become homeless," and I'm saddened that the streets I may have to live on are in wild, wonderful West Virginia, that of all places to *end*, it is going to be here.

I find a twenty-four-hour coffee shop a block and a half from the bar and figure it's the only way I'll make it till daylight. I wander in and survey the room for fear of repeating the bar incident. The place is old and the floor creaks with each step. There is a long bar along the right wall even though no liquor is served here, and the place is empty but for the exception of seven over-caffeinated students typing with speed that hints of unreachable deadlines. I walk to the bar and order their version of a Marble Mocha Macchiato and hand over a third of my remaining life savings.

I walk to a soft leather chair in the corner of the café and drop down and the leather deflates to the shape of my body. I nearly drift off to the gentle tinkling of plastic keys.

The weight of depression sets in because I realize this current batch of misery is of my own doing. Things really weren't that bad in Columbia, in retrospect. It was safe, suburban, upper middle class—in fact, the exact kind of place most young professionals aspire to call home, and it was handed to me, free of charge. My angst toward the feds had blinded me, allowed me to displace my boredom with a passive-aggressive infliction of punishment. And this is where my decisions have brought me: to a hopeless collapse. This is what rock bottom feels like. All of the fear and all of the insecurity and all of the sadness have got to stop and my only question now is, How is it going to end?

To my knowledge, the only real pleasure I've experienced ever came from Jonathan. He is, in the strangest sense, the only true thing in my adult life, the only person who doesn't require me to live a lie, my only chance at gaining a brief glimpse into what my real life might look like. The closest I can come to being myself, for better or for worse, is with him. He knows who I was and what happened to me. The fact that his father initiated the string of pain and misery in my life is beginning to matter less and less.

If I'm going to flame out, I want it to be with Jonathan.

I actually miss him.

The beer overpowers the caffeine and I hear Billy singing "White Wedding" and his truths about fairness and safety and sureness and purity softly echo in my head as I fade.

• • •

I wake to a guy in a business suit turning the pages of his newspaper in a manner that suggests he wants me to get up.

I rub my eyes and the sun is blasting through the window and I wince in pain. I glance around the room and the same students are pecking away but they have decelerated, spending equal time typing and twisting the kinks out of their necks.

I reach for my half-rate Macchiato knockoff as though I had only dozed for a few minutes and take a loud sip to key in the other patrons that I am indeed a paying customer; I could easily be mistaken for a homeless person at this point.

As clarity makes its way back, I reaffirm that there is only one way for all of this to end, and that is with Jonathan—and I am determined to find him.

There is a phone by my chair as though some subliminal force pushed me to this particular seat as part of a grander plan. I stare at the phone like it's a weapon of mass destruction.

A weapon of self-destruction.

I take another sip from my coffee drink (for no other reason than to rehydrate), then I pick up the receiver like I'm pulling the pin from a grenade.

I call information for New York City and run through all the boroughs until I find out there is an unpublished listing for an Anthony and Sylvia Bovaro in Brooklyn. I return the phone to the cradle and think. There are benefits to having lived in anonymity for almost my entire life; I tend to think outside of the box because I have never been inside the box.

I grab my coffee—my passport for staying in this café—and snag a pen from the bar and the last remaining computer. I try to Google Jonathan but it's as if the guy never existed. As for Anthony Bovaro, the best I can get is an address for a post office box in Brooklyn.

I grab the phone again and call New York information, requesting the toll-free number for the post office servicing this specific zip code. I look around the room to make sure no one is paying attention and I relax as they're all buried in their overdue term papers and their inferior West Virginia newspapers.

I dial the number and an older man leisurely answers.

"Hey, you guys are on thin ice with my mail," I say firmly, yet quiet enough that no one hears. "I want to talk to a supervisor."

"Ma'am, just relax. How can I help?"

"You can start by making sure my mail goes to my post office box and not to a residence. My husband and I want privacy, which is why we got a box in the first place."

"Certainly, ma'am. You say your mail was sent to your house instead of your box?"

"Worse, it was sent to my neighbors' house—and we don't want them knowing our, uh, business dealings."

"I understand. What's your box number?"

"Four ninety-one." He pauses for too long, so I add, "Name is Bovaro."

He waits a few more seconds, then says, "Um, are you Mrs. Bovaro?"

"What do you think? Why don't you just let me talk to your supervisor."

"No, ma'am, I'll be happy to help you."

"For starters, I want to make sure you have our correct home address on our information card, so if there's ever a problem again, the mail comes to *our* house and not our neighbors'. You have the Atlantic Street address?" I'm totally winging it now.

"No, we have the address on Hicks Street."

"You've got to be kidding. We haven't been there for years. How did you not get our new address but manage to send our mail to our new neighbors? What kind of operation are you running down there?"

"Ma'am, I—"

"Listen, next time you guys have a problem I want a phone call, you hear me? You probably don't even have our most recent number. What number are you showing for us?"

"Um, we, um—718-555-4369?"

Bingo. I scribble the number on my napkin and slam down the phone.

I walk over to the barista, a college-aged coffee slinger who does not appear to be in the mood for anything other than nursing her hangover, and ask to use their phone.

"Phone's by the chair over there," she mumbles, never making eye contact.

"I know," I say sweetly, "but I forgot my calling card number and my cell died this—"

"Sorry," she says and rubs her eyes.

"It's an emergency."

"Go call nine-one-one."

I grind my teeth as I reach in my pocket and ball up all of my money and put it on the bar. "This is it. This is my bribe. I can give you six dollars and change. So what do you say?"

She looks at me, though she might be seeing double. She steadies herself on the edge of the bar and says, "Oh, what do I care," and plops an outdated phone on the bar and the bell in the bottom dings loudly and all the patrons look our way. The barista stares at the money like she wants it to stop moving in circles, takes the five-dollar bill, and leaves the rest.

I pick up the phone and dial.

It rings six times and I am awash in failure; I fear an answering machine is imminent. And though this chapter of my life is coming to a close, it also happens to be the last chapter in the book.

After ring seven, someone picks up and all I get is an unfriendly, raspy male voice. "Yes."

"Um, oh, *hello*?"

"Yes."

"Hi, um, I'm . . . I'm trying to reach Jonathan?"

He pauses. "Who?"

"Jonathan."

Another pause and then, "Sorry, no Jonathan here. You got the wrong nu—"

"Wait!" I yell, loud enough to cause the procrastinators to stop typing. I know that if this guy hangs up the phone, I am done. Forever. I try to think of something to say, to extend the conversation, to *create* a conversation, until I can find a way to link myself to Jonathan without sounding like an undercover agent. Then it hits me. Jonathan. Who am I kidding?

He resumes. "Look, there's no—"

"Actually, I'm looking for Johnny. You know, Little John?"

"Oh, Little Johnny? Why didn't you say so?"

I *knew* it. Those Versace frames aren't fooling anyone.

"He's out of town," Raspy Guy says, "but he can't really be reached at this number anyway. Call his cell. 212-555-1214. Is this Carla?"

I finish writing the number on my napkin and consider lying and saying yes because, of all the skills I've acquired over the years, my most practiced is that of assuming an identity.

"Uh, no. Just an old friend."

"Oh, well, Carla will be happy to hear that."

I close my eyes and inhale loudly. "Yeah, we wouldn't want to upset Carla."

"Do I know you? Your voice sounds familiar." He might know me better by my scream. I consider belting out a few renditions of "Daddy! Daddy!" for him. "What's your name, dear?"

"Angelina Benedetto." See how easy this is?

"Hmmm . . . sorry, doesn't ring a bell. Angela, you said?"

"Angelica, uh, Berenetti." Good gravy.

"Well, if you're a friend of Little Johnny's . . ."

I think for a second and smile. "I am."

We have one of those weird endings where no one says good-bye, like in the movies.

I look for the barista again but she's disappeared. Who cares; I'm calling Jonathan's cell phone no matter what she says.

I dial and on the third ring he answers and I can hear the wind and I know the top is down and I am anxious to be with him, wherever he is, wherever he is going.

"Guess who?" I say.

"I . . . don't know." It's a better response than *Carla*. "Um," he says, fumbling with his phone a bit, "someone calling from the Mountaineer Coffee Mill?"

"Right. Now who do you know who could be so unfortunate to be calling from a coffee house in Morgantown, West Virginia."

"Well, that certainly narrows it down." I hear the rhythm of the concrete clicking under his tires. "How are you, Melody?"

I sigh and listen to the road and though it was only a day ago, it seems a lifetime ago (or, at a minimum, a persona ago) that I had the wind in my hair and I was feeling the irregularities of the highway in the seat of my pants.

"I'm cold, dirty. I'm exhausted and broke. I'm at the end, Jonathan." I whisper, "I didn't leave you. I hope you know I didn't leave you."

The lag of his cell phone delays his response, but it seems he might have hesitated anyway. "I know." I hear a horn blare in the background. "Hey, up yours, you fu—uh, fantastic driver."

"Always the gentleman."

"It's a challenge." A few more concrete seams distance us. "You have a . . . an unexpected, positive effect on my life, Melody."

I smile. "And for some reason you have the *only* positive effect on mine—which is why I want you to know that I didn't leave you; I was taken away."

"It seems no one wants me to have you, not the good guys or the bad guys. It's just one big—hey, how'd you get my number?"

"Your dad gave it to me."

He laughs. "Seriously."

"I might be. 718-555-4369?"

"Holy sh—"

"You mean that was dear old dad? The Disemboweler of Brooklyn?"

"Where'd you get *that* number? That's the private line for his office in Brooklyn. Not many people have it."

"I'll tell you later. So where are you? I'm a damsel in distress here."

"Distress?"

"West Virginia, Jonathan, West Virginia. People think I'm Billy Idol."

"I'm still in Baltimore."

I take a deep breath. "Will you come and find me?"

There is a long delay before he answers and I fear we're about to lose our connection. "Are you sure, Melody?"

The barista returns to the bar and glares at me. "I'm sure."

"I'm getting on I-70 right now. What's the address?"

"254 Walnut Street, outside the university."

"254 Walnut. Got it." I can hear his car accelerate and the wind increase into the phone. "Don't move."

We end our call and I push the phone back toward the interior of the bar. The barista walks over and returns it to its hiding place, then stares at me like she's possessed. "Anything else?" she asks.

"I have about four hours to kill. What can I get for a dollar and forty-six cents?"

She grabs a can of Pepsi and slides it over to me and clears the bar of all of my money.

I use some arithmetic to plan out my stay: twelve ounces, that's three ounces per hour, and at a half ounce per sip, that's one sip every ten minutes or a quarter-ounce sip every five minutes. The soda may evaporate faster. I open the can and walk to the free computer.

I consider killing time by visiting one of a dozen of my favorite math Web sites, but I'm just too shot, even for math.

I decide to Google Sean Douglas but I get over 33,000 hits and I'm not about to start narrowing the results. Then I try to Google some of my past identities—May Adams, Karen Smith, Jane Watkins—and sure enough, my aliases are even more mundane than Sean's moniker. Hundreds of thousands of hits and I am not tied to a single one, as though they made me vanish before I was ever created.

Which is exactly what I'm about to do right now.

$$7x = 6x + 8$$

Jonathan pulls up in front of the café, top down, and parallel-parks in one move, which is less about luck and more about having lived in the city his entire life; there are no parking lots, no lines. He looks around a little, pulls a sweater over his head, and runs his hands through his hair a few times.

I am waiting for him by the door.

Though certainly fueled by exhaustion and hunger, I can feel myself switching over, a conversion from allowing the good guys to do the work to the bad guys; I feel like I'm surrendering everything I've been brought up to understand as moral and right, giving the darkness a try to see if it can carry the weight more mightily. And at the same time, the lightness evanesces, passes me on like a baton, yanks from me my crutches.

Have you ever noticed that the end has a more distinctive feel than the beginning?

He walks in, sees me, and smiles, and I immediately start shaking. My legs go limp and just before I am about to crash, he catches me and holds me—not wrestles me back to my feet, but holds me, like a rag doll—and I tremble in his arms for many minutes. And though I can feel the eyes of all the patrons boring into me, he just hugs me tightly and whispers in my ear,

"It's okay. It's okay. I've got you." The last time someone held me this unconditionally was when I was eight and two boys bullied me on the playground, scaring me to the point that I'd wet my pants, and when my mother came to pick me up she held me and let me cry and didn't care about how my wet clothes were seeping onto her slacks or my relentless tears or the layers of mud the boys had put in my hair and down my shirt. And today I'm being held by this strong man and he doesn't care that I'm filthy and not smelling like anything that implies femininity or how I am broken in ways he could never comprehend. He just tightens his arms around me and whispers over and over, "It's okay. I've got you."

Indeed, he does.

What he doesn't know is that I don't have a penny on me, I have been living on a liquid diet for the past day, and I have not showered or washed my hair or changed my clothes in what seems like a week. I was at the end of the proverbial rope and had he not been there to catch me, I might've fallen into the abyss forever.

When I'm back on my feet, Jonathan steadies me and helps me walk out of the café. The temperature in the café and the temperature outside are identical, but the smell of the fresh air is wonderful, an arid and floral blend like nothing familiar to my senses. I take back everything I said about West Virginia.

He helps me into the car and I fall back against the seat and the leather wraps around me like the arms of an old friend. He gets in too, then reaches into the backseat and pulls out a bag.

"For you," he says.

I glance at him and pass him an emaciated smile. "You're always bearing gifts."

"Well, I had time to kill in Baltimore. Picked this up for you at the college bookstore at Johns Hopkins."

I open the bag to find a brand new copy of Barton Zwiebach's *A First Course in String Theory*.

"Not as useful as a sweater, I suppose," he says, then looks down.

I get a little misty. "Are you kidding? It's perfect." I reach over and give him a hug and he puts his arm around my back and pulls me in. When he lets go, I ask, "You pick this out on your own?"

"Get real. I would've thought string theory had something to do with the clothing industry. I called the assistant dean of the School of Math and asked what the next logical class would be after Differential Equations. Then he reeled off a list of titles that made my head spin. The only one I could remember was String Theory. The lady at the bookstore said this was the best for self-learning."

I shake my head in amazement. "I can't believe you called the dean to research this—and that you remembered that I was ready to move beyond differential equations. That's so . . . *romantic*."

Context is everything.

The sky fills with clouds as we chat. We both glance up and watch them move at the same time.

"Where's that useless fed of yours?" he asks.

"A few miles back."

"He managed to lose you twice in two days. That's gotta be a career killer."

I walk my fingers around the edge of my text and smile. I catch a glimpse of Jonathan and he's watching me—noticing me—and I can tell he's taking it all in, making mental notes, experiencing.

"You know," I say, "your dad called you Little Johnny."

He sighs and rolls his eyes. "What bugs me is there's no Big John. It's not like my dad's name is John or there is some bulky uncle in my family who goes by John."

"So, you're little because you're the youngest?"

"No, I'm little because I'm the *smallest*."

"What? You've got to be five-eleven and three-quarters."

He narrows his eyes at me. "Six feet, thank you. And a solid two-ten. Anything small about that?"

I don't answer; I'm imagining a family of Bovaro men towering over me in my final moments. To think Jonathan would be the smallest guy in a room full of Italian muscle is disturbing at best.

He starts the car, and as we pull onto the road droplets of rain begin to fall on the windshield and Jonathan raises the top while we're in motion. He navigates the town like he's driven through it every day of his life, and just as I settle into my seat, we're on I-68 and the sun is fading in the mirrors. He rolls up the windows and the tint of the glass keeps enough light out that I become drowsy.

I turn and stare at him for the longest time.

Jonathan clears his throat and asks, "Do you want me to take you anywhere?"

I breathe him in, unbuckle my seat belt, and slowly lay my head in his lap and say, "Yes, take me anywhere."

He gently takes his right hand from the steering wheel and places it on my shoulder, and I can feel it shake a little before it comes to rest. I put my hand on his knee and slowly curl it underneath until the tips of my fingers are between his thigh and the seat.

Sometimes there is something sexual about surrender, but not this time. Besides, it's hard to imagine sex could ever bring this kind of euphoria.

I wake to Jonathan speaking softly, and though the car is still in motion, there is no light. Not even on the dashboard.

"What'd you expect?" he says. "You think they'd keep her there forever?"

I try not to stir; I can tell I'm going to be in pain when I move from this twisted position. Right now I feel fine, so I decide to stay silent as long as possible and let the kinks out slowly.

He continues, "Yeah, well, good luck. She's probably in North Dakota."

I'm so comfortable and drowsy that I could probably stay this way forever. But Jonathan's side of this conversation—of which I am likely the topic—is bringing a rush of alertness.

He whispers his final statement, "I'll let you know what I find out." Then he quietly closes his cell.

I decide to let my wakefulness be known.

"Jonathan?"

He jumps and his leg slams my head against the bottom of the steering wheel and suddenly the car is swerving from side to side.

I suppose the kinks were inevitable. I quickly sit up.

Jonathan gets us back in our lane and steadies the car. "Geez—you scared me to death."

"Sorry," I say as I rub the back of my neck with one hand and my forehead with the other. "Why are the dashboard lights out?"

"I thought you'd sleep better. Well, that and I didn't want any passing trucks or cops to get the wrong impression."

"How long was I asleep?"

He turns up the lights on the dashboard. "About three hours."

"We must be getting close to Philadelphia."

"Baltimore, actually."

I rub my eyes and think. "Wouldn't it have been faster to take the Pennsylvania Turnpike?"

"We're avoiding Philly. For the moment."

I stop rubbing and try to focus. "What's in Philadelphia?"

"Some bad people—bad people who received incorrect information." He says this with a strained, wry smile.

I lick my lips and swallow hard. "*You* gave them the incorrect information?"

He nods, inhales awkwardly, and adds, "And there are some bad people in D.C. as well, so we need to snake ourselves between the two. And who knows where the marshals and FBI are at this point. They're a completely separate issue."

It seems Jonathan might have found this task tougher than he first imagined, that keeping me away from both the feds and his family simultaneously is proving to be an undertaking too arduous for one man.

It all sinks in rather quickly. At first, having approximate locations of the hit men brings on a wave of anxiety, a sensation bordering on vertigo. But the more I ponder the situation, the more I realize I'm actually on the proactive side of things for once. Most of the time, the marshals are just moving me around, waiting to see if anyone is coming after me; it always felt like I was barricading myself in a foxhole, waiting for opposing soldiers to find me before figuring out the next move. It's nice finally to be the one with a plan.

I try to watch Jonathan without him noticing. He focuses on the road, almost cataleptic, driving. Devising. When he finally sees me, he smiles, and it is casual and calm, as if nothing is wrong and everything is on schedule. He subsequently calms me as well.

He reaches behind my seat. "Thirsty?"

I adjust my seat a little and Jonathan hands me an Orangina. I shake it a few times but do not open it. "Who's Carla?"

"Who?"

"Your dad thought I might be Carla."

"Carla is my personal trainer."

Rough life.

"Sounded like it might be more than that." I twist the top and take a drink, as though the drink and the comment are equally casual.

"She'd like it to be more, I guess." He turns to me and says firmly, "But it's not."

"Why? What's wrong with Carla? I'm sure she's buff."

He looks at me and smiles. "She is, but . . . she wants to be with me for the wrong reasons—because of my family's influence and money. It's like being a rock star, sort of." He turns back to the road. "With a greater certainty of being murdered or doing time in prison."

I stare at the road and we're passing by the white lines with steady speed. "At least you *have* some form of certainty. You have an identity, a family, a before and after, a lineage and history."

He takes a deep breath like he's going to offer up some great insight, but he merely holds it for a few seconds, then lets the air come out in a rush.

"What?" I ask.

He hesitates again but finally drives it home. "You are beautiful, Melody, in more ways than one—but you would be even prettier if you'd stop feeling sorry for yourself."

I bite my cheek and turn in my seat to face him. "Come again?"

"Seriously, do you think you and I are so different?"

I consider his theorem but it's not working for me. "Yeah . . . I think we're totally different."

"Really? Well, let me tell you how we're alike." He scratches his cheek a few times, looks like a stereotypical mobster. "How often do you think I'm watched by the cops or the feds? If I get a citation for jaywalking, they'll be on me in a heartbeat, trying to get me to flip on someone in my family. I can't go anywhere without being noticed—and I'm a pretty stand-up guy by comparison. But regardless of how straight I am, I will never be rid of the Bovaro tag. I am anything but free. I will always be viewed as a criminal or as a criminal-in-training or, at a minimum, I'll always be viewed as someone with information on other criminals."

"Do you? Have information on other criminals?"

He looks at me and shrugs a little. "Of course. I mean, did you know the details of what your dad did for a living?"

Two police cars go flying by in the fast lane, lights and sirens blazing. Jonathan doesn't flinch. I watch until they are out of view.

"I see your point, but . . . we're still very different. I mean, you can be yourself. You can do whatever you want with your life. Nothing is keeping you suppressed, forcing you out of the realm of possibility."

He laughs and smirks at the same time, like I'd just told him a dirty limerick. "Wha—are you joking?"

I squint. "I don't think so."

"You think I can be a United States Congressman?"

"Okay, well, I—"

"How about a world-class surgeon? Would you want your prostate removed by the son of Anthony Bovaro?"

Despite his family's predisposed knowledge of internal organs, I answer, "No. But, you know, I don't have a prost—"

"That's not my point, Melody. What about being an FBI agent. Think I have a shot at getting into the academy?"

"I, uh—"

"Or a stockbroker? Would you put your financial investments in the hands of a Bovaro?"

"Well—"

"How about a disc jockey? Musician? Professor? I can't even be a Little League coach."

I let him finish; we stare at each other—at least, as long as we can before he needs to return his attention to the road.

"Maybe we are alike," I say. I turn and look out the window and mumble to myself, "Maybe that's why I feel I have this connection with you." As soon as I finish the sentence, I realize I said it too loudly. It wasn't meant for him to hear.

Jonathan smiles and takes my hand. He touches it with the same level of affection as a pat on the shoulder. His hand is warm, and it envelops mine completely. I place my other hand on top to keep him from pulling his back. We both stare straight ahead and swallow.

"But you *could* be a musician," I offer. "Isn't the Mafia involved in payola and all that? I mean, I saw *The Godfather*."

He shakes his head in amazement, as though I'd just guessed his favorite color. "You'll love this: When I was growing up, my brother, Peter, thought he was Jon Bon Jovi—minus ninety percent of the style and all of the talent—which led him to start a band called Shiver. My family pressured some execs at Columbia into releasing an EP of four songs titled *Piloerection*." He turns my way. "Sold four hundred twelve copies." Then back to the road. "Peter still has four hundred and eight of them in a storage locker."

Jonathan slows to the speed limit as we pass the now-parked police cars on the shoulder of the road. I watch as two officers shove a guy in handcuffs into the backseat of one of the squad cars, while two others empty the trunk of a dilapidated Dodge Neon. Jonathan never takes his eyes from the road. This event has nothing to do with me, with us—but my nerves are sparking like I'm overdosing on caffeine.

"So, anyway," Jonathan says once the spectacle has passed, "my family retreated in embarrassment and never entered the world of music again."

"And so ended your shot at becoming a rock star."

He tightens his grip on my hand. "Hey, people enjoy it when I sing in bars because I'm so *bad*."

The stress and anxiety caused from the police scene have instantly been snuffed out. "Hold on, a Bovaro who does karaoke?"

"I was *joking*, Melody." I stare him down. "Sort of. And I'd rather refer to it as open mic night."

I let go of his hand and clap a few times like I'm trying to get a dog to do a trick. "C'mon, baby, sing me a love song."

"Melody," he says, like I'm annoying him. Then, out of nowhere, he throws his fist up to his mouth like he's holding a microphone and belts out something that might've scared me under different circumstances. By the time I recognize his pitch-poor, a cappella version of The Scorpions' "No One Like You," he's mutated it into a medley of their greatest hits, giving me sour bits and pieces of

"Big City Nights," "Still Loving You," and some other tune with indiscernible lyrics.

He returns his hands to the steering wheel and says, "That what you had in mind?"

"Not exactly." His humor—at least I think humor was the intent here—hits me just the right way. My laughter comes out hard and loud. "I was hoping for a little John Mayer, but it's hard to lose when it comes to the Scorpions."

Jonathan's smile fades as it's obvious he's lost in thought.

"What's wrong?"

He sighs. "About you and I being alike . . . there's another thing that keeps me from being whoever I want to be: I got the cops and feds bearing down on one side, but on the other side is . . . my family."

"What do you mean?"

"Well, I always did well in school. Let me clarify: I was the *one* who did well in school. I got into some trouble here and there, not being immune to violence, but I always studied, got good grades. I pretty much could've done anything with my life. But, as a kid, you know, people would ask me, 'Hey, Little Johnny, what do you wanna be when you grow up, huh?' And I'd say something, like, 'An accountant.' My old man would nudge one of his flunkies in the side, laugh, and say, 'Hey, thank God—we need someone who can fix our books.'"

I groan; I know where this is going. Where my view of family has always depicted a blessing, he's going to explain the *curse* side.

Jonathan continues, "If I said I wanted to be a banker, they'd say, 'Finally, someone we can trust to launder the money!' If I said I wanted to be a pilot, they'd say, 'We can get Johnny to help us heist cargo right off his own planes!'"

"Oh, Jonathan."

"I tried for years to think of something I wanted to do that could not be tied back to my family's criminal behavior, but it became impossible. Social worker? Sure, great way to hook up drug connections and prostitutes. Pharmacist? Drug dealer! Photographer? Pornographer!"

Jonathan was right about me feeling sorry for myself. I've wanted a father again for so long that I forgot how miserable some fathers can be, all heavily weighted with abuses of disparate kinds: physical, sexual, or—in Jonathan's case—mental.

I wipe my face, suddenly feel cold. And what do you know: *piloerection*.

"So, what did you do?"

"Well, I thought I'd finally come up with the perfect solution. I went to culinary school, believe it or not. I love food. I love experimenting in the kitchen. So I bought a small place in Williamsburg and run a modest restaurant there."

"Legitimate?"

"The food is. And the waitstaff and the hostess and the reviews." He pauses. "I also managed to launder over eight hundred grand there last year."

I sigh; I can no longer deny that I'm starting to care about this man, because I'm genuinely disappointed. "Why, Jonathan?"

He says to me, weakly, "Because . . . he's my dad."

I bite my lip, suddenly brought back to the reality of his life, of my life, of this moment.

"So, Melody, we are quite alike. In fact, we are identical except for one thing: You would give anything to be who you were meant to be, and I would give anything to be anyone but who I was meant to be."

And that's it. We chew on his observation as the traffic on the highway builds. We stay in silence while the Baltimore skyline grows in front of us like a waiting monster. Jonathan takes the long exit ramp down into the heart of the city.

I do not ask.

•   •   •

Jonathan pulls in front of the Renaissance Harborplace Hotel in downtown Baltimore, across the street from the Inner Harbor. He pops the trunk, leaves the car running, and gets out. For a second, I wonder if he's going to rob the place. The next thing I know he's at my door and opens it for me and offers his hand.

I take it.

He pulls me out and keeps my hand in his grip a few seconds longer than one normally would, and I find it suggestive. I tuck my text on string theory under my arm. He goes to the trunk and removes a small suitcase and four shopping bags. He throws the suitcase over his shoulder and puts two bags in each hand. As we walk toward the entrance of the hotel, Jonathan asks the valet to pass the ticket to me, which the valet does, and as we pass through the front door, the Audi disappears.

This is not WITSEC.

Even though it's nighttime, my eyes take a moment to adjust to the interior of the hotel. Over the course of a lifetime of stays in three-story motels, I have never experienced anything like this dark and surreal entrance. The walls are paneled with mahogany and the millwork is opulent and elaborate. The walls, the carpets, the ceiling, the statues—all deep, lush tones; it feels like I'm walking through the belly of a living creature. Based on my appearance, it really couldn't get dark enough for me anyway.

We're suddenly at the front desk and Jonathan is fumbling with the bags.

A perfectly coiffured, middle-aged woman rushes to help Jonathan and stares him down with a smile that insinuates attraction. "Have you stayed with us before, sir?" the clerk asks.

"*We* have not," he says, rustling through his pockets until he finds a wad of cash.

I move a few steps closer to Jonathan.

The clerk's smile fades a bit, morphs into a more artificial I-am-here-to-help-you look.

I turn and watch Jonathan. This is the critical moment; his intentions will become completely apparent with the decision about the sleeping accommodations. If he rents one room, he's probably thinking he'll get lucky; if he rents two rooms, he's taking the path of the well-mannered and considerate. Had I more experience in the bedroom, I might view this as a win/win situation.

"I just need your name or reservation number," the clerk says.

"We don't have a reservation." He makes no eye contact, keeps counting the bills.

"Well, sir, there's a convention in the hotel. I'm afraid there are no—"

Jonathan chucks a wad of bills on the counter. If I had to guess, it was at least four hundred dollars.

He keeps his eyes down, still counting. "And we'd like two rooms, adjoining, facing the harbor, for two nights."

I'm impressed—and not surprised.

"Uh . . . sure," she says, "let me see." She types for a moment, then nabs a passing clerk and whispers, "Move the Mendels down to seven-nineteen." Suddenly, the printer under the counter goes to town and within a few seconds she places the page in front of Jonathan to sign.

This is *definitely* not WITSEC.

"Do you have a credit card, sir?"

Jonathan's response is the plopping of a second wad of cash on the counter—this time at least six or seven hundred.

He takes the keys and we walk away. I'm pretty sure he never even looked at the poor lady. As we head for the elevators, her voice fades. "Please enjoy your stay at the . . ."

We enter the elevator, alone. I turn to look at him, but instead I catch a glimpse of myself in the wall mirror. I try to turn away but the interior of the elevator is covered with mirrors, like some sort of torture chamber of self-analysis. What has made this man want to spend even a fleeting moment with me is beyond my understanding.

Jonathan shoves all the remaining cash into his pockets, sighs, and turns my way. He smiles, but I can't tell if it's a smile of happiness or of pity. He reaches over and runs his fingers through the stubbly hair on the back of my head and gently pulls me to his chest and holds me there. He slowly leans over and kisses me on the head and I can feel his lips, full and firm, pressing against my scalp, and everything I just felt, all the insecurity and sadness, is washed away. I always hear about how people want to have sex in elevators; this has got to be far better.

We exit the elevator on the eleventh floor, just one from the top, and wind down the hall to our suites. Jonathan opens the door to my room, and as I enter he remains close behind. He puts all four shopping bags on a table near the dresser.

"These are for you," he says. "I hope I wasn't being too presumptuous."

I sit on the bed and there are no squeaky springs; it feels like a hundred little hands are holding me in the air. The comforter looks new. There is no noisy radiator, no arguments coming from the next room.

There is no deputy marshal next door.

I lean forward on my knees, point my toes inward, and grin at him. "Why did you book two nights?" The truth is I wish he'd booked a couple of years. I have no idea where I'll be the day after tomorrow, whom I'll be meeting face to face, whether I'll still be breathing when the event reaches its denouement. All the days past and all the hours forward are just a flicker of indistinctness. This very moment is true, the one I'd like to put on pause or be forced to live over and over for an eternity.

He gently sits on the bed with me, leaving enough room between us for another body. "There's a great spa in this hotel.

I figured, um, you know . . . you'd like to spend the day getting pampered."

His generosity should astound me but I'm overwhelmed with self-consciousness. I look down and laugh. "I don't know what to say."

He slides over a few inches and touches my shoulder.

"Is this because you're going to take me to see your family? You know, to rid me of the bedraggled and unkempt look?"

"Melody, c'mon."

"It's okay if that's what it is, Jonathan. If I could leave myself, I would."

He slowly stands and says, "It's not about me and it's not about my family." He walks to the window and stares at the harbor. "When was the last time someone did something just for you?"

I figure his question is rhetorical but I give him an answer anyway. "When my parents went out of their way to take me to Vincent's for breakfast."

I fall back on the bed, grab my book on string theory, and hug it like a favorite teddy bear.

"There is nothing in this for me, Melody. We are not in the same room. You can leave anytime you want, okay?" He turns from the harbor and looks at me. "I'll be really sad if you do, but . . . it's totally up to you. You can leave anytime."

I nod and he walks to the adjoining door and opens it and throws his suitcase on the floor, turns back to me, and smiles. "I'm just one knock away, okay?"

I nod again and look toward the window so he can't see the emotion in my eyes. "Okay," I whisper.

"Good night, Melody."

He closes the door and I pull my knees to my chest and I begin to sense my body's petition for decent sleep.

I look around the room and it is rich, an exercise in luxury that I have neither earned nor deserve. I am here because someone *put* me here, the same way the marshals put me in various scummy motels on the banks of polluted rivers nationwide.

I am an object.

I pick up a pillow and bring it to my face. It is fresh and clean and smelling faintly of lavender. I pull it down over my face, hard, and fade out.

I wake to my numb arm under my textbook, a hungry belly, and a cold, wet pillowcase on my cheek. The clock reads 4:27 A.M. and my growling stomach insists on attention. I now know what a newborn baby feels like.

I switch on a light, grab the room-service menu, and order eggs Benedict—two orders—and sausage and a bagel and orange juice and an espresso *and* a pot of coffee. I get in the shower and wash off two days of traveling and dust and embarrassment and humiliation. I quickly dry off and slip into the terry robe in the bathroom. It is way too big, but it covers me like a blanket and warms me like a hug.

Breakfast arrives and I waste no time getting the food from plate to mouth. And with each bite I can't help but wonder if my moans of pleasure are penetrating the hotel walls.

I am finally satiated—and full of caffeine—and I sit back in bed and watch the clock. Then I start reading about how Louis de Broglie earned a Nobel Prize by way of his doctoral thesis on particle-wave duality of the electron that he delivered at the Sorbonne.

Light breaks and the clock reads 5:49 A.M., and it turns out electromagnetism is deduced or inferred from gravity in a grand unified theory if, instead of three space dimensions, there are four, where the fourth is transformed into a diminutive circle.

At 6:22 A.M., I'm pretty sure I hear Jonathan moving around in his room; I put my ear to the adjoining door and keep it there for many minutes but hear nothing more, so I soon find out that three independent particle theorists determined that the dual theories that render the particle spectrum similarly evoke the quantum mechanics of oscillating strings—and there you have it, the veritable conception of string theory.

There was a war going on, stimulant versus sedative, and the basic summation is this: Caffeine wins.

The clock turns to 8:00 A.M. exactly, and within a few seconds there is a gentle knock on my door. I hop up (I had three cups, not including the espresso) and run to the door and see Jonathan through the peephole. He's wearing jeans, a white tee, a navy V-neck sweater, and he appears fresh showered and clean shaven.

I open it and laugh. "You could've come through the adjoining door, you know."

"It seemed a little . . . inappropriate. Like I had some right to be in here anytime I wanted." He looks down and notices me in the robe—or rather, that I am wearing a robe and nothing else. He bites his lip and looks down the hall.

I smile, pull it tightly around me, and allow him to enter.

"I'm sorry to disturb you so early, but I got you in at the spa at eight thirty."

"They had an opening?"

He shrugs. "I made an opening."

"No wonder Carla wants you."

"It's all smoke and mirrors. In New York, it's my name doing the work; otherwise it's just a matter of throwing money around."

"You say that like you have no respect for yourself."

He glances around the room for a moment, like he's thinking about how to answer, then, as his eyes return to my face, he says, "I don't."

I giggle, longer than I normally would at such a comment, and I can't stop smiling.

Caffeine wins again.

"You seem like a decent guy to me, Jonathan."

He shakes his head a little. "I've never really had to work hard at anything in my life. I'm *trying* to work hard, though. I want to be fair and honest." He rubs his nose and sighs. "It would mean so much more if the cash I was throwing around was money I'd earned from being a talented chef or a successful restaurateur. Or even if I'd legitimately won it at the track. I mean, most of my income does come from above-board sources, but the other money poisons the whole wad. Do I smell sausage?"

I slide in front of the room-service tray coquettishly. "I took the liberty. Sorry."

"No, good move. We won't have time to eat before your spa appointments anyway."

"Appointments. I have more than one?"

He smiles and says, "Today is all about you, Melody."

I smirk. "What do you mean, today?"

He moves toward me, like he's going to plant one on me, but he just pats me on the shoulder a few times and says, "Today, as in all day. You're getting the works: massage, facial, hair, mani-cure, pedicure, some sort of upper-echelon skin treatment, and a couple of things I didn't really understand and probably cannot pronounce correctly."

I stare at him blankly. "So, I'll be done around . . ."

"Dinnertime."

I bridge the distance between us, stand on my toes, and throw my arms around his neck. I close my eyes and gently, carefully press my lips to his, hold them there for three seconds, then move my mouth to his ears and whisper, "Thank you, Jonathan. Something this wonderful could only come from the money you *earned*."

As I hug him, I feel my robe fall open; I keep my arms around his neck anyway. The cool air hits my body and my skin comes alive with goose bumps. Piloerection has become a regular part of my life. I hear Jonathan gulp as he carefully reaches down to my waist—and I mean *carefully*; his hands never brush my skin—and takes the ends of my robe and deftly places them together. I release him and we both watch as he slowly ties the belt.

When we pull apart our eyes are locked on one another.

Jonathan presses his lips together like he's savoring the taste of me. Then, after a moment, he says, "I'm picking up a hollandaise."

I squint. "And to think I let you in my room at such an unscrupulous hour."

"Worst of all, it tastes like those bastards used tarragon vinegar instead of fresh lemon. In a hollandaise? If one of my chefs did that, he'd be at the bottom of the East River. You want me to have the chef eliminated?"

"Drawn and quartered."

"Eh, my horses are at the stable. But if you let me borrow your spoon, I can file it into a shiv."

Our smiles fade a little. His self-deprecation is humorous, but it's hard to ignore the obvious references; a person can only disparage or undervalue himself so far without the truth getting in the way. He looks away and sighs. I am about to ask the question he knows I am about to ask.

"Have you ever killed anyone?"

Jonathan looks around the room like it's bugged, like this has all been one big setup. Then he leans toward me and says loudly, "No."

I grab his shirt in an amateurishly seductive manner and say, "You mean, I would've been your first?"

He sighs and touches my hand. "That was the plan."

I look up at him and smile. "Well, if you keep treating me this way, you may end up being *my* first, too."

Thinking out loud may have finally done me in.

He drops my hand and backs up a step as though I'd just told him I was fourteen years old.

"You mean, you're a . . ."

I sigh and give in; there's really no point in trying to pretend I didn't say it. "Yes, a *virgin*, Jonathan. What's the matter, you've never killed a virgin?"

"I told you I'm not gonna kill you."

"It was a euphemism. Would you prefer I use the term *deflower*?"

"How is this possible?"

"What do you mean? You think there's some right of passage that occurs when you're a teenager? I kept my legs closed, Jonathan."

He scratches his neck. "How old are you?"

"Depends on what persona you want me to use. If I use Linda Simms, I'm about to turn thirty. If I use Shelly Jones, I'm a spry twenty-four." He waits me out. I tilt my head a little and sigh. "I'm twenty-six."

Jonathan sits on the sofa near the window. "And you never . . . you never found someone you loved enough?"

I sit across from him on the bed and tuck my legs under me and cover myself with the robe. "I'd love to say I was being morally responsible, but the truth is I never allowed myself to get close to anyone—physically or emotionally. There was just too much risk."

He bites his lip as he considers my comment. Eventually, he asks, "Risk for whom?"

For everyone should be my answer, but I get lost in a memory and I'm not sure how much time has lapsed but Jonathan never snaps me out of it. I stare at the pattern in the carpet and my eyes become unfocused. Rather than trying to explain my purity, I let the memory flow from my mind to his ears.

Softly, like I'm trying to keep it between the two of us, I tell him how, when I was a teenager, I thought I'd found the love of my life—like, I suppose, most kids do around that age. Mine was a boy named Brian Basinger, an athletic, pockmarked lad with electric eyes and tight blond curls that I would twist whenever he would kiss me. He was funny and cute and smart and for whatever reason he seemed to like being with me. We'd go to the movies and eat junk food and take long walks and talk about our futures and what we wanted to be, mostly because I'd never really mastered the art of talking about a false past.

One night, Brian and I were snuggling in the basement of my home in Powhatan, North Carolina, a third of the way through *Silence of the Lambs*. I'd grown to love scary movies, not because I was some fan of the genre as much as it gave me a valid excuse to jump into Brian's arms. Around the time Clarice and Hannibal were getting down to the nitty-gritty, I heard a rumbling upstairs, a looming malignity, and my instinct was much like a Kansan sensing a twister not far afield. I immediately went cold and clammy, and I closed my eyes and buried my head in Brian's chest. And I remember how he put his arms around me as though he wanted to protect me—but he could only safeguard me from the characters in the movie; he could never protect me from what was coming.

Then came the stomping of booted feet, the loud voices, the frantic vibrations of things being moved around, the now unmistakable music of people in a hurry. I buried myself in Brian, deeper and deeper, praying that what was coming would go away. Though, just as certain as I was, you too know what was coming.

The feds.

Many miles and days later, I found out that someone had left a message on our answering machine stating we'd all be dead in twenty-four hours. They say it sounded like a kid calling from a pay phone and that it was probably a prank, a horrible coincidence, but they could not and would not take the chance.

But that night I kept the faith, holding on to Brian with all my might, eyes closed, praying silently. The movie was raging on while men shuffled quickly down the steps to our basement. I pulled my face from Brian's chest and watched him. His eyes were locked on the television, totally engrossed in the picture.

He turned to me and said, "I hate this part."

And as the marshals pushed open the door to our rec room, I stared back at Brian and said, "I hate this part too."

Brian had no idea who my family really was. I kept my arms around him, latching on with all my strength, but the marshals just kept yelling, saying we had to go now. I hugged him with everything I had in me, but the marshals must have been through this before and they grabbed my body and pulled me off Brian. He tried to hold on to me, too, but the marshals pushed him back. Brian was just screaming at me, "*Terry, Terry*—what's going on? What's happening?" And as one of the marshals picked me up and threw me over his shoulder all I could answer was, "I love you, Brian. I love you."

Brian Basinger was never a part of my life again.

Jonathan and I sit in silence for a moment, then he says, "Literally pulled from the arms of your lover."

"Within the same minute I was yanked from Brian's grip, I was tossed in the back of a Chevy Impala and I watched our home disappear through the rear window." I sit up and play with the belt of my robe. "I still wonder to this day what must have run through his mind, watching my family scramble out the back door, being driven away by the Marshals Service, leaving him at our house and no one else, all the lights on, back door wide open, television still blaring Clarice and Hannibal. I always wondered if Brian took in our pet bird and kept him from starving to death."

"So," Jonathan says as he walks over and sits next to me on the bed, "you never tried to find Brian after that? Never tried to call him?"

"No. I mean, I wanted to, but . . . I figured it was pointless. It would be a brief, awkward conversation, mostly just an explanation, and then he would move on with his life and I would move on with my life. My *lives*."

I clutch the robe to my chest and lie back on the bed.

"Does that answer your question? I never saw a reason to love, Jonathan, because it meant that one day I would either leave someone behind or take him with me and put him in equal danger." I laugh a little. "Besides, how betrayed do you think my lover would be once he found I had lied to him about who I really was for all of our days together? It's a real mess. I've thought about this for years and years, and as far as I can tell there's no loophole."

Jonathan gets up and walks to the window but merely looks down at the floor. "I'm sorry, Melody."

"For?"

"Everything. For every single moment of suffering and heartache you've been through—because it all comes back to my family. If I had a father who did something legitimate with his life, we wouldn't be here."

I turn my head to catch his eye, but he's still staring at the floor. "True, but . . . you realize we never would've met if your dad hadn't gutted that guy at Vincent's—and, of course, if they hadn't sent you to knock me off."

He finally spins around. "Well, regardless of why we're here now, I'm happy to say that my first memory of you is that little girl with bouncing curls who held her mother's hand on the sidewalk in front of Vincent's." He comes over and kneels on the floor and rests his arms on the bed. "I'm glad I got to see your innocence—even if it was just for a few seconds—and that you were once happy and at peace."

I smile. "I don't think I'll ever be at peace again, Jonathan. I mean, what are we doing? Where are we going? I'm not exactly at peace with meeting the people who want me dead." I laugh a little. "But I'm happy now . . . oddly, because of you." I reach out and touch his hand.

He looks down, then quickly turns his head to the clock. "Well, if you think you're happy now," he says, "just wait till you've had a full day of being pampered! We better get moving."

It's as though the mere mention of my lifelong abstinence has convinced him my body will explode if he tries to explore it. Little does he know that I am the New World.

I catch up with Jonathan in the hall after a few minutes. I perused the bags he left in my room but I did not have time to start removing all the tags and labels from the clothes, so I put on my worn jeans, a new T-shirt, and the green sweater, which, at this point, is more about feeling good than looking good.

We take the elevator down to the second floor and he presents me to the ladies at the front of the spa like he's bringing in a foreign diplomat. When the ladies see him, they're all smiles and coo "Good morning, Jonathan" as though they've known him all his life, but I understand it's probably an even mixture of his looks and charm and a mighty fistful of dollars.

The spa is chic and warm and smells of sweet chemicals. One of the clerks takes me by the arm like I'm some long-lost friend and Jonathan follows a few steps behind. She asks me whether I've been here before and I tell her I've never been anywhere even remotely spa-like and she assures me the experience will be memorable. She has me sit in a room with an elegant though noisy waterfall in the corner, soft classical music playing, and plush seating. She points to a buffet of food across the room: breads, yogurts, cheeses, pastries, and an assortment of fresh fruit that keep my attention while she goes on and on about what they are going to do to me and how I am going to be transformed and how they will create a new me and all I can think is "I want the original me, not another new me" and "Do people really eat star fruit?"

She leaves and I watch Jonathan examine the food. "Ever eat carambola?"

I stand and walk to his side. "I was just thinking about that. No, never had one."

"Well, don't start with any of these; they're too green. They'll be horribly sour." He walks a few steps. "This pineapple, on the other hand, must have been cut just moments ago; it hasn't oxidized at all." He picks up a chunk and places it to his lips and he sort of kisses it instead of taking a bite.

"What are you doing?"

"I'm checking the acidity. Amazing." He places it in his mouth and moves it around like a taste of wine. "This you must try. Sweeter than sugar. Only God could make something this perfect."

He picks up a piece, carefully selecting one that will not be too big for my mouth, and brings it to my lips. I keep my eyes on his and when he puts the wet fruit in my mouth, I bite down on his fingers a little and suck. He slowly lowers his hand and I chew slowly and smile, my lips still wet. "Well, you were right about that."

He is about to say something when the masseur and one of the clerks come in to get me for my massage. We all walk out, and when we get to the massage room, everyone looks at Jonathan like he needs to leave.

"What," he says.

"Sir," the clerk says, "she'll be getting her massage now."

Jonathan peeks into the room and studies the masseur; in comparison, he really is Little Johnny. And from the look on his face, it seems he might've been expecting a woman.

"He's gonna . . . do the . . . thing?"

"Yes, sir," the clerk answers.

Jonathan turns to me and whispers, "You have to take off your clothes?"

I smile and whisper back, "I think that makes it easier."

"Well," he says in full voice, "as your bodyguard, I need to stay by your side today and guard your . . . body. Literally."

"Jonathan," the clerk says, suddenly dropping the *sir*, "she'll be fine in our care."

"But even better in mine." And he walks in.

The masseur laughs and nods to the clerk that it's okay. "Why don't you disrobe and put this towel around you and I'll be back in a moment." He pats me gently on the back a few times and squeezes my shoulder, as though it should signal my getting used to his hands on my flesh.

The door closes and Jonathan sits in a chair and covers his face with his hands. I take off my jeans and my sweater and my shirt and my bra and drape the towel around me, and as I reach up under the towel and pull my panties off, the sound of the fabric sliding against my legs makes Jonathan's Adam's apple bob a few times.

"Okay," I say, "it's safe."

He cracks his fingers a little, peeks, then drops his hands. "Great," he says, casually crossing his legs.

I slowly crawl atop the table and lie on my stomach, pull the towel to my waist and put my arms above me. I can feel my chest slightly spilling to the sides. I turn my head to face him. The look on his face is sweet and distinctly red; he is a cherry Life Saver.

Jonathan's voice jumps a little as he says, "Maybe I should wait outside."

I frown like a child. "But how will you guard my body?"

"Huh, yeah, true. How could I . . . yeah." He fumbles around his pockets and I can tell by the way he's feeling himself up that he's trying to find his cigarettes. He reaches under his sweater and removes a small box and taps it a few times like he's going to pull out a smoke. But instead he opens the lid, clumsily, like he has yet to master some new routine, and taps a small white tablet into his mouth.

I laugh. "Is that Nicorette?"

He noshes it like a dog chewing a bone and he gets this sad look on his face, like he recently buried a close friend. "What can I say? You make me want to be a better man."

I lose my smile. "Are you serious? You stopped smoking for me? But . . . I never asked."

"Well, you shouldn't have to."

The surrender of an addiction might be the noblest of all gifts. "You . . . you really are full of surprises." I look away. "I mean, we don't really know how much time we're going to have together."

"Which makes it even more important that I stop now, you know?"

We stare at each other.

His chewing slows.

And so it happens again, another moment where I have forgotten where I am and who I am with. I am not a kid who sneaked out of her parents' house one night to make out with her boyfriend. I am on the run in the wrong direction with the wrong guy. Yet he's giving me gifts, physical and emotional, that I don't fully understand. And for some reason I want him, and certainly need him. So around I go, back to being the kid, and now I want the physicality that marries the emotion. The clock is ticking, yes?

"Have you ever given a woman a massage before?" I ask. Jonathan adjusts his glasses. I close my eyes and say, "Come here."

He clears his throat. "What do you mean?"

"I mean stand up, take steps in my direction, and stop when you reach the table."

He hesitates, but does as I have asked.

I raise my arms even higher and say, "Now, place your hands on the small of my back." My sexual inexperience brings a glint of anxiety, but Jonathan's determination to preserve my virginity actually relaxes me, allows me to be uninhibited—and, ironically, allows me to pursue *him*.

He takes in a long, steady breath and says, "I'm not sure this is a good idea."

I repeat more softly, "Place your hands on the small of my back."

He does nothing, remains motionless. I am about to open my eyes and give up when I suddenly feel his hands slide down the lower portion of my back and land on the small of it. His hands are warm and he puts his thumbs together at my spine and spreads his fingers over my skin and he is able to cover my entire lower back. The skin on his hands is rough and it tugs my skin slightly as he moves his fingers.

Directions are no longer needed as he digs his hands into my body and he squeezes my flesh and I wince and I keep taking air in my lungs but can't seem to let any out and my body rises off the table as he tightens his grip on me and I can feel the towel has shifted lower and the cleavage where back meets bottom is exposed. Jonathan glides his hands to the base of my neck and pulls them back down, dragging them across all my muscles, and I can feel myself loosening up, twenty years of fear and tension being squeezed from every muscle, every bone, and I do not want him to stop, and before I can catch myself the air finally leaves my lungs in the form of a request.

"Oh, Jonathan, that feels so good. *Please* don't stop."

He responds by digging in harder, tugging at my muscles, and I can feel all the experience he's had with violence as he twists my body around. He keeps moving me and pulling me and the roughness of his palms is scraping me and my towel is shifting farther down and I can tell his face is getting nearer to my skin as he excavates. He moves closer and closer and I can feel his breath on me and I arch my back because I want to feel his lips on me and he rubs harder and his hands are sweating and just as he is about to kiss my back and I am about to flip myself over on the table and pull him down, the door opens.

"Uh," the masseur says, "that's not what we mean by hourly rate."

Jonathan and I look at each other, then at the masseur as we say in unison, "We're done."

"Are you sure? That looked more like the middle."

I sit up and hold the towel to my chest. "Uh, you know . . . I think I'm finished with the massage portion of my day. I'm sort of spent."

Jonathan just stands frozen with his hands at his sides, like he's never been caught doing something illicit—which, again, I find impossible.

"I'll just . . . wait . . . outside," he says.

After I get dressed, I walk back to the room with the food and Jonathan is waiting there. I smile and hug him and whisper, "I loved having your hands on my body."

He trembles a little and says, "There is really no other place they'd rather be."

We hold each other for a moment and he is the first to pull back. "Listen, I'm gonna make myself scarce."

"No, I want you here."

"Well, so far my presence seems to have clouded what I wanted to be a day of relaxation for you. And I need to make some phone calls. I need to set some folks straight. Or unstraight."

I give him a quizzical look.

He clarifies, "I need to buy us more time."

I nod a little, even though I don't understand. "Why do we need more time?"

He gets a faraway look on his face, then runs his fingers through his hair and says, "We just do."

He gives me a quick peck on the cheek and if I'd known he was coming in like that I would've intercepted with my lips.

"I'll see you at five o'clock, okay?" He steps backwards. "Meet you in the hotel bar?"

"I'll be there." I say this like it's a certainty but it seems there's really no way to know.

I like the fact that Jonathan trusts me to spend the day here, that he's self-assured enough to know I'll be waiting, especially after I was pulled away last time.

I've heard people mention the term *day spa* before, but usually only on television or in the movies. People who are stuck in—or put in—jobs that pay in the entry-level range typically do not get to experience such luxuries. But the entire process is addictive: the unfettered care and attention, the high-end hair and body products, the knowledge. The experience is enough to make me want to find a high-paying job just so I can maintain a regular fix.

The hours flew; when I wasn't having my skin treated or my nails done, I was being pampered and fed and treated like a movie star. With each person who helped me, I could see myself changing—changing *back*—to the person I was supposed to be.

The ultimate transformation came during my time with the hairstylist. She spent twenty minutes just *discussing* what I wanted my hair to look like. I didn't know, of course, other than to say natural.

Which was a problem.

The stylist asked me what my natural hair color was, but all I could offer was "some shade of blond."

I truly have no idea what I should look like.

But the stylist did. She matched a color to my skin and cut my hair into a shape that accented my face, feminine and, perhaps most important, intentional. It took two women to get my hair beautifully colored and conditioned to where it was a pleasure to run my fingers through it.

It's just after one o'clock and I'm a new woman. A *different* woman. I stare at myself in the mirror of the spa lounge for a good five minutes before someone comes over and asks if there is something wrong.

"No," I say, "everything is finally right."

I can't take my eyes from the mirror. "Welcome, Melody Grace," I whisper. "I've missed you."

I truly think no one would recognize me right now. Perhaps it's the greatest disguise of all—simply to be myself. If I didn't recognize the person in the mirror, how would the Bovaros?

The food on the bar has changed for lunchtime and I eat a few finger sandwiches. As I am about to leave the room for my one-fifteen appointment for something called a body polish, a clerk walks over and tells me a gentleman is waiting for me out front. Since I know only one gentleman, I double-time it to the entryway, ready to show Jonathan the new me and throw my arms around him. But when I reach the entrance to the spa, there is no one there.

I step into the hall of the hotel and look around and just as I am about to ask the clerk where this gentleman is, I hear a familiar voice from behind me.

"Hello, Michelle."

Turns out the new me looks a great deal like the old me.

$$f(x) = 2x + 1, \ g(x) = x^2, \ (f \circ g) \ (-2)$$

So here is how pathetic I am: I actually turn around and look at this man and say, "I'm sorry, but you must have me confused with someone else." I walk back toward the spa and as I get within striking distance of Sean, I add, "And you're no gentleman."

"Michelle," he says. I keep walking.

"Michelle," he repeats. I enter the spa.

"Melody."

I stop. Then I turn and glower at him and he throws his hands in the air and quickly drops them to his sides.

"Look, I'm not tossing you in the back of a government vehicle, am I? You're not being hijacked by two or three feds, right?"

The people in the spa have stopped talking and I can feel them watching over my shoulder. Without turning to acknowledge their attention, I slowly walk toward Sean.

"All I want," he says, "is to talk."

We stare at each other for a moment and I can feel all of the tension returning, the muscles tightening, the bones aching.

"How did you find me?"

"What?" He gives me a condescending laugh. "You're kidding,

right? The job of a U.S. Marshal is to hunt down fugitives. How hard do you think it was to find *you*?"

"Take any heat for losing me twice in one week?"

Thus endeth the laugh.

"Look," he says, stepping close enough to whisper, "we know who you're with. And based on how you're spending your day, I'm assuming you went with him willingly."

I can't look him in the eye any longer. I meagerly answer, "I did." I stare at my freshly painted toes. "I hope I didn't get you in trouble."

"Don't worry about me, okay? I'm here because I'm concerned about you."

My eyes return to his face. "It's okay, Sean. Jonathan is okay. Everything is okay."

He gives me a restrained smirk. "*Nothing* is okay. Do you know who you've put your trust in?"

"I know about his family and . . . I'm all right with it."

Sean leans in and whispers louder. "Am I to understand that you're all right with the people who had your parents murdered? The people who ruined your life?"

Over the recent days, I have subconsciously converted my units of rage for the Bovaros to units of affection for Jonathan. In any case, he's got a point and it angers me, so I hit back with the only ammo I've got. "No, Sean, *you* are the people who ruined my life. All the morons from the Justice Department are the people who ruined my life."

He sighs. "How long have you known Johnny?"

"He goes by *Jonathan*." I sound like a little kid.

"Not to his friends and family back home, he doesn't. Do you have any idea who this man is, the kinds of things he's done?"

My instincts tell me that I'm right to be with Jonathan and right to distrust Sean, but no matter how many times I try to convince myself, at the end of the day, Sean is wearing the white hat and Jonathan is wearing the black.

"What is it you want?"

"I want you to come with me, Melody. I want you to talk to some people." He moves back a little. "Look, I'm not the right guy to explain things or cook the deals or even pamper you. I'm a marshal, and that means I have a specific job: to hunt and to transport and to protect; I leave everything else to the other folks."

I glance over my shoulder and the spa employees are still staring at us. When my eyes meet theirs, they all turn away quickly. I had friends for half a day.

I turn back around. "I made a promise to stay here. I'm not going to break it."

Sean looks at his watch. "When are you meeting him again?"

"Five o'clock."

He nods. "All I'm asking is that you come with me now for a few hours. And, if after these folks have talked with you, you still want to return to this hotel, well . . . I'll get you back here by five."

I stare at Sean and his gaze is oppressive and I can see how he manages to intimidate.

"Not one minute past five, you understand?"

He nods and his shoulders slump a little, like this is the first deal he's ever closed.

I reluctantly walk back into the spa, clear my throat, and quietly say to one of the clerks, "Um . . . something sort of came up and I won't be able to meet the rest of my appointments." I glance at myself in the mirror behind her and I look and feel cleaner and more natural than I have in my entire life. I do not want to go.

"Well, I, uh," the clerk stutters, as though her service was really for Jonathan and not me, "I hope you enjoyed your time with us . . . and that you'll visit us again." She says this like it's half statement/half question.

"Yeah, well, here's the weird thing: I'm coming back in a few hours and I'm going to pretend I was here all day. Is that okay?"

Her smile sours, warps into a friendly frown. "Sure."

"Thanks." I turn to walk away. "You were paid for all my, uh . . . ?"

The smile returns. "Handsomely."

I'm not sure if she's referring to cash or the guy who gave it to her, but I don't have time for a discussion; the sooner I leave the sooner I can return. And I am determined to keep my promise to Jonathan.

Something is not right. Sean drives us out of Baltimore and does not say a single word. Not only that, but I'm seated next to him in the front seat, like they understand I've given up on them and they have no intention of genuinely protecting me.

We drive half the distance to Washington and just as I am about to break the silence and ask him what is going on, he takes one of the exits for Columbia, Maryland. We drive by my old neighborhood and I see where I worked and where I lived and where I eavesdropped on little Jessica and where I purchased pizza every Tuesday night. It's like returning to the scene of a crime. My body involuntarily shakes and though it seems like I've been gone forever, it's only been a few days.

"Why did you bring me back here?"

Sean says nothing and before I know it we're on some parkway that leads us to the countryside, where the estates get larger and larger and the road gets narrower and narrower and the land on each side eventually turns to miles of corn and soybeans and before the road nearly ends, Sean pulls into a parking lot for an abandoned Baptist church and waits.

"What's going on?" I ask nervously. "Will you answer me? *Why are we here?*"

In the distance, I see a rolling dust cloud, and at the head is yet another Ford product, this one bigger than the Explorer Sean and I are waiting in. It zooms up the road and pulls right next to us and two men get out and open the doors and I am pulled from one and pushed into the backseat of the other. And just before they close the door, I see Sean staring at me and he smiles a little. Then, as the door shuts, everything goes black.

Literally.

It is a black Ford Excursion with black leather seats, a black interior roof, and black controls. And the windows are black—not tinted, black—and there is a window in front of me, like in a limousine, and it's black too. I can't see a thing.

"Light?" I ask.

A few seconds later, the man next to me flips a switch and says, "I'm Deputy Marshal Williamson and we're taking you to the WITSEC Safesite and Orientation Center. We'll be there in approximately eighteen minutes."

I stare at the heavyset, middle-aged man with a fresh high and tight. "Come again?"

"You've never been there, according to your file."

I continue my staring but I'm not really looking at him at all; I'm confused. "The Safesite and Orientation Center?"

He keeps speaking but looks straight ahead, as if he's watching the road instead of the dark void. "It's where people are . . . reborn, I suppose."

"Well, why the black windows? I'm not that much of a threat, am I?"

"The black windows aren't to keep people from seeing in." He finally turns to me. "They're to keep you from seeing out."

I look down, pretty much because there is nothing else to look at, and I'm amazed at the quality manicure and pedicure I received hours earlier. I can't help but think they'll be destroyed before Jonathan ever gets to see them. I have a brief fantasy of digging my freshly painted fingernails into the side of Sean's neck.

After a solid fifteen minutes, the car shimmies and I can tell we're going down, fast, and we hit concrete and suddenly the car's wheels are crying as we make repeated sharp turns. Then we stop and the engine goes off and the doors unlock and everyone exits the vehicle, except me; I've learned to wait for instructions.

And, sure enough, the marshals converse for a moment—they're all business—then ask me to step out of the car. I do.

They escort me down a long carpeted hallway and into a receiving area that looks almost as classy as the entrance to the Renaissance. There are one-way mirrors spaced sporadically in the walls and cameras whirring inside black globes. I slow my pace. I'm sure my mouth is ajar; I just hope there isn't any saliva running down my chin.

"What is this place?" I finally mumble.

"It's where we bring everyone entering the program. It's a one-stop shop, a state-of-the-art center designed to protect and re-invent."

Williamson points at various items in the facility as we walk, commenting on all of the hidden benefits, selling me on it like I'm a child reluctantly dumping a parent off at a nursing home. He explains how the doors here are bolted and can only be opened by WITSEC inspectors, how the hallways are monitored with video cameras and motion detectors, how one witness will never know that another is here, and how they've housed up to five families at a time. He tells me how the center has a solid exterior and another completely separate interior so that nothing can get through, explosives or otherwise, and how they have gates and fences that keep out intruders and uncleared vehicles.

He tells me how they've got document specialists and trained personnel to help people get all their new IDs and records in the fastest manner; psychologists and psychiatrists in residence to

help folks being relocated better understand the changes ahead—
and to help with any outstanding fears and issues they may have;
lawyers who build a contract into what they call a Memorandum
of Understanding—that is, the details of the specific agreement
for a relocated witness and his or her family so they can be certain
what they're getting in return for their help; inspectors available
to discuss and develop a plan for where the witnesses would like
to be relocated, where they can watch videos of the targeted areas
and get a better understanding of terrains and expenses and lifestyle options.

If this was why Sean wanted me to come here, that he hoped
this spectacle might turn my tide, he was way off. I am certainly
impressed by the facility—by the government's forethought, com-
prehensiveness, and commitment. But right now I am nothing
more than a paroled prisoner strolling through the halls of the
penitentiary that once housed me. And all the chimerical, fancy
detail work cannot change the predestined outcome of another
cycle through the system. This place is nothing more than a
Porsche with the engine of a Buick.

Deputy Williamson continues his comprehensive coverage
until I ask the burning question. "Where was this when my parents came into the program?"

He pauses and looks at the marshals beside me. "It wasn't completed until 1988, after your family was already in the program."

I consciously have to remove the bewildered look from my
face. "No one ever gave us psychiatrists or relocation options or a
Memorandum of Understanding."

Williamson touches me on the shoulder and tilts his head as
if to say *Yeah, yeah, I know, but I'm just a marshal and you need to
complain to someone else.* Now more than ever I wish I hadn't come.
Even as I have dismissed the lot of them, they seem to find a way
to get under my skin. And rankle.

As my blood pressure rises, I'm ushered into a dark, plush

conference room where four men are waiting—no one I recognize—and they stand when I enter like they're the surest of southern gentlemen.

"Hello, Melody," the first man says, equally practiced and sinister. I stand with my hands at my sides and Williamson nods to the group and leaves me. "You're looking well. Very healthy."

"I wasn't six hours ago." I give a snide smile. "You caught me on a good day."

"Can we get you anything? Something to eat or drink?"

"Let's move this along. I have to get back to Baltimore."

First Man frowns and looks at the others. "Very well. Please have a seat."

I sit, but am quickly annoyed that four pairs of eyes are observing me at once.

First Man says, "My name is Hugh Donovan; I'm the assistant director of the U.S. Marshals Service. This man next to me is Miguel Sanchez, Justice. Next to him is Special Agent Lou Foncello with the Federal Bureau of Investigation. And the man at the end is Abraham Greenberg, our chief psychiatrist here at Safesite."

"I always wondered what happened to stooges four through seven."

Donovan sighs a little and looks over at Agent Foncello.

"It's our understanding," Foncello says, "that you've not been satisfied with your experiences inside WITSEC."

I chuckle. "Dissatisfaction lends itself more to buying a blouse with a hole in it or eating a bad cheeseburger." I stare at him like I'm trying to make him burst into flames.

"Right. Well, either way, we'd like to make it better."

I sit back in my chair for a moment. "What are you guys, some hybrid customer-satisfaction panel?"

Donovan gets this supercilious look on his face. "Melody, you are in the presence of some of the smartest and greatest minds at Justice."

"Oh, yeah? What's the square root of negative four?"

"Two. No, wait . . ."

"Chew on that for a while. I'm going back to Baltimore."

"Melody," says Sanchez, "the purpose of this panel is . . . well, we're here to make your life better."

"Did you say life or *lie*? If the government lifts a finger to my lips one more time, I swear I'll bite it off. I do not need another artificial life." I turn and look at Donovan, who is squinting toward the ceiling, still pondering how to derive the square root of a negative number. I decide to set him free. "It's an imaginary number, Hugh. I thought for sure you'd grasp that concept considering your recurrent influence in the lives of the imaginary."

Sanchez picks up where he left off. "What we're offering is an artificial life, yes, but a *wonderful* life. Anything you want—within legal reason."

I pause to think. "Meaning?"

"You would stay right here, at Safesite, while we re-create who you are, so that when you leave, there is no waiting. The whole process would take less than two weeks. No months of hotels and waiting for work. We have folks who'll draw up a memo—a contract, if you will—outlining exactly what we have offered, right down to the job, location, and subsistence checks. And we're willing to be generous."

I swallow. "Why?"

Sanchez leans forward and smiles in a way that makes me feel like a perp. "You can help us, Melody."

I widen my eyes. "Thank goodness, because keeping you guys happy is my deepest desire."

"Jonathan Bovaro," he says, using the name as a knife to cut my sarcasm. "He seems to have manipulated you quite a bit."

"Interesting you put it that way. Maybe we should focus on how he managed to find me in the first place. Might be time to officially change the term from *witness protection* to *witness relocation*." I clear my throat. "Besides, no one has manipulated me."

"Really? Are you saying Little Johnny didn't push himself into your life? He didn't woo you with money and luxuries and who knows what else?"

"I called *him*." My answer is childish and poorly thought out. I can feel myself sinking.

Sanchez loses his aggressive smile and says, "Let me tell you about Jonathan Bovaro. He's a liar and a crook and a violent man."

Jonathan has told me about items two and three, which sort of defuses item one. "He's not a liar."

I am not helping myself.

"Really? You find him to be a truthful and forthcoming kind of guy?"

"Yes."

"So I guess he told you about what goes on at his restaurant in Brooklyn?"

"Yes, he was totally upfront about the money laundering."

How stupid am I?

All four men sit back and smile simultaneously.

"That's what we thought."

I close my eyes and shake my head. I have never felt protected around these men, reinforced by the types of actions they are committing right now. I am a pawn—*again*—in their quest to bury the Bovaros. Taking that family down will make one or more of the careers of these guys. But all it means for me is another town, another alias, another stint of life on the run and wondering when my car is going to explode. And the satisfaction in their collective eyes, the warmth in their faces at getting closer to a showdown, tells me one thing and one thing only: They really couldn't care less about me.

I look up at the ceiling and softly offer, "Jonathan is a good guy. He's not like the rest of—"

"*Right.*" Agent Foncello slides a folder across the table and says, "Take a look."

I put my hand on the folder gently, like I'm placing a flower on the coffin of a loved one.

"Take a look at the kinds of things *Jonathan* is capable of."

I open the folder and I get only as far as the first picture before my stomach turns. It is the image of a young man with the bottom half of his face bloodied and listing to the left, his mouth protruding as though pushed from the throat outward, with several teeth broken or missing. The man in the picture is conscious, and the look in his eyes is undisputed terror.

"That's Gregory Morrison. Jonathan gave that man what the Bovaros call a *souvenir*—something to remember the event, as it were."

I swallow. I can't take my eyes off the picture. "What, um . . . what did he do?"

"Well, once he was done smashing the guy with various objects, he took off his belt, placed the buckle inside Morrison's mouth, making sure the guy's top and bottom teeth were in the buckle. Then Johnny pressed his foot against Morrison's chin, wrapped the belt a few times around his fist, then yanked up like he was pull-starting a lawn mower."

I close the file and slide it away and fall back in my chair and everything gets light and gray. "May I have a glass of water?"

Nobody moves.

"We need you to help us, Melody."

Nothing has changed in twenty years. They are employing the same wear-down, fear-inducing tactics they used on my parents. I cover my eyes, wish the room would stop spinning. "Why do you need my help? Looks like you have plenty of evidence against him."

"You think Morrison's going to testify?"

I lurch forward and slam my fist down on the table. "Why don't you put *him* into Witness Protection? Bring him here and tell him what a great life he's going to have in Nebraska as a fertilizer deliveryman!"

"You can get us a lot more information. You would be a great asset to—"

"Don't you *dare* try to play on my patriotism."

Donovan steps up to bat again. "Listen, Melody, you're already *in* the program. You're not giving up anything *new*."

It's hard to believe those words actually came out of his mouth. The other three guys look at Donovan.

Sanchez quickly tries to stop what is about to happen. "What Donovan meant was—"

"Wait," I say, but I can't help laughing with all my might, all my heart. It does not bring relief; what I've needed all these years is a good laugh, not a good hysteria. "You know, you guys are a bunch of low-life losers, scumbags of the highest order, a bunch of self-important dicks who are just as bad as the bad guys but you pretend to be the good guys, which makes it so much worse. You have no face value. You have no worth to speak of. You promise hope and deliver ruin. And my last, undying prayer is that each of you will live a life of pain and anguish and misery, that some new and excruciating cancer will emerge and fester in your bodies where you will rot for years on end." I stand and adjust my clothes. "And you got it all wrong, Donovan. I am *not* in the program. And I never will be again."

I turn and leave the room and though I hear a little rustling in the chairs, one of them says, "Let her go."

I walk down the hall where Williamson is waiting and I angrily say, "Take me back to Baltimore."

He nods and says "Yes, ma'am" like a soldier, an entity entrusted to do as it is told; I have no doubt he will complete the mission.

Within minutes I am back in the blackness, zooming from the building, onto the rural roads back to the parking lot where they open the door and point to Sean parked fifty feet away. I step out

, of the vehicle and before I am three feet from the door, the Excursion spins its wheels and disappears. I turn and watch it fade away, along with my last chance.

Sean gets out of the Explorer and casually walks over to me, as though he knows that there is no need to protect me, that I am no longer in the program.

"They told me not to wait," he says. He smiles and adds, "I knew better."

The dust catches in my throat and though my response is delivered weakly, I am firm in my belief. "They just wanted to use me, Sean. No one has my best interests at heart. And honestly, how could they? Unless you're emotionally bonded to someone, how can you ever *really* protect that person? In my case, no one at Justice cares."

He shrugs and looks into the distance. "You think John Bovaro does?"

I shrug back. "At least I know what he is, you know? You guys are just . . ."

He sighs and folds his arms in a nonaggressive way. "It's a good program. Don't knock it, Melody. Just because it didn't work for you doesn't mean it doesn't work at all. We've been able to put hundreds of horrible people away for life because of testimony generated out of WITSEC. And the recidivism rate for criminals that went into the program is not even a tenth of what it is for people who get *rehabilitated* in prison." He pauses and stares back into the distance. "It's made a difference."

I want to believe him but his genuineness is one dimensional, like he's repeating statistics from a recent briefing used to invigorate an increasingly disenchanted force of marshals.

I nod a little, throw him a bone. He can spew the facts at me all day long, but what I know is that my mother and my father and I fell through the cracks, and instead of pulling us out, they sealed us over with a fresh layer of cement.

"They're not heroes," I say.

He smiles and shakes his head. "Heroes are *exactly* what they are. You cannot imagine how many people are alive because of the good things these guys have done. I know you think you're a victim—which you are—but so are these marshals and agents. You think *they* don't get threatened all the time? Or their wives and kids? They do, believe me; I've been on those details, protecting government officials and their families. It's not perfect, just like the entire criminal justice system, but it's all we have. And sometimes good people, like you, get caught in the middle."

I step up to Sean and he bridges the gap and pulls me in for a hug and my head falls right into the valley between his pecs; it's a warm, inviting place to dwell.

Sean lightly strokes the back of my neck and says, "If someone had testified against the Bovaros decades ago, your parents would never have been involved. They'd still be alive today." I pull back and look at him. "Your parents saved someone else's life. You see? The system works in a chaotic way."

"But the feds lost the case my folks testified in."

"Yeah, they did, but other guys—lower-level guys—folded because of the pressure of that case, which led to more arrests down the line. It did more good than you probably know."

We stare at each other while we remain partly embraced and for a moment I imagine what it would've been like if my little brother had survived. I'd like to think he would be strong and protective, like Sean, but without the tunnel vision.

"You still want to go back to Baltimore?"

I leave his grip and look down the road. The dust from the Excursion is long gone. "Yeah, I do."

"Because you have no place else to go?"

I exhale slowly. "No, because it's the place I want to be."

Sean walks around the side of the car and opens the passenger door. "Listen, I'll take you wherever you want to go, but please know that Jonathan Bovaro will *never* be your hero. There is no way he can rescue you from the life you have to live."

I say the words I've practiced, but the mantra is losing its effect: "He's not the same as the others."

I get in and Sean closes the door. After he walks around and sits down on his side, he says, "There is only one type of Bovaro— and Johnny is his daddy's boy."

As Sean accelerates, I stare ahead blankly, unable to get the image of Greg Morrison out of my mind. But the thing that haunts me, that scares me and brings about a sudden faintness, is the rage one must be capable of to inflict that kind of torture on another person.

Sean pulls in front of the Renaissance and puts the Explorer in Park. He turns and leans on the steering wheel as I open my door and get to the sidewalk.

"I guess this is good-bye," he says, but I hear a question mark in his tone.

I turn and rest against the frame of the door, sort of casually, but my stance is mostly derived from fatigue. "I suppose so."

Sean smiles and all of a sudden he's human again, all McConaughey-esque and whatnot, as though our parting is a signal for him to be a decent, caring guy for a moment. "You're a beautiful woman, Melody."

I smile a little and look down.

"And I don't mean just today, from your spa thing. You were already beautiful."

I look up again. "Thanks, I—"

"And you're worthy of more than John Bovaro. Don't think that by switching sides everything will get better. It doesn't matter which team you play for; the game remains the same." I stare at him. Just like that, Matthew is gone and Sean has returned, like he's suffering from dissociative identity disorder. He puts the car in Drive and slips away.

My body and mind are now conditioned to toss me into worry whenever instability or loss enters my life, and I begin rubbing my temples as I walk through the lobby of the hotel. I glance at the clock on the wall and see it's nearly three o'clock. I take the elevator to the second floor so I can return to the spa, and the image I see in the mirror of the elevator is a vaguely familiar one, a weathered, exhausted woman with mascara-smeared eyes and patchy makeup. I'm struggling to maintain this morning's conversion; I've become a close, rivalrous sibling of my former self.

As I walk through the entryway of the spa, I'm greeted by the same clerk as earlier in the day, and I finally notice a little name tag on her sweater that reads KIMBERLY. I liked her better as Clerk. She takes one look at me and says, "Oh, dear. When is Jonathan coming back for you?"

"Five."

She looks over her shoulder and checks the time. "We better hurry."

In an instant I'm tossed into the chair for a facial, and two estheticians go to town at once. I want to ask how much Jonathan gave them to be this attentive, but I'm probably better off not knowing. Besides, it's more fun to pretend they're doing this because they want to help me, as my friends, look good for my boyfriend.

The hairstylist passes by, glances my way, stops, and says, "Oh, dear," and before I know it she's grabbing chemicals and re-applying them to my hair and scalp.

One of the estheticians nods to someone behind me and instantly the manicurist is looking down at my fingernails, then my toenails, and then she says, "Oh, dear," and my arms are out and my sandals are off and my feet are propped up like I'm seconds from giving birth.

I am a movie star. Right down to the broken home and the perpetual insecurity, I am a movie star.

Sixty minutes pass and by some wave of a magic wand, all hands are removed from my body at the same time, their faces and bodies parting like the Red Sea so that I may finally witness the glory of their concerted labor. I see myself, but it's hard to recognize me. They finished the job and finished me off at the same time. May Adams and Karen Smith and Anne Johnson and Jane Watkins and Terry Mills and Shelly Jones and Linda Simms and Sandra Clarke are gone forever. And so is Melody Grace McCartney.

I may never look this good again. The only thing missing is the halo.

That such health and comfort are delivered only to the rich and privileged seems horribly askew, so unfair, and for the briefest of moments, while I am staring at my silky hair and my soft, powdered skin and my glistening nails, I think it might be okay to be a criminal if the fruits are this sweet and juicy.

I stand motionless, frozen, a deer with an introversive beam of light in my face. I can't stop staring at this sight, but the image before me is so beautiful, so sexy, so elegant, that I cannot help being rude to myself. And all at once I see decades of missed opportunities fall to the sides of my history.

My eyes begin to moisten.

"Oh, dear," I hear in unison.

I lunge for a box of tissues and start pressing them to my eyes. "It's okay," I say.

Tears of joy are so much easier to stop.

I turn and thank each one of them individually—and confirm they've been taken care of, financially speaking. They say they have been, like they just finished some daylong lovemaking session; my dark side wonders what Jonathan gave them for currency.

As I walk away and stroll out the front of the spa, I hear Kimberly say to someone, "She is simply lovely."

Twenty-six years in the making.

On the journey back to my room, up the elevator and through the halls, the eyes of men are casually upon me in a way they've never been before; they are covetous. I smile at each but I keep walking; I've got a deadline to meet.

I enter my room and turn on the Weather Channel and find out tonight is going to be warm, in the mid-seventies. I finally start going through the bags of clothes that Jonathan filled with his purchases, and I spread it all out on the bed. He managed to buy something of just about everything, and in an array of various sizes: jeans, blouses, sweaters, various colored T-shirts and camisoles, a skirt, a sundress, a pair of strappy sandals, even two bras and three panties. He is an all-inclusive kind of guy. And I'm impressed at what must've been difficult purchases, embarrassment-wise, for a man of his character.

I carefully remove the tags from the sundress—a blue and white dress with a questionable pattern until I see the manufacturer, after which I'm quickly assured of its good taste—and slip out of my clothes. I hold the dress up to my body in the mirror and the colors bring out the natural tones of my skin and the new (original) color of my hair.

I stare at the bras on the bed, but—one advantage to being flatchested—I decide to forgo one altogether. I slip the cotton dress on *carefully*; it does not touch my hair or my face. It fits on the tightish side, clings to my body as though it were tailored specifically to my figure at a younger, slightly thinner age, and the fringe of the dress meets my legs at mid-thigh. And what do you know: it's a size six; there are advantages to starving oneself on the run.

I slip on the sandals and they're the wrong size by a half, but as luck—or Jonathan's hidden skill—would have it, this maker runs big, so they fit well enough.

It is three minutes till five and I grab one last look in the mirror. I'd primp myself a little, but at this point I could only do damage. I snag my room card and proceed to the elevator, get off on the second floor, and walk toward the bar.

I approach cautiously because I am not a veteran of such scenes, and the last time I spent any significant time in a bar, I ended up going home with the nipple-twister. The place is quiet but the traffic, for the most part, is going in now that the workday is ending. The lounge is massive, could easily hold five hundred people, with floor-to-ceiling windows that offer views of the harbor and Pratt Street. The entire bar is dark and sort of dreamy and I slither in as I scan for Jonathan. I do not see him.

It is exactly five o'clock.

I walk to a series of low, empty tables by a window in the corner and I face the doorway. I try to send off a leave-me-alone vibe, but I've never been very good with vibes. A waitress comes over and carefully places a napkin in front of me and asks what she can get me.

I say, "Um, can you recommend something?" I smile like I'm something more than the nitwit I'm portraying. I lean forward and slide my hand down my calf to appear casual and I'm distracted by a delicate softness not known to my skin since I was a toddler.

She starts whipping off a stream of mixed drinks and martinis that hold no future in my bloodstream.

"I'll have a glass of red wine. A Shiraz or Cabernet or something?"

She smiles and nods, walks with a determined pace that has her delivering my beverage in under a minute.

Two guys at the bar, about thirty feet away, are chatting and smiling, and one of them keeps glancing my way. I pretend not to notice, but they are sort of in the path of the entrance, where

my eyes are fixed. I'm waiting for Jonathan to come to my rescue.
Again.

The bar guys are smiling more intently. The first nods in my
direction for his friend, then they both look over, then lots of smiles.
Now the first one is on the move and it occurs to me that all I had to
do was order two glasses of wine and I would've been left alone.

The guy is aiming for me, like an arrow from a bow, and he
shows no signs of stopping or slowing until he pierces my flesh.
He is a young professional wearing a dark business suit, mid-
twenties at best, built, short hair, with glasses so trendy they
scream of overcompensation, good looking, and obviously practiced in what he is about to do.

All I can think of are the frat boys back in West Virginia.

I consider looking away, though now it would be obvious. As
he approaches, he studies me from head to toe. If he asks to join
me, I'm prepared to tell him I'm waiting for someone.

He doesn't ask; he sits. Now, I'm annoyed.

He smiles—the smile he's likely practiced in the mirror every
day since he turned thirteen. "I'm Marcus."

I rub my forehead a little, and instead of offering a name or a
hand, I sigh quietly. "Hi. Look, um, I'm sort of expecting someone."

His smile weakens and he casually looks across the room at his
buddy and suddenly I feel I am once again the balancing point of
a bet. He moves his influence from his smile to his shtick.

"You are the most beautiful woman in this bar."

I frown and glance around the lounge. "There are, like, eight
women in here."

He stops and readjusts, like he's pulling from a random point
in his overworked algorithm. "Your eyes, they're just amazing. I've
never seen color so—"

"Drab? I have drab hazel eyes, Marcus. For future reference, if
you want to blow a woman away, compliment her lips."

He smiles again and starts going on about how beautiful and sensational I am, how he has never witnessed such splendor, and the words flow with increased speed and triteness.

From the corner of my eye, I see Jonathan's physique appear in the entryway. He pauses to look around, spots me, and heads in my direction—first at full pace, then slower, then full pace again.

Things are going to take an ugly turn for poor Marcus.

I am not hearing a word, but the guy is really trying hard, so hard that I'm convinced there is at least a hundred bucks on the table. I turn and look at Jonathan, and he walks up behind the guy and places a hand on his shoulder.

"A friend of yours?" Jonathan asks.

I smile a little, as I can only imagine what clever thing Jonathan is going to say to this guy. I shake my head no.

Jonathan does not use words. Instead, I see Marcus quickly yield under Jonathan's grip and he slides down in the chair in immediate pain.

"Wait, wait, wait!" I yell.

But it's too late. Before I can even leave my seat, Jonathan has already grabbed the guy by the collar of his suit jacket and dragged him several feet across the room. And as he tosses him back toward the entrance and over a table, Marcus goes limp and the room falls silent.

The friend at the bar is not coming to the rescue. Again.

I'd like to say my present concern is for Marcus, but the only thing running through my mind now is that black-and-white photo of a fright-filled Gregory Morrison—and an attempt at understanding what made Jonathan capable of that brutality. This scene feels like a precursor to a more savage event.

Jonathan hurries back to me. "Are you okay? Was he trying to hurt you?"

I take a few clipped breaths as I feel this room full of strangers turn into a room full of witnesses. "You're supposed to ask that *before* you come to my aid."

He studies me, takes a step back. "Oh, Melody, you are stunning. It's hard to imagine you could be more beautiful than before, but I'm nearly breathless. I cannot tell you how proud I am to be at your side this evening. You look like an angel."

Angelina. Angelica.

I throw my hand up and say, "Uh, thanks, I really, um, appreciate—shouldn't he be getting up by now?"

Jonathan shrugs without looking at the guy. "He'll be fine."

Marcus comes to life with a weak groan.

Everyone stares at us as Jonathan pulls out his wad and drops a handful of bills on the table. He gently takes my arm and says, "We should get going."

I cover my eyes and walk with Jonathan, hand in hand, a few paces ahead of him, like I'm dragging my son through a crowded mall. Once we reach the hallway of the hotel, I punch him three times in the chest; he does not move.

"This is *not* New York!" I whisper loudly. "You cannot just walk into a bar or restaurant, render a person unconscious, and drop some cash on the table like it's some MasterCard with an unlimited credit line for felonies!"

He simpers. "Technically, you can't do that in New York, either."

I am not in the mood. I look at him in a way that conveys this notion.

He clears his throat. "I'm sorry. Look, I can never know who's after you, right? I'm just trying to protect you." He takes a deep breath and we both start walking very quickly; now he's dragging me.

"Was he bothering you?" he asks.

"Not really."

"Was he hitting on you?"

"Yes. But he was *only* hitting on me, okay? Just like those kids were *only* spitting on your car. They're offensive acts, sure, but there's no reason to overreact—and certainly no cause for violence."

He looks down. "Right."

We get to the elevator and as the doors close I feel some relief. I move toward him and gently place my hand on the spot I'd punched. "Sorry I hit you."

He takes my hand, brings it to his lips, and kisses it softly. The blood rushes to my face.

I pray Sean is wrong; I *need* Jonathan to be my hero.

$$C(5,3) = \frac{m!}{(n!)(m-n)!}$$

We leave the hotel, and the closer we get to the harbor—and the farther we get from the hotel bar—the safer I feel. Part of my anxiety is from Jonathan's propensity for violence; the rest stems from an underlying fear that I'm going to get nabbed by the police in conjunction with one of Jonathan's outbursts, and I will have to explain who I am and why I am voluntarily with my captor, and I can just imagine Sean standing behind a one-way mirror, shaking his head in disgust, muttering, "There's your hero, Melody."

Jonathan makes a phone call on his cell, the first call it seems he is deliberately trying to shield me from hearing. He waited until we were in the midst of a loud section of Harborplace, the strip of shops and restaurants on the water, before deciding to use his phone. And his head is constantly turned away from me. My concern dissipates, though, as he shuts his phone and clenches his fist and smiles, like his team just covered the spread. He looks at me and his whole body droops with relief.

I stare at him and he scrunches his chin. "Just making sure we're buffered," he says. "I managed to get us one more night."

Of safety, is what I'm sure he wanted to add. Because, you know, tomorrow . . .

This day of pampering and this last-supper sort of evening have me wondering just how confident Jonathan is in his plan; I feel my hours are potentially numbered—in the single digits, no less. A stress-based shiver overcomes me, and he gently takes my hand and somehow pulls the torment right out of me. Like a drug, he is.

We hold hands and walk around the harbor; he steals glances at me and I believe he is truly proud to be with me. The air is warm and moist and there is a gentle breeze that has the edge of my skirt tickling my thighs. We walk for many minutes without saying anything to each other.

I look down at my new dress and sandals and say, "These are lovely clothes, Jonathan. Thank you."

He tightens his grip on my hand and looks at me for a few seconds before saying, "They're only lovely because you're wearing them." We stop and I turn and look up at him. He stares into my eyes and without hesitation or embarrassment or premeditation, he says, "You are flawless, Melody. Beautiful, smart, funny. Everything about you is right in every way: your height, your hands, your skin, your hair, your eyes." He slows his list, speaks softer. "Your smile, your laugh, your . . . legs, your body, your lips . . . everything about you." And finally, in a whisper meant only for my ears, "It's the kind of thing men live and die for."

Oddly, it's sort of the same speech Marcus was delivering just before he was flung over a pub table. But there is one thing lacking in the Marcus version: genuine words from a genuine heart. And to be told this from a man who seriously and convincingly means them—well, it makes all the difference.

I am suddenly self-conscious and cannot look him in the face. Through nervousness, I begin to dilute his compliments, as I did with Marcus. "My, um . . . my eyes? They're a drab hazel that—"

"It's more than the color." He lifts my chin a little and our eyes reconnect. "They have a dark line around the edge of the iris, a thing of natural beauty that brings your eyes to life. And they are intense; they shine like they're reflecting the light of a thousand stars, and they reflect me, too, and they make me want to be everything to you. And when you get angry, they dance a little, and every time it weakens my heart and makes me smile."

I am tipsy. My recent days and nights have been a miserable blur, but I could not be more certain of how I am weak with affection for Jonathan. I have known him for a few days—hours, really—and my life has never felt so complete.

He holds me and kisses me and I feel like I could let go, yet never drift away.

He is inside me.

Eventually, after some unknown passage of time, our lips move apart and we begin walking again, like we have some important destination. We watch the boats slowly float into the harbor as others pass them on their journey out. Parents run after escaping children and the entire waterfront is filled with giggles and laughter and the smell of beer and diesel fumes. The skyscrapers look down on us like protective deities and it feels like we are here for a reason, safe among the visiting suburbanites and the urban affluent; it feels like we're the normal people we long to be.

We start to run out of sidewalk as we approach Federal Hill on the south side of the harbor, and as we do, the foot traffic recedes.

"Should we eat?" Jonathan asks.

I grab his arm with both hands and curl my wrists around it, like I'm holding on to a pillar. "Okay," I say, leaning my head on his shoulder.

"Seafood?"

"With Little Italy on the other side of the harbor? What would the other Bovaros think of that?"

"They'd think what they've been thinking for thirty years now: that I'm the unpredictable one."

I'm sure Gregory Morrison would concur. And though I feel like this evening is on the verge of impeccability, it also feels like Greg is right behind us, tapping me on the shoulder or whispering in my ear, "Look what Prince Charming did," and suddenly I'm staring at caked blood and horizontal teeth. I'd give anything to get rid of these superfluous pieces of Jonathan's puzzle.

As we turn around and begin walking toward the masses, I try to clear my mind of these thoughts. Though apparently I'm hopelessly stuck because I ask, "How old were you when you realized your father—or family—was involved in, um . . . you know."

He glances at me briefly and laughs. "Well, looking back, I probably should've realized it earlier, but the understanding came in little chunks." He scratches his forehead and says, "Like how we always had large amounts of cash around the house. I mean, the eighties were all about credit cards, yet my parents didn't have a single one. Whenever my mother needed to go shopping, she'd go into one of several boxes in our house and grab a fat stack of bills. My friend, Billy Barone, showed me a credit card when I was twelve. I didn't know what it was. I thought he was pulling my leg. The whole concept made no sense to me."

I stare at him and smile. His story, in a way, is a story of innocence; I wish these were the only ones he had to tell.

He continues, this time with a vignette about how, as a kid, all he did was casually mention that he might like to learn more about baseball, and the next thing he knew he was sitting behind the dugout at the World Series.

"There was a lot of stuff like that," he says. "But there was other stuff, too, odd things—things I thought were supposed to be funny but were really a subtle preparation for my upcoming life as a grown-up Bovaro."

He says no more. He seems to have a real problem with dropping off at critical points in his delivery. I have to nudge him. "Like?"

He clears his throat. "Well, here's a little something I heard quite a bit growing up: 'Sticks and stones may break your bones and everything after that is irrelevant.'"

I laugh. "Get real."

"How about 'The pen is mightier than the sword, huh? Well, how're you gonna use that pen after my sword cuts off your frigging hand?' Then, of course, they'd throw in a reference to the person being an incestuous bisexual."

"Naturally."

"You know Rock, Paper, Scissors? Turns out nothing beats Rock."

I stop—because I'm really laughing too loudly for a public place. I bite my lip a little. I make it look like I'm being sultry, but the truth is I'm trying to suppress further laughter. "So, what was the event that finally brought it all home?"

"It wasn't one single event. I just finally realized my father did nothing *real* to generate income. When I asked my mom what my dad did for a living, she'd always reply, 'Tell people he's in investments.' I'm like, why do I have to *tell* people anything? What's the truth?"

"They never told you?"

We start walking again.

"Not really, because what my family does is . . . dabble. If you really want to know, we handle a lot of carting, we run numbers, we do some fixing. I don't get involved in the action end, thank God; all I do is launder some of the money. Just as guilty, mind you, but at least I don't have to see much blood."

He tells me this like he's discussing the difficulty of running a convenience store. "So," I say, trying to keep the conversation informative but light, "your dad wasn't in investments at all?"

"I suppose, a little." He shrugs. "He used to fix races up at Belmont."

"How does that fall under the umbrella of investing?"

"Pretty simple, really. You spend, say, twenty grand fixing a race, paying the jockeys to back off and/or getting the horses drugged up. Then you bet half that on the horse guaranteed to win, spread over ten or twelve bets. You make five to ten times what you invested, more if the horse was a long shot."

"Better performing than a good Scudder fund?"

He glances at me casually. "I have no idea what that means. But I can tell you there is really no guarantee of anything. Ever."

"Who would dare override a win for a race the Bovaro family had predetermined?"

Jonathan giggles and shakes his head, seemingly thrilled that the memory he's recalling actually occurred. "Two years ago, my dimwit brother, Peter, wanted to move all the family's actions toward fixing races across the country. He was obsessed. If he could've influenced the lawmakers in New York to change the road markers from miles to furlongs, he'd have created a political action committee. Anyway, he fixed a race at Belmont, and it was gonna be a huge payoff, the biggest yet. All the jockeys were in on it—a very difficult and risky venture—and we were looking at a quick mid-six-figure payout."

He giggles again, like there is some sibling rivalry behind the reverie.

"On the second turn," he continues, "the horse pegged to win slips and falls against the rails and sprains its ankle. Suddenly, all the jockeys back off and start looking at one another, like, what do we do now? No one—and I mean no one—wanted to be the guy bringing his horse across that finish line. The other eight jockeys pulled back on their horses and they all sort of strolled past the finish line in what was the slowest finish to any seven-furlong race held at that track. It was the talk of all the sports shows in the city and before you knew it, investigations were coming from every direction. And that was the last the Bovaros ever set foot near Belmont or Aqueduct or any other racetrack in New York ever again."

So far, the Bovaros have turned out to be utter failures in the areas of music and the equine. Jonathan is emerging as the star player on a team of bunglers. "I didn't realize crime was so complicated."

"You have no idea. That's why it's *organized* crime. Without the organization, we'd never get anything accomplished."

A breeze pushes us forward and my sundress flitters and the chill reminds me of how little I am wearing. We walk a few paces before I ask, "You ever get involved in any wrongdoing beyond the laundering?"

He looks my way quickly, like he's going to frisk me down for a wire, but it seems like it's nothing more than a default reaction. He turns away and quietly answers, "Sure."

I swallow and ask hopefully, "Carting?"

He smiles but makes a face like I'm cute for asking, and that I'm now old enough to know there is no Santa Claus.

"Trash has never really been my thing."

"Running numbers, maybe? Which I could totally respect, by the way."

"No numbers."

I gulp again. "Murder?"

"You asked me that before."

"I know. But I need the truth, Jonathan."

He shakes his head a little. "I have never taken a life."

"What about—"

"We're here!" He points toward a seafood restaurant a few paces in front of us.

"We're *where*? We've passed this place five times already. Suddenly it's our destination?"

"Look, I've never murdered anyone, okay? Besides, no family

is in the murdering business, per se; it's more of a required action when other business dealings go awry, like firing an employee."

"Permanently."

He rolls his eyes.

"What, you're justifying it?"

"Absolutely not," he says, "just explaining why it happens."

Jonathan keeps looking over his shoulder at the restaurant; he's preparing for another segue.

"Have you ever *wanted* to murder someone?"

Jonathan grunts a little and wipes his face. "Sure. Haven't you? What do you really want to know, Melody? Have I ever beaten someone within an inch of his life? You bet. I've done what needed to be done, to protect myself, to protect my family. That's what you do for the ones you love! It's what I would do for *you*."

A few people turn and stare, but keep walking. His comment about beating someone within an inch of his life is offset by the fact that he sort of said he loved me. I step closer and say, "Tell me the story."

"Why?"

I hesitate. "Because I have very intense feelings for you, okay? And I need to know this side of you. I need to know what you're capable of."

He stares at me for a long moment, then looks down. "There was, uh . . . one guy in particular. Turned out very badly."

"Who?" I silently pray that the name he utters is Gregory Morrison, that I have already seen the worst-case scenario, that I can finally move on.

"Maybe we should get a table in the restaurant and—"

"That's fine. If you want to slurp down some crab bisque and sip a nice Pinot Grigio while you tell me how you dismantled someone, that's just super—but I want to hear a name first."

Jonathan shifts in his spot a little. He pushes his glasses up the bridge of his nose and studies me, like he's slightly more convinced I might be wired. He glances at the folks around us, then farther and farther away, all the way to the top of Federal Hill, where I imagine he expects to see an unmarked van, envisions federal agents sitting inside who are listening to our conversation, ready to descend.

Really, why else would I be so obsessed with having Jonathan tell me who the guy was. Wouldn't the actions be the more important details?

I turn his face back to mine. "Jonathan, I would never get you in trouble, okay? Now, for the first time, I need you to trust *me*."

He licks his lips a little and says, "Gregory Morrison."

I close my eyes and I hug him and whisper, "Thank you."

He returns my hug and buries his face in my hair, but it's only a few seconds before I can feel him looking around again.

We make our way to the hostess of a large but cozy seafood restaurant with window views of the harbor and the Baltimore skyline. She smiles and welcomes us, and before Jonathan can utter the word *two*, he's reaching into his pocket and pulling out bills. I grab his hand and shove it back into his pocket, give him a look like he's nuts.

"What," he says, "it's impolite to tip a hostess?"

She grabs two menus and walks us to the back of the restaurant, far from the windows, a few steps from the kitchen.

I sit. Jonathan does not.

He starts reaching for those bills.

"Sit," I say.

"But—"

"*Sit.*"

"Is there a problem, ma'am?" the hostess asks. I tell her we're fine; she nods and walks away.

I look up at Jonathan and say, "It's just a table."

"You deserve better. You deserve the best—"

"*Sit.*"

Finally, he does. And I can tell he wishes we'd gone to Little Italy after all, where a young, amorous couple would be sniffed out and given the highest priority.

"Just a table," he mutters to himself a few times.

The waiter arrives, a guy named Herman, who has the build of a young boy and hair making an aggressive exit from this world. He introduces himself and asks if he can get us something to drink. He makes the mistake, however, of glancing at my chest for a few seconds and I can see Jonathan begin to seethe.

"First the table and now *this*?" he says to me.

"Jonathan, it's just a—oh, for Pete's sake." I turn to the waiter and say, "We'll share a bottle of Chianti."

The waiter tries to pretend it didn't happen. "We have several different—"

"Just go. Run along, Herman."

The waiter backs up a few paces, then scurries away like a rat.

"This is all wrong," Jonathan says. "I just want the best for you, Melody. The best food, the best table, the best waiter—preferably one who isn't lecherous."

His intense concern for the quality of my day and this meal has me further persuaded he thinks they may be my last. I'm banking on his Italian heritage being the real motivator. I reach over and touch his hand. "You're here, so I have the best table, the best window, the best waiter. It's the classiest meal I could ever imagine."

Someone drops a tray of dishes in the kitchen and the sound reverberates to our table. There is some brief arguing.

Jonathan grips my hand and sighs. "If you're sure."

Herman returns with the wine and shows the label to us.

"Ruffino," Jonathan says. "Acceptable, but predictable—sort of like you, Herman."

"Yes, sir," he answers, staring straight ahead like a plebe who's one day into basic training.

"Leave us." Jonathan snags the corkscrew from Herman's hands just before our waiter hurries off, then opens, pours quickly. We hold up our glasses and he says, "To the best table in the house." We smile and we clink and we drink.

I wait for him to continue the story he started outside but he stares at me, like he's trying to hypnotize me. It doesn't work.

"Gregory Morrison," I say.

Jonathan rolls his eyes and takes another drink. "Greg Morrison was one of a bunch of guys who used to hang around my neighborhood, thought he was real tough. We never paid them any mind; they were just neighborhood kids. Then one night, my brother and I catch him and his buddies trying to break into one of our establishments. My brother confronts them. Well, it's like six of them and only me and Peter, so they start talking it up all cool, like they're going to rough us up. My brother, he likes to throw our name around, and when he does this time, all the kids turn and look at Greg, as if Greg is the one who's going to decide how this goes down.

"Now, the proper thing for Greg and his buddies to do would have been to apologize, to show respect. I know that sounds corny and all, but it's true. We would've let them all walk away. All *anybody* wants is some respect, you know? Not just the Mafia. Some respect and a decent white clam sauce, which is getting harder and harder to find in New York."

"Greg Morrison."

"So Greg stares at Peter and tells him to his face how he's gonna hurt him. Well, Peter turns to me and laughs, like he's sort of been looking for some action anyway, and starts rolling up his sleeves."

He stops again, like nothing else happened. This is getting old. I kick him under the table and he picks up where he left off like a malfunctioning tape recorder.

"So things get very ugly. Peter gives him a pretty good pounding. Nothing major, just an old-fashioned beating."

"You can't beat an old-fashioned."

"Yeah, it was pretty easy. His friends did nothing. Just watched—and learned."

Like the friends of the frat kid in West Virginia.

Like the friend of Marcus at the hotel bar.

I'm feeling a connection here, but the story seems to have come to a nebulous end. I'm hopeful that all Jonathan did was watch, and fail to prevent Greg Morrison from getting beaten. "So you never actually harmed Greg yourself?"

"Well, not *that* time."

I sigh.

"See," he continues, "the whole time Peter is going to town, Greg just keeps saying Peter is going to pay, that our family is going to pay for this." Jonathan starts playing with the cork from the wine bottle, and I can see the tension increase as he starts breaking off chunks of the cork with his thumbnail. He stares at his wine-stained fingers, so entranced in the memory he converts it all to present tense. "I go to my folks' home one evening, about a week later, and I find my mother rocking in my dad's arms on the couch and she is weeping and my dad is . . . he's, like, staring into the distance with tears running down his cheeks. He has this look I've only ever seen him have a few times, and I know someone is going to have to die."

"What'd happened?"

He clears his throat and drops the cork and wipes his face. He looks me in the eye and says, "Greg Morrison raped my mother while she was putting groceries in the trunk of her car. Just shoved her body in the trunk, lifted up her dress and . . ."

One thing is certain: To have raped the matriarch of a crime family, Greg Morrison had to be either a sociopath or the stupidest man on earth.

I can tell Jonathan is fighting the retrospection, that he does not want to show this side of himself.

"The whole time," he says, "Greg just kept repeating, 'Tell your boys payback is hell.'"

I gulp and bite my lower lip. I touch his hand gently; it's shaking. "I don't know what to say, I . . ."

Herman starts heading our way. I wave him off.

"My father put my mother down for a rest in their bedroom and told me he needed to stay with her—and that I needed to go make things right."

I hold my breath. "And did you?"

He sits up. "You better believe I did. I went to Morrison's scuzzy little apartment and kicked in his door. He was just sitting there in a stained La-Z-Boy with a pistol in his hand, waiting for me or Peter or whoever. He held it up, pointed it at me, and said, 'Payback' and pulled the trigger—but nothing happened. God knows why, but nothing left the barrel of that gun. I jumped on him and the gun went sliding across the floor. I picked up a chair from his kitchen table and smashed it over his head." He snaps his fingers. "Out immediately."

I wait a few seconds. "And that's it?"

"No. I sat in his apartment for over two hours, waiting for that piece of crap to return to consciousness."

"Why?"

"Because he needed to live through what I was gonna do to him, the way my mother had to live through what he did to her. I wanted to make sure he would never forget, for the rest of his life, the mistake he made."

"For screwing with a Bovaro?"

He leans forward and his face goes completely flush. "For messing with my mother, Melody. This has nothing to do with my family's name or my family's history. I would've done the same thing if my name was Schwartz."

I sigh again, but this one is a sigh of relief. It turns out Jonathan's one bad act—or at least his worst act—was not because he was a Bovaro at all; it was because he was a human being.

We sit in silence for a minute before a thought occurs to me. "So, your dad was proud of you, I guess?"

He laughs a little, cracks his knuckles. "He was livid."

"Livid? Why?"

"He wanted Morrison dead, gone forever. He wanted to send a message to the entire community that if you ever mess with our family you will die."

"I'm surprised your brother didn't go back and finish the job for you."

"Oh, he wanted to. And my dad wanted him to, as well. It was the source of many arguments we had as a family." He goes back to playing with the cork. "But I told my father and my brothers and the other 'made' men that if we killed Morrison, he'd be forgotten in a month and someone would fill his place. But this way, with him being a living, breathing example that people would see day after day, the event would never be forgotten."

It was a good argument. Jonathan is either very smart or very lucky. I'm glad he's on my side. "But what if he heals?"

"He won't."

"Well, it's possible that—"

"He won't."

I watch Jonathan and the tension slowly leaves his hands, then his face, then his body. He is transforming back to the guy I have fallen for, from the Hulk back to David Banner, and I can see that in his own violent, perverted way, he has made peace with what happened. And, having convinced his family not to kill Morrison, I feel he might actually be able to pull off the greatest swindle in Bovaro history: presenting me to his family and asking that they let me live in peace—with amnesty.

Herman returns for our order and he approaches the table like it's wired with explosives. "Can I, um, take your order?"

We play with our menus, opening them for the first time. I can feel Jonathan watching me.

Jonathan smiles at Herman and says, "She'll have the best of everything."

I chuckle. "Make that two."

Herman must've been scared to death that he'd fail the crazy couple seated by the kitchen, so he takes Jonathan's "everything" comment rather seriously. He has two additional servers come over to our table and cover it with an array of dishes from every section of the menu: mussels; scallops; lobster tails; three different blue-crab dishes; fresh littleneck clams, still steaming, with a bowl of melted butter at their side; two different bowls of pasta, including their version of a Chesapeake Alfredo—which is essentially regular Alfredo with Old Bay dashed on top; and a massive bowl of Caesar salad, which Herman nervously prepares table-side.

I lean over the dishes a little, trying to catch the aroma of the garlic rising from the mussels, and my left strap falls from my shoulder. Herman pauses his salad-making as he attempts to catch a glimpse down the front of my dress.

Jonathan snatches one of the utensils from Herman's hand and whispers, "Guess what I'm gonna do with this?"

Herman nods and says, in a quick falsetto, "Let me know if you need anything else," and scampers off.

"What," Jonathan says to me. "I was just gonna finish tossing the salad, is all."

I sit back and fix my strap. "I'm not that hungry."

Jonathan puts the salad utensils down. "Me either."

"I'm nervous."

"Me too."

We both swallow.

"Why are we nervous?" I ask.

He bites his lip, then answers, "Because that's how you feel when you're about to experience one of the best moments of your life."

Or: one of the *last* moments of your life.

But the truth is hard to deny. I've entered one of the manic cycles of my bipolar interplay with Jonathan. He's got me convinced again that his plan will work and that some great ending is hours from unfolding. Or maybe I've convinced myself. Either way he's right: The nervousness—for the moment—is anxious pleasure.

I stare at the shellfish and the creamy pasta and the bottle of wine. "We've got a table full of aphrodisiacs here."

"I don't need them."

I cock my head and sigh. "Neither do I."

Jonathan stares at the wine but does not pick it up. "More wine?"

"No." He looks at me. "I . . . I don't want anything to interfere with the way I'm feeling." I reach across the table and run the tips of my fingers across his hand and wrist. I keep my eyes on his. "I don't want anything to impair this night. I want to experience you, Jonathan."

He turns his hand over and I gently drag my fingers to his palm and he closes his fingers around mine.

Jonathan holds my hand very tightly, seemingly intent on preventing my escape. He takes his fork, sneaks it between the shells of a clam, deftly pops the meat out and submerses it in the butter, dabs the excess, and carefully brings it to my lips.

I laugh a little and look around the room, then look back at Jonathan and say, "Okay." I put the clam between my teeth and take it from the fork. It is salty and tender and a little grainy— sort of like Jonathan. I try to keep from laughing with my mouth open.

I take my fork and plunge it into the Chesapeake Alfredo and begin twisting a huge spiral of fettuccine—humorously big, actually. I hold it up to Jonathan and cream drips on the table.

"You've got to be kidding," he says.

"Take it like a man."

He squints and says, "Bring it on."

I deliver it to his mouth, timing the drips to avoid any mess, and he opens as wide as possible and I manage to push it all in and he winces as he noshes.

Jonathan grabs his fork and extracts the meat from between the shells of a mussel and holds it up.

"Oh, but the garlic," I whine.

"You've lived on the run most of your life and you can't handle a little garlic?"

I roll my eyes. "Bring it."

I chomp down on his fork in feigned anger and the mussel is wet with olive oil and studded with flakes of sautéed garlic and crushed capers and for a second I roll my eyes again, though this time from a prandial rush.

We continue this journey around the bowls and platters of food on our table until we both hit the dish with the blue crab au gratin. We get stuck there and alternate feeding forkfuls of it to each other until it's gone, which takes several minutes, and we each take a deep breath and sigh and loosen our grip on each other slowly until our hands drift apart and we rest back in our chairs.

I guess we were hungry after all.

We cleanse our palates with a single swish of the Chianti. We rest our glasses back down, leaving two-thirds of the bottle unconsumed.

"I've got one thing on my mind right now," I say.

"Passion?"

"Garlic."

"Afraid I won't want to kiss you?"

"Afraid of what you'll think *after* you kiss me."

He smiles. "Want me to fix it? I've got a lot of experience with fixing things."

I'm not sure what he means but I nod like I know.

Jonathan carefully reaches into his glass of water and removes the slice of lemon, cuts two narrow slices across each end, and lets it drip on his bread plate for a moment.

"Come here," he says. I lean forward. "Tilt your head back just a little." I do. "Now open your mouth." I part my lips. "A little more." I open wider. "A little more." Then, just as I begin to feel self-conscious, he squeezes the lemon and a narrow spray of citrus splashes onto my tongue. He squeezes more firmly and it takes five seconds before all of the fluid is in my mouth.

"Swirl it around," he says, "and swallow."

The lemon is fresh and sweet and the tartness makes my nose burn. I swallow and my tongue and my throat feel alive—and clean. I laugh as I bring my fingers to my lips. "Oh, *wow*—that's amazing."

Jonathan nods and puts the lemon slice on his plate. "As a member of a Sicilian family, you grow up with almost every dish starting the same way: sautéed garlic in olive oil. By the time you enter adolescence, you find ways to cope. It's one of those things that seems odd and trivial but is incredibly necessary, it turns out."

"Hmm, like a Fibonacci number."

He flips his hands out. "Am I supposed to understand what that means?"

"Oh, um, a Fibonacci number is formed from a sequence defined recursively where, after you select two starting values, the number is the sum of the two preceding numbers—like, 3, 4, 7, 11, 18, 29—and it's just the kind of thing you try to comprehend and think, How would I ever apply this in real life, and, judging by the look on your face, I'm guessing you weren't really that interested."

He smiles. "I'm interested in everything about you, in all the pieces I was never able to grasp by watching you from a distance. You're like this beautiful painting where the colors become richer and deeper and more captivating with every step closer to the canvas."

I can feel myself blushing. "That is so not something I would imagine coming from the mouth of a Bovaro." I nod a little. "But it's something I will remember for the rest of my life."

We stare at each other for the longest time, like we can read each other's minds. All I can think is how happy I am that I don't have garlic on my breath anymore.

We skip dessert and coffee and agree to head out into the night air. Jonathan takes his stash and shows it to me, for permission, and I sort of shrug and he peels off a bunch of bills and drops them on the table. Then he sees Herman across the room gawking at a different customer and Jonathan curls his lip and takes one of the bills back.

He reaches into his pocket and takes out his Nicorette, taps it on his hand a few times like he's trying to ready the tobacco of a fresh pack of smokes, and lets two little tablets fall into his hand. He stares at them and sighs and pops them into his mouth.

We walk back to the harbor and the temperature has dropped at least ten degrees. I briskly rub my shoulders with my hands. Jonathan wraps his arms around me and not only do I warm, I melt.

"So," I say, "want to find a karaoke bar? You can serenade me with vintage Scorpions."

He tightens his arms around me as we watch the water taxi glide across the harbor. "We should probably head back to the hotel."

Though he cannot see my face, I grin. I nudge him in the side a little. "You're not going to take advantage of me, are you?"

"Actually," he says, pulling away, "I was thinking we should get some rest. We have a big day tomorrow."

I turn around and face him. "You're serious?"

He shrugs and says, "Tomorrow will be a very serious day."

We both walk northward, in the direction of the hotel.

"Jonathan, are you sure you want to do this thing tomorrow? Are you sure you've thought it all through?"

His answer comes slowly but is firm when it arrives. "I have."

I shiver and Jonathan pulls me closer.

"C'mon," he says, "let's take a shortcut so we can get you back safe and warm."

We pick up our pace and quickly find ourselves on the edge of Pratt Street. From our position, Jonathan points to an alley sandwiched between two skyscrapers just up from the hotel. He leads; I follow.

We cross eight lanes of traffic and sneak down the alley, nearly jogging now, and we're both laughing as we go. Suddenly, as we hit the darkest depth of the alley, the sound of four feet turns to six.

I slow down, an odd reaction to thinking someone's following you, I suppose, but I want my balance steady and sure. I start to turn around to see who's behind us and Jonathan nonchalantly says, "Just ignore it."

I watch the pavement move beneath us, and my heart is pounding hard—not from running, but from fear. I know this because this is the fear that has been regular in my life since I was six years old.

I whisper panic-based comments to myself and Jonathan puts his arm around me and says, "Hey, it's okay. No one is going to hurt you—now or ever. I'd never let it happen."

We slow our walking even more, and I close my eyes as I hear the footsteps get closer and closer.

My mind fills with all the possibilities—and certainties.

Sean Douglas or some other marshal.

Peter Bovaro or some other assassin.

The FBI.

The police.

The person catches up to us, grabs me by the shoulder, and shoves me into a grouping of trash cans. I go tumbling and end up on my back with my legs apart, with scrapes and cuts on my arms and shoulders, and I can taste blood.

I regain my bearings, and as I look up I see Jonathan standing with his hands at his sides as an enormous man holds a knife to Jonathan's neck. The guy looks dirty, so dirty that I can't tell if he's white or black or something in between. All I know is he's the adversary.

Dirty Guy glares at me, then between my legs and says, "That's it, you stupid bitch—stay *just like that* for me. When your man is done giving me his money, I'll make him watch while I take you on the ride of your life."

I leave my legs as they are; I'm frozen anyway.

He returns his attention to Jonathan and presses the blade into his neck enough for a thin stream of blood to trickle out. Jonathan does not budge.

"Gimme your wallet, asshole. *Now!*"

Jonathan cocks his head my way and turns his hands up, like he is again asking for permission.

"*What,*" I whisper.

Jonathan smiles and says, "Just a mugging?"

I study Jonathan and in this instant all the fear I have from this scene—and my entire life—is cast aside. What a thousand marshals could never achieve in a thousand versions of my life is what is happening right now. Finally, *I am totally secure.* There is not a doubt in my mind that I will be perfectly protected.

I smile and give Jonathan a thumbs-up and say, "Rock him like a hurricane."

Dirty Guy looks at me and says, "You dumb bitch! You better keep those legs spread, you ugly slut, 'cause I'm gonna give you the hardest fu—"

That's all he gets out before Jonathan slams the guy's Adam's apple into the center of his throat. One single thrust with the back of Jonathan's fist and Dirty Guy can't stop making this ugly gurgling sound. It's only a few seconds before he drops to his knees, hands clutched to his neck.

Jonathan leans down to Dirty Guy and says, "I'd appreciate it if you refrained from using profanity around the lady." He turns to me and asks, "You okay?"

I rest back against a Dumpster, close my eyes, and nod.

Jonathan chomps his gum, wipes the blood from his neck, and returns his attention to our assailant. "And now for the entertainment portion of our evening: Lessons in being a wise guy."

I sit up a little and watch Dirty Guy choking on his blood.

Jonathan says, "Lesson one: Silence." He reaches down and grabs an old shoe from behind a trash can and jams the toe in Dirty Guy's mouth.

Jonathan says, "Lesson two: Impair. In the movies, the good guys always give the bad guys too many chances to get back on their feet and fight again." He walks over to a pile of loose trash and grabs a broken two-by-four and rains blow after blow down on Dirty Guy's ankle until all three of us hear it snap. Dirty Guy shakes like he's being electrocuted.

Without Martin Scorsese at hand to animate this scene, it's a little awkward; there is little noise, no loud punches, no punctuated profanity, and the whole event is sort of sloppy—though Jonathan is certainly getting the job done.

"Now," Jonathan says, "all he can think about is that ankle. He's not as focused on running away or retaliating."

I smile; this is some seriously entertaining vengeance. After a lifetime of fearing this specific violence, I have found a sudden safety in it.

"Third," Jonathan says, after catching his breath, "we get rid of the weapon. You leave it around and it could find its way back into the hands of the bad guy. And we kick it, never touch; finger-prints are our enemy." He kicks the blade down into the sewer and Dirty Guy tries to get back on his feet but what's left of his ankle is certainly posing a problem; his calf is at twelve o'clock but his foot is at six o'clock.

Jonathan blows a little bubble with gum. "Poor guy," he says, studying Dirty Guy's body. "It appears our friend has lousy blad-der control."

"Good to know I'm not the only one."

He wipes his hands on his pants. "And now for our final lesson."

"Yeah, give that bastard a souvenir!" I quickly cover my mouth, like I just belched at a high tea.

Jonathan stares at me for a few seconds, confused. He pulls himself away, though, and finishes off Dirty Guy. Jonathan stands over the man's chest, pulls him up by his shirt, and whispers, and I can hear all the profanity he has held back come rolling out like thunder, slamming down on the felon like additional swings of that two-by-four.

Jonathan is whispering and screaming at the same time, over and over, "Remember this face. Remember this face. Look at me. Look at me." Then he leans over, takes the shoe from the guy's mouth, and whispers one more thing directly in his ear, and, though I cannot decipher a single word, it leaves Dirty Guy weep-ing, curled up in the fetal position, moaning through a simple repeated sentence.

"I promise. I promise. I promise."

Jonathan stands above him and his fists are clenched and he displays the most disturbing scene of the evening, of our entire time together: He watches Dirty Guy struggle. I mean, he *really* watches, for at least thirty seconds.

He never says a word.

Finally, Jonathan brushes the dirt and dust from his clothes and jogs to my side and carefully helps me to my feet. We simultaneously analyze my situation: The straps of my sundress are broken and my dress is torn on the side and there is an apple-shaped bloodstain near the bottom; both of my hands, forearms, and shoulders are cut and bleeding, as well as my right thigh; one of the heels of my sandals is broken and missing.

"You want me to take you to a hospital?" Jonathan asks.

I smile and attempt to smooth the wrinkles in my dress. "I've been in worse condition."

I try to walk a little but my ankle buckles. Without asking, Jonathan picks me up and carries me. I'm suddenly so small, so protected. It feels a little goofy, but it feels lovely, too; I throw my arms around his neck and enjoy the ride.

I stare at Jonathan and suddenly I am changed, full of clarity and closure, as though the final piece of my life's puzzle has been put in place. His security, his strength, his ability to *have the answer* is what I've been lacking—and the fact that it's bundled up in this attractive man is just icing on the cake.

I surrender.

$$\sqrt[3]{1331}$$

JONATHAN CARRIES ME THROUGH THE LOBBY OF THE RENAISSANCE and people stare and I smile and say, "We just got married," and everyone starts clapping and whistling and passing approving glances. We get into the elevator and one of the guys who'd been whistling looks at me oddly.

"You know you're bleeding?" he asks.

"He dropped me on the sidewalk," I say, then whisper, "He's a bit of a *weakling.*"

We exit on our floor. Jonathan carries me to his room, throws me over his shoulder like a sack of potatoes, and tosses me onto the bed—carefully but playfully.

I go flying back and my dress rises up to the top of my thighs and the top falls down easily without straps to hold it up or full breasts to fill it out and as a result my chest is exposed. I reach up to cover myself. Sort of.

Jonathan looks at my face, then my body, then my face, then the ground.

"Come here," I say. I am slightly anxious and very serious.

"We should get you cleaned up."

"I'm too dirty for you?"

"That's not what I meant."

He won't lift his eyes from the floor.

"Okay," I say, and slowly get to my feet. My ankle is feeling better already, but I still have to hobble to Jonathan.

I walk up to him and say, "I'll draw a bath," and I slowly raise my arms and let my dress fall to the ground.

Jonathan blinks a few times and swallows, then he finally lifts his eyes—skips my body completely—and lands on my face. I will never mistake him for Herman.

"Melody," he says, grabbing a blanket from the closet and wrapping it around me, "you don't need to seduce me." He takes a step closer and cups my face with his hands and says, "I'm yours already." I exhale excitedly, about to move in for a kiss, when he says, "*I'll* draw your bath."

I fall back on the bed and I am hot, literally and figuratively, and I just sit and wait and think of how my life is changing again.

Jonathan returns and cautiously looks my way. "Your bath is ready."

"Will you stay with me?"

"I was gonna fix your wounds."

"You don't need an excuse."

He looks away and smiles. "Yeah, I think I do."

I walk into the bathroom and it's full of steam and the water is full of bubbles and I drop the blanket and slip off my panties and slide into the water and I feel blasts of pain in a dozen different places.

"You can come in now," I say.

Jonathan peeks around the corner and enters with reticence, carrying a small leather bag. He kneels by the tub and looks at my arms and hands. He removes a few small bottles and some cotton balls. "This is gonna hurt," he says.

He soaks a cotton ball with alcohol and applies it gently to my forearm; I try not to show the pain. I watch him tend to my wounds and I start to think warm things, silly things, like how he would make a good father—if he could discard the Bovaro legacy.

"You're good at this," I say.

"Well, let's just say I have a lot of experience at fixing wounds—my own, at least."

I stare at his body through his sweater and I try to imagine to no avail. "Show me one."

Jonathan stops and studies me, can tell I'm serious. He looks down sheepishly and raises his sweater around his stomach. I sit up a little as I spy a six-inch diagonal line across his stomach. But what I notice more is the six-pack he's been hiding under his clothes. I reach out to touch the scar—to at least make it *look* like I'm interested in the scar—and rub my fingers over his stomach muscles. It's sort of hard to believe a knife could penetrate something this firm.

Carla is worth her weight in gold.

The scar leads up toward another healed wound, a small puncture between two ribs; I move his sweater out of the way. I rub my fingers over this one, too.

Jonathan swallows, hard.

Higher on his chest I see another cut and I pull his sweater up to the point where it's obvious I want it off, and rather than having me sit all the way up and expose my naked body, he preempts the effort and takes it off himself. He looks away.

I'd like to say what is running through my mind is pure desire, but once his sweater is completely removed, I'm actually aghast. I'm looking at a minimum of a dozen scars. This historical road map of a life of violence brings a flash of my meeting his family to my consciousness; I see my body being dumped into a pre-dug hole, feel a blanket of cold dirt being spread over my flesh, hear the squeal of a getaway car. And this fear for my own well-being awakens me, for I cannot fathom what he has experienced in his life.

I sink back down in the tub and mutter, "Oh, Jonathan." I stare some more. "I thought you didn't see much of the violence in your family."

"Not seeing much means I haven't been around much death, but . . ."

I force myself to look away. "There are just so many."

He nods nervously; quickly puts his sweater back on. "Well, the best part is all wounds heal, I guess. You can get through pretty much anything."

My stomach knots a little as I remember what I am going to need to *get through* when I meet his family—and the fact that this evening, this moment, may be the last instance of calm in my life. I gently brush Jonathan's hand and I can sense his strength and the knot loosens.

He says, "Remind me to get rid of this sweater, by the way."

"Because of the bloodstains?"

He chuckles at my innocence. "Because of the DNA."

I stare at him and can't help passing a tearful smile. He catches me.

"So, Ms. McCartney," he says, back to fixing my wounds, "enough about my childhood. What was yours like?"

I shrug and close my eyes and let him do his thing. He hits a new wound and I squirm. "It was a cavalcade of lies."

Instead of showing empathy for my miserable upbringing, Jonathan earns points by saying "Well, there's a story there, then. What was it like to live a constant lie?"

I open my eyes and think about it for a moment. "Honestly, the younger I was, the better it was. Back then, I always thought the next time we moved would be our last, that I might be able to establish some friends and relationships."

"Never happened?"

"You know the answer. You were there, right?"

Jonathan rubs my hand gently with some sort of balm that was already in the hotel bathroom. It smells like apples and brings with it a distinct hotel quality. No matter how expensive the room, you always get apples.

"So how did you cope?"

I take in a deep breath and let it out like cigarette smoke. "I isolated myself, basically. Kept myself from getting too involved with people."

He nods, then looks me in the eye. "You ever tell anyone the truth about who you were?"

Another deep breath. "Yeah," I say, envisioning my mother and my father and me being whisked from yet another home in the middle of the night. "Once."

He finishes one arm and moves to the other. Every dab of those cotton balls brings a shudder of pain and a wince.

We do not talk as he works on that arm; the only sound is the hum of the bathroom vent and droplets of water falling back into the bath. When he finishes, he says, "What was bleeding on your face?"

"My tongue, I think." I stick it out and he nods.

"I see a red mark. How's your foot?"

"It's still sore."

"May I?"

I pull my foot from the water and he takes it in his hands gently, like he's holding a newborn infant for the first time. He caresses it and asks me how it feels.

He has no idea.

After I've been in the bath for almost twenty minutes, the water has cooled and the bubbles have popped and if he wanted to look, he could see all the details of my body under the water.

He remains a gentleman.

Jonathan stands up, goes over to my room, and returns with the terry-cloth robe. He opens it for me and looks away. I step out of the water and into the robe and pull it tight around me.

He says nothing and leaves the bathroom.

I dry off and rub some body lotion on my legs—more apples—and peek into the room. Jonathan is sitting on the edge of the bed with his head in his hands. I tighten the robe around me and sit next to him.

"Beating up that guy take it out of you?"

He turns and looks at me and smiles. "*You* take it out of me."

I move a little closer to him so that our knees touch. I slide my hand up his leg, then push it between his thighs. I am wired, like I've been drugged against my will with an inimical amount of adrenaline. In an unprecedented event, the manic and depressive cycles have somehow become synchronized, parallel, and every emotion is coming to the forefront of my existence. What is left of my life?

"Listen," I say, "I'm tired, Jonathan. I'm tired of waiting and I'm tired of lying and I'm tired of not living and, um . . . I'm just going to come out and say it." I tremble. "I want you to sleep with me tonight. I mean, I'm not even sure what I'm really asking, but I want it to happen."

Jonathan clears his throat. "I want you, too, Melody. But you're a . . ."

"Virgin? Yes." I turn more in his direction. "Why is it so hard to say? Technically, it should be harder to find out a girl's a slut."

"It's just that . . . my family has taken so much from you already, I don't know if I can take any more."

I laugh, still shaking. "You're not taking it, Jonathan; I'm giving it."

He turns my way and kisses me, but I can tell it's not the start of something; it's the conclusion.

"We should wait, Melody. We should wait until after tomorrow."

My shaking levels off. "Why?"

"I don't want to take that perfect thing from you only to have us be apart afterwards."

I can barely get the question out: "Why would we be apart?"

"Remember? There are no guarantees."

I can feel myself cooling, finding that place Jonathan has already reached, a point of anxiety derived from a future reality. And wouldn't you know, not only has Jonathan protected me from the outside world, he's managed to protect me from myself. Now there's something the U.S. Marshals Service can never add to their motto.

Justice. Integrity. Service. Virginity.

"I may be the unpredictable one," he says, "but I come from a long line of capricious and impulsive behavior." He reaches up and runs his fingers through my hair, looks at me and adds, "I know what I'm doing. I need you to trust me. I'm just preparing for the worst."

I nod and smile, but my smile disappears quickly. "What *is* the worst, exactly?"

He laughs a little. "You haven't considered the worst?"

I prop my knee up on the bed to face him more squarely. "I hit rock bottom a few days ago. I haven't considered the worst since I was experiencing it." I reach up and put my hand around his neck. "But I have a big reason to want to stay alive now—and to live well. Do you understand?"

He nudges my leg. "Don't worry, Melody. I'll never let anything bad happen to you again. Okay? I made you that promise and I intend to keep it. I'll always do what needs to be done to keep you safe."

I take my robe and wrap it tighter around me; I'm suddenly cold. I stare at Jonathan and wish I could read his mind, but this subtle distance between us, the distance between now and tomorrow, is like an impenetrable fog. I want to journey through it, but I'm simply out of strength.

"Will you sleep with me?" I ask again. "I mean, literally?"

He purses his lips, like he knows it's a bad idea, but after a gentle sigh he slowly nods. "I'll be over in a minute."

I leave him with a warm, soft kiss, hoping it will serve as some sort of commemorative of the invitation.

I walk back to my room, through the adjoining door, and slip into bikini panties and a white camisole from Jonathan's shopping bag of goodies. I wash my face, brush my teeth, and comb my hair, and when I exit the bathroom, Jonathan is standing before me in pajama bottoms and nothing else. It takes all my energy to avoid focusing on his body.

"I feel funny," he says. He glances at me and the camisole fits me tightly and he presses his lips together as he notices my body, and for the first time since we've met I may actually be the stronger one.

"You don't *look* funny." I walk up and take him by the hands and lead him backward toward the bed.

I sit on the edge of the bed and pull him down. I slide under the covers and he reluctantly slips in next to me. He takes off his glasses and I reach over and turn out the light and the room goes completely dark. I begin to notice the other things about him: the way he smells, the texture and warmth of his skin, the timbre of his voice.

"What now?" he says.

I snuggle up against him and we begin to kiss, and after a few minutes, we realize simultaneously that we do not stand a chance unless we stop right now. I turn over and push myself back into him and it's like having my body enveloped by a life-size heating pad. I press my lower back and bottom against him harder. I reach behind me, grab his arm, and pull it over my body to my belly, and sneak his hand under my camisole. I go no further; this is how I want to fall asleep.

Jonathan puts his other arm above his head so he can touch my hair, and he strokes it softly and I can feel myself drifting. I am warm and secure and happy and—finally—at peace.

After a few moments of silence, I cave in to a simple desire: the desire to amplify the most satisfying moment of my life. I ask, "Do you speak Italian?"

He pauses, so long that I wonder if he heard my question at all. "A little." He keeps stroking my hair.

"Whisper to me," I say, almost asleep.

He pauses again and slows his stroking. He moves closer and I can feel him breathe his words against my hair and my neck.

"*Ti voglio bene, non solo per quello che tu sei ma anche per quello che io sono quando sto. Mi innamorato di mia principessa, mia angioletto . . .*"

I want to ask what he is saying, what the words mean, but I hear *principessa* and I smile as I dissolve. I drift into a deep, restful slumber.

I slept for twelve hours and I'm pretty sure I never budged. I feel relief from getting what was the best rest of my life, but everything about me aches: bruises, cuts, and lumps.

I crawl around the bed, trying to get some blood into my stiff muscles, and I immediately start looking for Jonathan. I prop myself against the headboard and I can hear him chatting in the next room. I wipe my face a few times and try to listen to his side of the conversation.

"Yeah, I know," he says. "I just want to make sure he's gonna be there. I want everyone there." He pauses. "I'm thinking early afternoon." He pauses again. "Yeah, it'll be a surprise, all right."

I stumble out of bed and rush for the toothpaste. Jonathan catches me in mid-spit.

"Good morning, gorgeous," he says.

My response is a hearty smile with white foam at the corners of my mouth; I look like a scantily dressed clown. I quickly pat my face with a washcloth.

He tries to kiss me but we kind of bob and weave at each

other, ultimately settling for a peck on my cheek and a hug usually reserved for grandparents. This awkward attempt to pick up where we left off not only hints at the immaturity of our intimacy, but the fact that more consuming events are about to unfold; the dreaminess zeroed out at daybreak.

Nevertheless. "Since you seem so convinced you'll be keeping me safe from harm, I'd like a time and place where we can consummate this relationship, so I can be sure you're not going to renege."

He gives me a cockeyed look. "You know, pressure only impairs performance."

I kiss him on the lips and pull his lower back to my body.

He clears his throat. "Though I do not anticipate it will be an issue in this instance."

We remain in each other's arms for a few seconds until I feel something vibrating in Jonathan's pocket. He reaches down and pulls out his phone.

"Yeah," he answers, and as the voice on the other end begins to speak he pulls away completely.

"That's great," he says, but the look on his face is not one of happiness. He flips his phone shut quietly and stares at the floor.

Jonathan's phone call—and his immediate detachment—act as a slap back to reality. Like a libidinous adolescent, I've been concerned with *where* and *how* I am going to lose my virginity, an insensate thing to scheme, in general; I should've been most concerned with the *if*. With the Bovaro men staked out at irregular intervals along the Atlantic megalopolis, and with me about to head right for them anyway, I should be asking Jonathan to love me right now, in my potential final moments. Alas, the opportunity is gone, vanished and sucked into a void of stress and imminent disaster. Sometimes a phone call is all it takes.

"What's great?" I ask.

"Uh," he says, still looking down, "my whole family will be there today. Just as I'd hoped."

I sit down on the bed and stare at the same spot on the floor as Jonathan. "They know I'm coming?"

"No."

He doesn't stir. "They have any idea what you're about to do?"

"No."

A movie is running through his mind, a vision of the upcoming event and the potential outcome. He starts grinding his teeth.

I get up and walk to him and lightly stroke his arm and say, "Remember, you're the unpredictable one. They should be prepared for something surprising."

He looks at me and smiles and kisses my forehead. Then he hugs me and says, "They can be surprising at times, too."

We retreat to our respective rooms and shower. I do my best to turn myself back into the woman the ladies at the spa created the day before, but I have not been given the same tools; if I had industry-leading hair gel, makeup, and body creams, not to mention a decent hair dryer, I might stand a chance.

But as I gaze at my reflection in the mirror, I get a vague sense of what I might be like, feel like, if I'd grown up a suburban kid, or at least a kid tied to a single suburb, and wound up awake and fresh on this average day. And I pretend how my biggest event would be running off to the mall to do some shopping or planning a trip for some purpose other than survival.

Alas, today is not that day.

Considering how many times my hair has been colored, it's in remarkable condition; it's soft and silky and I find it implausible that it's actually attached to my scalp. My fingernails and toenails have survived well too, along with the color and texture of my skin. My friends at the spa managed to deliver a long-lasting product. The issue I can't seem to get past is all the dried blood and scratches speckling my upper body.

Jonathan knocks and I slip on my robe and open the door for him. He is clean-shaven, wearing jeans and a tight-fitting navy tee, with a slightly darker navy sweater draped over his arm.

"So what does a girl wear when she's going home to meet your folks?"

He studies me. "Armor."

Jonathan starts rummaging through the bags of clothes he purchased for me. I'm hoping he's going to select the skirt and one of the light blouses, to sort of suggest classiness—or that he might be hoping to impress his family.

Instead, he selects the pair of jeans and a red, formfitting knit sweater; he went one hundred percent practical.

"Red," I say. "Hides the blood better?"

He frowns as I grab the clothes and take them into the bathroom. As I put them on, I'm amazed at how well everything fits—not perfect, but surprisingly close. And there is something so alluring, almost amatory, about a guy who buys clothes for a woman. It requires so much more thought—and attention—than buying something static, like perfume. It's as though Jonathan already knows who I am and the terrain of my body, every curve and line, that he has it all memorized, and finding something to cover it is not only simple, it's sensual.

When I exit the bathroom, Jonathan is waiting by the door and quickly checks me out. I throw my arms in the air, smile, and say, "So what do you think?"

"You are . . . amazing. You look great wearing anything."

I lower my hands and put them in the pockets of my jeans. "So do you," I say. I sound juvenile and passive, but I mean it.

"You want some breakfast?"

Despite an increasing anxiety of the coming day, I do, so we go down, exit the hotel, and walk toward the harbor. The air is cold and crisp but the sun is quickly heating the pavement and I can tell today will be warm.

We find a restaurant with outside seating and let the sun keep us from getting chilled. Jonathan orders various foods for us—eggs, bacon, sausage, french toast, and a dish that is essentially eggs Benedict but the Canadian bacon has been replaced with backfin crabmeat—and we immediately dive in. There is no playfulness this time, no buttery forkfuls of pasta or aphrodisiacal shellfish; it seems we have taken more of a breakfast-is-the-most-important-meal-of-the-day approach.

Or a *last meal* approach.

"Do you ever wonder what your life would be like if you'd grown up in a normal family in suburban Cleveland?" I ask.

Jonathan grins a little and says, "Yeah," and leaves it at that. I guess he's not in the mood.

"You know," I try again, "when I was a little girl I would draw pictures of big houses but never with anyone inside. I always struggled to draw pictures of people."

"Really?" He swirls a yolk around his plate with a fork.

"Hey," I say, annoyed at his disinterest, "you've got a big green thing in your teeth."

He keeps swirling. "Okay."

I sigh and wait for him to realize I'm relatively pissed. I get nothing. "Wanna *talk about it*?"

"About what?"

"The doom that is clearly emanating from your entire presence here."

He puts his fork down, takes off his glasses, and pinches his eyes. Then he reaches into his pocket for his Nicorette. He shakes the box up and down but there is no rattle of relief. "You've got to be kidding me." He rips the thing apart, verifying there are no pieces left, then narrows his eyes at it like he's trying to destroy it by way of some occult power. Suddenly, he slams the box on the table and starts stabbing it with his spoon.

I just watch and say, "I find this . . . disconcerting."

He drops the spoon and it bounces on the brick patio a few times and everyone is staring at us. Again.

Jonathan buries his face in his hands and says, "I'm sorry."

I reach over, pull his hands away, and force him to look at me.

"I just . . ." he says, "I just wish it could be easier. For *you*."

"What do you mean?"

"Your entire life has been ruined by my family. You've been deprived of a normal existence because my family refused to break from our world of crime and find a way to become upstanding citizens. And now . . . now, here *I* am, asking you to face the people who wrecked your life—who had your parents killed—so that they will, God willing, cut you some slack and let you live in peace. Here I am asking you to trust me and my cockamamie plan."

I take his hand in mine and tighten my grip. "First of all, I totally trust any man who can use the word *cockamamie* in a sentence with complete seriousness. Second, I agreed to your plan because, well . . . I really had no place left to go; it was either this or death." I squeeze his hand as tightly as I can. "But most importantly, I've come to trust you, Jonathan. And I know that you'll take care of me. I truly believe it—and no one could be more amazed at that than I am. The last few days, however many hours it's been, have been the greatest of my life. I feel like the person I was born to be—*meant* to be—is waking for the first time and I have you to thank for it. And if God had this difficult life planned for me just so that I could find you and be with you here, now, then it was worth every minute of misery."

Jonathan shakes his head and looks away. "Don't say that."

"Why?"

"I'm not a good man, Melody. Don't settle for me."

"What do you mean? Everyone has flaws, Jonathan."

"Felony-level flaws? Mine are more extreme than most, you know? I mean, what will become of us?"

I tug him a little to my side of the table. "We'll figure that out as we go, okay?"

Jonathan sighs, then stares at me. "I'm sorry, Melody. I only want the best for you."

"Don't you see?" I slide my chair around to his side of the table and put my hand on his leg and say, "This *is* the best."

$$x = ((((7(3/6)) + (1/2)) \times 5) - 8)$$

For the first time since I've met Jonathan, he is reserved and quiet and dark. We do not speak much for the remainder of our meal, nor during the walk back to the hotel. We remain close, holding hands and the like, though the purpose of his grip points toward pulling me away to safety at any moment, but the words have all but disappeared.

We pack our things (all of my clothes go in his bag) and return to the lobby, where Jonathan disperses random bills and things happen with speed and attention.

We make our way outside and the sun shines hard on the side entrance, where we wait for the Audi to be delivered from the underground garage. The valet pulls the car in front of us and has already put the top down, adjusted the interior car temperature, and turned on the radio; I guess this is part of the service. Jonathan slips him a twenty, opens the door for me, and helps me in, then gets in on his side and immediately undoes everything the valet set.

We fly through the city streets; the lights remain green for us as though they understand the urgency of our mission. As we exit the downtown area, we are delivered into a dizzying mixing bowl of beam bridges and trestles that could only have been developed as a response to repeated population spikes. I try to imagine the math required to make this scene a success, and realize, for the first time, that while math can solve everything, it demands a creative mind to make it useful. The understanding of what makes these bridges exist and work—the compression, the tension, the torsion were all contrived by a creative engineer or architect—was *then* cycled through mathematics to make it real.

All my life I've been lacking the vision. Jonathan, you see, is my engineer, my architect.

Within one minute we are booming out of the city on an exit ramp elevated two hundred feet above the water and we are heading north on I-95 and it is now only a matter of time.

Before we are out of time.

Once we're through the Fort McHenry Tunnel and on a stretch of highway free of traffic, Jonathan grabs his CD case and selects a disc by Death Cab for Cutie titled *Plans*—as dimly entertaining as my choice of the Killers disc days earlier. He pushes it in the player and the mellow music drifts around the interior of the car and he reaches over and rests his hand on my thigh and says, "Three and a half hours and you'll be in the presence of the Bovaro clan."

I gently place my hand on his and ask, "So what do I need to know?"

He turns to me and sighs, throws the car into sixth gear, and punches the accelerator.

White Marsh, Maryland, 91 m.p.h.

"My brothers," Jonathan says, "all live in New York, one of them still at home. I'm the third of four, and the most independent. I'm the only one who reads literature; my brothers think reading is noticing the ads for Dewar's and Tecate in between the pictorials. Let me give you some background . . ."

• • •

Elkton, Maryland, 88 m.p.h.

"Jimmy is the youngest and a bit of a stooge to his older brothers. He'll do what they say and has made no real effort to understand what our family does or why we do it. I love my little brother, but he's a total slob—and a caricature of a Mafia member. He's got the thick black hair, magnified New York accent, is overweight, and always has some kind of food in his hand, like a cannoli or a Twinkie. He's muscle and not much more . . ."

Brookside, Delaware, 82 m.p.h.

"Gino is two years older than me, and probably the closest to being as sane as I am. He's smarter than the rest of us. But he weakens under pressure from my father and will do whatever he says—or whatever any of my father's associates say—to stay in his favor . . ."

Swedesboro, New Jersey, 76 m.p.h.

"Now, Peter . . . he's the oldest. And the cockiest. And the most vicious. And the most antisocial. And the best looking. Frigging Frank Sinatra with a boxer's build and the mind of a crook. He's a real bastard. He's the quintessential mob leader, and he quite obviously wants to take over for my father when he's gone. He sees everything my family does as his legacy but fails to realize that it actually takes a lot of smarts and a lot of self-control to succeed the way my family has—and he has neither. If he weren't my brother he'd be my nemesis . . ."

Cherry Hill, New Jersey, 69 m.p.h.

"My brothers' spouses? Peter is not married and does not seem to show any side that might be even remotely interested in carrying on a relationship beyond the two or three minutes it takes him to gain some sort of physical pleasure. As for Gino and Jimmy? Their spouses would be Connie and Roberta, respectively. Cosmetologists, gossips, gaining weight by the day. But they'd take you out if you ever disparaged their husbands, regardless of the horrible things their husbands do on a daily basis . . ."

Trenton, New Jersey, 65 m.p.h.

"As for my mother," he says, then hesitates.

This is a telling moment, because there is something about men and their mothers—and I imagine it must only intensify within a Mafia family.

Finally, he says, "She died last year."

I'm glad I didn't make a joke.

"Long story short, she had aggressive ovarian cancer, eventually making its way to her lymph nodes, and she was gone in a matter of weeks."

Jonathan stares forward, not necessarily watching the highway as much as blanking out, merely trailing the car in front of him.

"What a life she had," he says eventually. "The wife of a mob boss, raised four boys into men, threatened countless times, raped once, then died a painful and miserable death." He sniffs a little but is not tearful. "You can look back and say, 'Why me? Why have my family and I been forced to deal with such misery?' But . . . the truth is we all *know* why." He turns and looks at me and says, "No one deserves it more."

Rossmoor, New Jersey, 63 m.p.h.

"And then, of course, there's my father, a man who's probably done everything wrong in his life, who's entered virtually every aspect of crime considered by man since day one. And other than maintaining a faithful marriage to my mother, I'd say he broke the other nine commandments on a regular basis for the vast majority of his life. All this is true about him, yet I cannot help but love and respect him.

"He is still, even in his older years, someone who is feared, not only by the public and by his peers, but by his sons, which is why most of us cave in to his every request. That and the fact that he's managed to be a successful criminal for almost five decades—and you can count on one hand how many people have been able to pull that off . . ."

East Brunswick, New Jersey, 60 m.p.h.

"You may get to visit some of my extended family, which really amounts to cousins and outside associates and, to be honest, it gets kind of hard to tell the difference. Everyone beyond my immediate family gets grouped into this olive-skinned mess of psychological problems."

I close my eyes and inquire casually, like I'm asking for a tissue, "Will your cousin who killed my parents be there?"

He glances at me briefly, then answers, "Uh, *no*. He was killed a few years ago." He points to his neck. "Bullet right through the throat, choked on his own blood for a long time before someone found him."

I am neither unhappy nor disgusted in the slightest.

"You know who found him? Peter. And he let him die right there in an alley in Midtown Manhattan."

I grimace. "Why?"

"Well, uh . . . it's kind of complicated, but we let him get killed. It was payback for a mistake we made against another family. The whole thing is sort of ridiculous."

"*Sort* of."

"Look, I don't make these asinine rules, and I certainly don't like playing by them, but we're talking about life or death here."

"Well, I can't say I'm sorry he's dead."

"You shouldn't be. But the truth is, he just pulled the trigger. My cousin really had no more stake in the murder of your parents than the bullets that killed them. All he did was follow orders."

I scowl; I'm furious that the man responsible is still alive. If I wasn't taken with romantic emotion and a vague sense of a hopeful end to all this, I'd be seething with rage, focused on violent retaliation. "*Whose* orders?"

Jonathan shrugs and sighs at the same time. "My father's."

Bayway, New Jersey, 58 m.p.h.

While Jonathan has been in a slow deceleration for almost three hours, I'm confused as to why he's not slowing down more abruptly, putting on his blinker and moving toward the exit.

He passes right by the exit for the Staten Island Expressway.

"I'm not the greatest with New York geography, but wouldn't that have been the shortest way to get to Brooklyn?"

"Sure. Why?"

I look at him like he might be denser than his little brother. "Doesn't your family live in Brooklyn?"

He frowns a little and says, "When did I say that? *I* live in Brooklyn but my family lives in Tenafly."

I twist in my seat. "*Tenafly?*"

"It's in New Jersey, just north of the George Washington Bridge."

"I know where it is. Tenafly is barely twenty miles from where I lived before my parents and I went into Witness Protection. You kept saying we were going to New York."

"Melody, my family's house is, like, a mile and a half from the Hudson."

I'm all befuddled. I was expecting an old brownstone full of thugs in dark clothes with five-o'clock shadows; now I'm envisioning an English Tudor and golf clubs and comfy slippers. "You never said Tenafly. I'm certain you said Brooklyn. I mean, geez, Jonathan, a New Jersey address would've stuck in my head."

"Well, my folks grew up in Brooklyn. Maybe that's where you got it from. Or maybe because you called my father's business line in Brooklyn. Or maybe we just got our signals crossed." Jonathan looks at me and laughs and says, "I mean, we've only been together for a couple days."

His words echo through my head, on and on, and his laugh makes them all the more poignant. He's right; we've only known each other a few days. So what in the name of all that is holy am I doing? Who is this guy? Why am I in this car, right now, right here?

I throw up.

"Whoa! Are you okay?" Jonathan carefully navigates the Audi to the shoulder and rests his hand on my back and tells me to relax, which is pretty admirable.

This is not *just saliva*.

Newark, New Jersey, 95 m.p.h.

Regardless of what was causing Jonathan to slow the journey to his family's house—fear, nerves, anxiety—there is a new motivator getting us moving: a stench. We roll down the windows but the scent coming back in as we progress closer to the Meadowlands is almost as offensive.

Jonathan, ever creative, reaches behind his seat and finds a half-consumed bottle of Coke and hands it to me. "Shake this up and cover the mess with it. If it works on dissolving battery acid, it should work on stomach acid." I glance his way. "Don't ask."

I take the bottle, shake it, and spray it all over the floor mat.

We wait a few moments as Jonathan continues his hearty pace. The Coke seems to work, but not enough.

He points to the mat and says, "Pick it up and toss it out the window."

"What? You're joking. I'm not going to litter!"

"Look around you, Melody. We're in the armpit of the Garden State."

He's right; it would be hard to notice a floor mat amongst the mattresses and blown-out retreads.

He slows down and pulls to the shoulder, and out it goes. No one notices or cares.

"That's one bad scent down," I say. He looks at me and I point to my mouth.

He reaches over and pops the glove compartment and two unopened boxes of Nicorette drop to the floor. I open a box and give each of us a piece.

"I'll take two," he says. I deliver. "Actually, make that three."

I take three myself, because I'm not paying attention to dosage and Jonathan is too busy swerving around cars to notice what I'm doing. The gum is minty—FreshMint, to be specific—and the cool flavor coats my mouth and cleanses my palate. Then the nicotine kicks in and, considering I've never placed a cigarette to my lips, the sensation, the relaxed and calm feeling, makes me consider starting the addiction should I survive the afternoon.

The Manhattan skyline approaches and fades over my shoulder.

Englewood, New Jersey, 75 m.p.h.

Everything has cooled: the air, the road, Jonathan, me. The images on the side of the road become soothing, a blend of suburbia and opulence; it's hard to imagine real criminals living in a place like this.

I've developed such a skill for lying that sometimes I even believe myself.

Jonathan reduces his speed and the clicks of the concrete seams under the wheels are like a love song fading out, readying me for the next track.

Jonathan keeps stealing glances of me and telling me (and himself) that everything is going to be fine.

Tenafly, New Jersey, 15 m.p.h.

As though I'd had some sort of vision, the neighborhood is just as I'd imagined. We drive past the strip malls, the Pathmark, the small businesses and mom-and-pop stores that somehow managed to survive despite the Wal-Mart a few miles away in Saddle Brook.

We twist through a series of crumbling streets, where the trees get taller and the houses get older—and larger.

And, as if on cue, Jonathan turns onto a curved driveway leading up to a brick-and-stone Tudor that sits inside an acre of ancient oaks and maples, a beautiful home that has clearly not seen a woman's touch in some time. Though the lawn is well manicured, the trees and bushes have started to engulf the house. It is just the kind of place you'd envision might be full of creaky wood floors, high ceilings and cross beams, and smoke-stained fireplaces.

The driveway is long, with a string of vehicles parked on it, all large, all American, each with seating for eight—if you include the trunk. Jonathan's red Audi sticks out like a pimple on an otherwise blemish-free strip of asphalt.

We sit in the car and face the house. Jonathan leaves the engine running.

"Looks like everyone's here," he says.

I take a deep breath and let it out slowly, quietly. "What did you use as an excuse to get everyone together?"

"I didn't really have to make an excuse," he says. "It's Sunday."

"What's that mean?"

"My family usually gets together for a big meal here. My dad, he, uh . . . he likes to cook. It seems to have a calming effect, so we give him a lot of latitude." He shrugs a little. "It was a long-standing tradition when my mom was still alive, and I think we all want to see it continue . . . you know, to honor her, I guess."

We both stare ahead, eyes locked on the house.

"You know, you guys sound so normal sometimes," I eventually say. "That is just the thing I would've loved as a kid, and especially now—a family to spend Sundays with. Even just a *family* would be nice." I swallow and hesitate to ask my question because it's going to sound silly. "You think, um . . . your family might accept me? I mean, into the family?"

Jonathan breaks his stare at the house and turns to me. "I honestly hope so, Melody." He smiles a little. "More than you could ever know."

We wait some more but I can feel the unrest rising, the subtle need to stop looking at the water and simply take the dive.

"This is a very confusing moment for me. Half of me wants to kill your father," I say, "and the other half desperately wants his acceptance."

"Hmph." He grins.

"I'm sure he's a good man, though. He raised *you*, after all." I turn and look at Jonathan and put my hand on his shoulder and say, "I'm sure he would've done anything to protect you over the years."

Jonathan's smile slowly fades.

I add, "I'm sure he would've left the world of crime if he'd needed to for one of his sons, right?"

He stares at the dashboard.

Nothing.

"Right?" I ask again.

We sit in silence for a full minute while it seems Jonathan is playing another set of tapes in his mind.

Tapes of failures.

I've hit a nerve and I certainly didn't mean to. Not here, not now.

"My family has never been very comfortable with the notion of sacrifice." All of a sudden, Jonathan sighs and opens his door. "Let's do this."

I'm not ready; I'm still in stare mode.

"Wait, I . . ." Jonathan comes around and opens my door. I grunt a little and flip the visor mirror down and check my hair and my teeth and the collar of my sweater. I flip the visor back nervously.

And now we are taking steps, closer and closer, to a moment I am not only unprepared for, but one I could never comprehend. Three squirrels bolt in different directions as we stroll up the brick sidewalk. Jonathan takes my hand, and his is warm and firm, and I glide to his side so that we are almost one person. Bushes spill over the walkway and broken branches and dead leaves are strewn over the path, and the crunching under our feet announces our arrival. We approach the front door, an ornate oak masterpiece with a round top in need of refinishing. Jonathan grabs the handle, pushes the latch, and opens the door. He pulls me in by my hand.

It's *home*.

The first thing I notice is the smell, the same scent that hits you when you enter a decent Italian restaurant. I close my eyes and inhale and I can tell Jonathan's dad has a pot of marinara cooking. And by the lingering, nutty aroma in the air, it's clear something has been recently breaded and fried, like eggplant or veal. It even *smells* warm.

The house is open and airy, and there are pictures of the Bovaro boys and their parents everywhere: fireplace mantels, up the staircase, on end tables, on a baby grand piano in the living room. The floors are all wide-plank maple and have a history to them—probably more history than they ever wanted to know. And then there's the music floating from a distant room.

Jonathan pulls me down the hall, to the back of the house. "Tony Bennett?" I whisper. "That's actually sort of trite, isn't it?" My feeble attempt at trying to appear casual.

"It's trite when the Olive Garden plays it. When a Sicilian family puts him on, it's as noble as a Scotsman wearing a kilt."

As we approach the kitchen, voices become audible and just before we enter, I hear someone say, "So I told him, 'Hey, relax; you still got nine fingers. That's nine more lessons!'" A half dozen people break into labored laughter.

Jonathan walks up to the brother doing the talking and smacks him on the back of the head and says, "Yeah, except what you really meant was that he had seven fingers and two thumbs left, right?"

His brother whacks him back and they hug briefly.

I stand directly behind Jonathan.

Everyone stares at us and the room falls silent, except for Mr. Bennett, crooning.

Jonathan's father, Tony, is chatting in the corner with another older man, thumbing through the contents of a manila folder. Finally, he gets up from his chair and slowly walks over to us, tugging up on his waistband as does. He is at least 250 pounds—a good fifty heavier than when I saw him gut that guy at Vincent's over twenty years ago—and totally gray. He looks weathered, like he's been a beach bum for most of his adult life. I peek around Jonathan to get a better glimpse, and I immediately match his face to the man who wrecked my life years ago, the man who caused so many nightmares in my childhood that I could never forget him, the man who ordered my parents dead.

There is a small paring knife on the kitchen counter, and for a moment I consider snatching it and jabbing Tony's neck with it a few times, even though the odds of my survival would be zero. But weirdly, I'm not consumed by that stress; I want to make this work. I want to see it through as Jonathan has planned, potentially to live in peace with him forever.

"Who's this?" Tony asks.

Jonathan steps to the side and suddenly I can see everyone and their micro-images; the snippets that Jonathan gave me in the car all come clear: Peter, drop-dead gorgeous, just as described, stands to the left and is the brother Jonathan just hugged; Jimmy is presumably the overweight one with his untucked shirt and the meatball sub in his hand; Gino is sitting down with his elbows on his knees and is the only one smiling at me; the wives are here too, both size-sixteens and casting a disapproving eye my way; a few other men linger.

"This," Jonathan responds, "is my new girlfriend."

Jimmy nudges Peter in the side and says, "That's fifty bucks. I told you he wasn't gay." He goes in for another bite and takes a third of the sandwich in his mouth.

"Yeah, but those friggin' glasses he wears. I had to go with the odds."

Everyone laughs and Peter steps forward and smiles. "You're way too pretty to be with this clown," he says, offering his hand. "Peter Bovaro."

I swallow and shake his hand limply. "Melody McCartney," I say.

Jonathan looks at me like I just farted; apparently, Jonathan was going to *ease* his family into the reality of my presence.

After a hushed moment, everyone bursts into laughter—everyone except Tony and the older guy standing in the corner. Tony squints a little, opens the manila folder, and reviews the contents again, then slowly closes it and places it on the kitchen counter.

Peter walks up to his brother and shoves him a little. "You dick! You thought you'd pull one over on us like that?"

"Good one, Johnny!" yells Gino.

I laugh a little too, like I'm such a clever actress. Jonathan wipes his forehead. I try to act natural, but I can feel a set of eyes locked in on me the way a tiger looks at a deer; Tony is fixed on me.

"What's your name, dear?" Tony says, very quietly and clearly.

The room falls silent again.

I glance at Jonathan and he smiles at me, sadly, like I need to do the right thing and turn myself in.

"My name is, uh . . ." I say.

I've had so many. I could whip any of them out and pick up right where I'd left off. Sandra Clarke, May Adams, Linda Simms. But what would be the point? I left WITSEC so I could finally be myself.

The running is over.

Forever.

"My name is Melody Grace McCartney." I pause and take in the slack-jawed images before me. "I'm exactly who you think I am."

Now Tony laughs. He is the only one.

Jonathan takes a step closer to his father and says, "Yeah, this is Melody McCartney." He looks around the room with purpose. "She's not six years old anymore. Surprised she managed to live this long?"

"That's enough, Johnny," says Tony. He rubs his eyes and leans against the counter. It shimmies. "Have you lost your friggin' mind? I can only imagine how much she knows."

Peter peels his eyes from me and scowls at Jonathan. "Holy hell, John. What have you done?"

"I've done nothing," Jonathan says. "I've fallen for a wonderful woman."

"A hundred million women in this country and you pick a federal witness, one who has every reason to take this entire family down?"

This is not the warm welcome I had hoped for.

I remember Jonathan's comment about just wanting respect and try to turn the tables; I look at Tony and say, childishly, "All I know is that I adore your son, Mr. Bovaro."

He looks at me, then looks down, then looks at me again and smiles—that same sad smile that Jonathan had a few moments ago. I now know where he gets it from.

"You're a good liar, young lady," Tony says.

I stiffen my posture but am careful with my tone. "I'm not lying."

Jonathan stands by my side, puts an arm around me, and says, "She's telling the truth, Pop. She just wants a chance at a normal life. With me."

Everyone in the room is still, only their eyes darting around to whomever is speaking.

Tony sighs and says, "I believe the part about her wanting a normal life, but not about it being with you. She has every reason to want us to pay for what we did to her, and she's played you in getting sweet revenge." Tony turns to me and adds, "And I'll tell you, kid, you're tough—for coming into my house and thinking you could pull this off."

"Pull *what* off?" Jonathan and I say in unison.

"Pop," Jonathan says, "look, I don't need you to teach me a lesson here, okay? I know what I'm doing. I—"

"This isn't about teaching a lesson, Johnny; it's about serving life in prison. I'm an old man. I'm not ending my life that way. And you got to think about your family, your brothers and their wives and their children."

"Melody's not going to—"

"Melody's not going to *what*, Johnny? *Huh?*" He grabs the remote and angrily points it in the direction of the stereo, as if firing a bullet into Tony Bennett's temple. "Why don't you ask the love of your life what she did yesterday."

Jonathan raises his voice. "I *know* what she did. She spent the day in the spa at the Renaissance Hotel in Baltimore. I've got five women who'll testify to that."

"Yeah? I got something better than your five women." Tony turns around, snaps his fingers, and Older Guy—the only person yet to smile—slides that manila folder across the counter. Tony snatches it up and removes a handful of photos and presses them against Jonathan's chest.

Jonathan and his father stare at each other and no one says a word. Jonathan slowly looks down and begins to view the pictures. I slide over so I can see them too. They are light and grainy but I can tell the one on top is a vague image of me in the arms of Sean, my head pressed against his chest.

Older Guy moves next to Tony and says, "Your girlfriend spent the day cooking up a serious deal with the feds. They took her to some operations center and apparently offered her the deal of her life. Any town, any job, any money. Isn't that right, sweetheart?"

My mouth opens but I cannot find any air. I feel weak, and my initial response is to grab Jonathan's hand, which I do, and begin pleading, but he pulls away and stares more intently at the pictures.

Peter closes his eyes and says, "Geez, Jonathan, please tell me you did not discuss what this family does. Did she ask you about our family? Did she ask you to talk about our personal business?"

All those incessant, probing questions I'd asked him about his life! This is like the diametric opposite of serendipity.

I try to grab his hand again but his fingers are hopelessly locked around the photos. He flips through them with increasing speed.

"Souvenir," he whispers. "That was how you knew what a souvenir was."

I finally find oxygen and my pathetic response piddles out. "Oh, God, Jonathan, no! No. I didn't make any deal! I—"

"How did you pull this off? I thought you were at the spa." His eyes become red and wet. "I thought you were waiting for me."

"I *was*. I *was*. They came and found me and took me to some place called SafeSite and they wanted me to play you, they did, but I told them I wouldn't do it!"

"Then why didn't you tell me?"

I stare at him, blank. The truth is I have no idea why I never told him. What can I say? I was afraid you might not believe me? We were too busy chatting about other things? I didn't want to ruin our nice evening?

My answer comes out weak and self-destructive. "I don't know."

Tony turns to his sons and associates and laughs. "She doesn't know! She's quick, this one."

The brothers smile nervously.

"What you mean to say," Tony continues, "is that you tricked my son into thinking you were at a spa all day, managed to sneak out with some federal agents for a while, then slip back in before he ever knew you were gone. And this didn't seem, I don't know, *shifty* to you?"

My gaze glides across every face in the room and my eyes fill with tears, and by the time my journey ends at Jonathan he is nothing but a blur. "I just . . . I-I don't know why I didn't say anything, Jonathan. We were living minute to minute and I didn't . . ."

Jonathan looks away and drops the pictures on the floor. Peter scoops them up and starts flipping through them, verifying that the person in the images is standing before him. He passes them along to his brothers, one at a time, each carefully examining them, like jury members viewing crime photos.

I feel a cold distance emerge between Jonathan and me and I am suddenly guardianless in a room full of killers. But, oddly, the fear I have is not of death; an ending to all of this is sort of welcome. The fear I do have is losing Jonathan, that he has been tricked by a handful of bad coincidences, that an end has come to the only true moments of freedom and fulfillment I have ever experienced.

And so my pleading begins. "Jonathan, please—I love you. I *do*. There is nothing I wouldn't do to keep you safe. I don't want to get you into trouble, or anyone in your family. I just want to be happy, for *us* to be happy."

My crying turns to a mess of tears and mucus and spit, and all of my emotion comes gushing. I turn to Tony and Jonathan's brothers and yell, "Please forgive me for making a mistake, okay? I didn't tell Jonathan about meeting with the feds and I am sorry. I don't want to hurt any of you! Please, just forgive me!" I drop to my knees. "I forgive *you* for having my parents murdered, for ruining my entire life, for making me the wreck you see before you! Can't you please, *please* give *me* one chance? I just want one chance! I just want one . . ."

I fall forward and rest my head on the floor.

No one says a word. Jonathan does not come to my rescue. I am alone. Again.

Forever.

I sob uncontrollably. Finally, I hear Peter say, "That sounds like the plea of a woman facing certain death."

I sit up and wipe my face. Peter is not joking.

I look at Tony and he walks over to his pot of marinara, stirs it a few times, and says, "Take care of her."

If I hadn't thrown up an hour ago, I'd be doing so now; Tony said "Take care of her," but I know he meant "*Get rid* of her," careful of his words as though I might've been stupid enough to wear a wire in his house.

I slide over to Jonathan and grab his leg like I'm holding on to a tree in a hurricane. "I love you, Jonathan. Please know how much I love you!"

Tony puts the lid back on his sauce and says, "Take care of it, Johnny, okay? Enough is enough. We've let you play this game for years." He steps up to his son and finishes with this: "No more."

Jonathan stares at his father for a few seconds, wipes his eyes, then looks down at me and gives me the same look he gave Dirty Guy in the alley in Baltimore. He reaches down and pulls my hand from his leg, grabs my arm and twists it, and yanks me up on my feet, nearly lifts me off the ground.

He gets two inches from my face and breathes down on me, betrayal fueling an anger I'd never envisaged would be turned my way. He twists my arm some more and it really hurts, makes my whole body ache. Jonathan slams me up against the wall, then shoves me in the corner and I fall to my knees again.

"Come here," he says, and grunts as he reaches down and picks me up by the other arm and drags me to the door. I cannot fight back.

His family just watches and, judging by their inaction, approves.

Jonathan opens the front door and manhandles me to the Audi, where he opens the passenger side and shoves me in. By the time I regain some composure, he is already on the driver's side, has started the car and locked the doors.

"Geez, Melody," he says, "I hope I didn't hurt you."

He speeds away from the Tudor.

"I'm so sorry," he says. "Are you all right?"

I look at him and shake my head, nervously wiping my face free of moisture. "I'm okay, I . . . think. Wait, you're . . . you're not mad?"

He waves me off. "Here's the situation: I know my family and they're gonna send someone after me, to make sure I close the deal."

"To kill me?"

"Yes. I don't have the greatest track record, if you recall."

I swallow. "But you're not going to kill me?"

He pulls back on the accelerator. "Oh, Melody, I love you. I promised I would never hurt you—*never*. Remember? I promised you that when we first met."

"Yeah," I say and smile. "But that was only, like, three days ago."

"I don't know how or why you met with the feds or how you managed to get to their operations center, but I know in my heart that you love me." He bites his lip. "Right?"

I reach over and touch his knee and say, "Yes, completely." I pull my hand back and rub my arm where it hurts.

Jonathan looks in his rearview mirror and shakes his head. "Predictable."

"What?"

"It's Peter."

Jonathan hits the gas and we're flying down the city streets at a speed that will surely grab attention.

"I'm never gonna be able to outrun him with that monster engine he's got." He thinks for a second, then adds, "Though we do have one advantage."

I rub my arm, trying to make the pain dissipate. "Which is what?"

He glances in the rearview again and says, "We can outmaneuver him."

Suddenly, he turns the car down a side road and begins weaving around the cars in front of us like he's playing a video game. I look in the side mirror and I can see Peter losing speed as Jonathan zips around the obstacles before us. He takes another turn and we're on a winding road that traverses a small grouping of hills. Jonathan is right; we're riding on rails.

Peter fades quickly.

Jonathan makes another turn and we're on a six-lane highway and headed for the Palisades Parkway.

Peter is merely a dot.

Jonathan zooms in and out of traffic, ignoring the speed limits and the safety of other motorists, and by the time we get to the New Jersey Turnpike, Peter is gone.

We are heading south.

I am still aching and my head is spinning and I am shaking because I have no idea what is going on or what Jonathan is thinking.

"Now what?" I ask.

Jonathan just stares at the road, hands at ten and two; he looks like a crash test dummy, right down to the blank expression on his face.

I try again. "Now wh—"

"Why do you love me?" he asks.

I turn to him and squint. "What do you mean? There's no *reason* I love you. It's an emotion, tied to—"

"No." He blinks a few times. "You love me because I gave you freedom, Melody." He turns and looks at me and sniffles. "I freed you from the bondage you've been in your whole life. That's why you feel this emotion for me. Only because I gave you freedom."

"What? I—no, that's not true. I love you because of who you are, the man you are. I love you because of what you're doing right now." I reach over and touch his leg again and it makes him sigh nervously.

"Are you sure?"

I lean into him and whisper, "Of course." I rub his chest while he drives. "Do you love me?"

"The way I feel about you, Melody, makes me realize I've never known love before." We drive for a few miles before Jonathan adds, "Oh . . . what are we gonna do?"

I sit up and kiss him on the cheek and whisper my scheme. "We could get married. That way I couldn't testify against you."

Jonathan laughs. "You're cute in a naive way. The feds would be watching you and me twenty-four hours a day. And you'd still be able to testify against my family, which would almost ensure a bullet in the brain. Besides, you're not ready to marry me; you've only known me for a few days."

"Jonathan," I say sternly, "I've only known *myself* for a few days." I sit up and look at him and wish he could make eye contact with me. "It really is like I'm just a few days old, like I'm finally understanding who I am and who I was meant to be. And I realize that I want to spend my life with you."

The reaction I was hoping to see in Jonathan is not coming. He is not smiling, not touching me, not hopeful. He quickly swerves into the slow lane and exits the highway and pulls off the road completely. He puts the car in Neutral, pulls up the emergency brake, and turns to me.

He lets out a sigh that could easily be mistaken for his final breath.

"We just played the only hand we had, Melody. It's over."

I shake my head in disbelief. "What do you mean? What's over?"

"This. Us. It's over."

My lips start to quiver. "Over? It's barely started. I don't understand."

"Don't you see? You had two days of freedom and you became a new woman—the woman you should've been your whole life. You're about to lose it all again."

"No," I plead, "it doesn't have to be that way." I touch his sweater and ball my fist up in it. "We can get married." I try to sound strong. "Marry me, Jonathan."

I can hear him holding back tears through his words. "You know we can't. No one will ever leave us alone. The feds. My family. Everyone will be hunting us down. There won't be a single day that passes that you won't wonder if your car is gonna blow up or I've been murdered."

I can't stop shaking. I reach for the nearest possibility. "Then let's just run away together. We can run away and no one will ever find us."

Jonathan strokes my hair, tries to be tender as he brings me back to reality. "Melody, you've been running for over two decades, and you had professionals helping you. How long before they find you—*us*—again?"

I try to wipe my face of tears, but it's pointless. "Then we can both go into Witness Protection together. You can testify against your family and—"

"Melody," he says, pulling me close, "*it's over*." He holds my head to his chest and we slowly rock back and forth. "Don't you see? If I go into Witness Protection with you it will be even worse than before, with more lies, with an even bigger threat of being killed. It will never end, Melody. You will never be free."

And he's right. The running would never stop. Every slip of the tongue, every mistake, would mean we'd be off to another town, another job, another resting place until the next blunder.

We cry in each other's arms.

After we calm, Jonathan says quietly, "My family was going to make me kill the woman I loved. They didn't care at all about what I was feeling. It was all about business. And they'd kill *me* if they thought I chose you over them. Seriously, Peter wasn't just following us to make sure I got the job done." Jonathan shakes his head and rests it on the window. "You see? We're running already."

He sits up and I pull my head from his chest and we stare at each other for a moment.

Then he looks down and I know this is the beginning of the end.

Jonathan puts the car in gear and we speed away, quickly returning to the interstate. "What are you going to do?" I ask.

He wipes his face with the sleeve of his sweater. "I'm gonna do what I promised you, Melody. I'm gonna *do what needs to be done.* I'm going to keep you safe and free forever."

I hold on to the door as he flies down the highway. "Why are you driving so fast?"

"Because Peter or someone else affiliated with my family is

probably heading for my house or my restaurant to see if they can find me—and I need to beat them there."

He passes cars like they're parked, weaving in and out, topping a hundred miles per hour. If a cop spots us, we're dead. And if a car pulls in front of us, we're *really* dead. His maneuvering and speed have taken the words from me. The only breaks we get—and the only chance I get to catch my breath—are the toll booths, like commercial breaks to some insane, unrealistic flick. All I can do is hold on.

We're over the George Washington Bridge and before I can even get my bearings, we're on the BQE. If it wasn't a Sunday we'd be sitting in gridlock.

Jonathan's eyes dart from the road to his mirrors and back, like he's fighting some tic, though he seems assured that no one is following us. He zooms around the city streets and begins to calm as we reach whatever destination he has in mind; he obeys the lights and speed limits. We reach Grand Street in the Williamsburg section of Brooklyn and he pulls the car in front of an Italian restaurant named Sylvia near Wythe Avenue. He looks around and reaches for the door.

I stare at the front of the meticulous bistro and ask, "Is this your—"

"Stay here. Keep your head down. If I'm not back in sixty seconds, you drive away. Understand?"

I gulp and nod.

Jonathan runs into the restaurant and I slink down in my seat. I watch the door and hope and pray that he comes dashing out with some great solution to our problem: an arsenal, a team of federal agents, a cloaking device.

He comes back at full speed, with no more than five seconds to spare, carrying what looks like an old medical bag.

Jonathan hops in the car and as the tires spin, he says, "They're here, coming in the back just as I ran out the front."

The pavement goes whizzing by and I'm holding on with all my strength.

Berry Street.

Metropolitan Avenue.

Meeker Avenue.

The BQE.

I think I've figured it out: LaGuardia Airport.

Jonathan slows, and suddenly we are moving away from the airport and just as I get a handle on where we are, he pulls onto Livingston Street and right up to the Greyhound bus terminal.

"Jonathan, what's going on? What are we doing?"

He stops in front of the entryway, turns the car off, and puts the flashers on. He gets out, comes to my side, pulls me from the car, and leads me inside the terminal. The station is dirty and noisy. We stop about thirty feet from the counter. It is Sunday and the terminal is going to close at 4:00 P.M.—six minutes.

"You wouldn't get anywhere on a plane without identification. This is the only way out. Not to mention my family would never think of coming here. They probably sent someone to LaGuardia, Kennedy, *and* Newark."

He hands me the pouch and I peek inside. Money.

"It's about nine grand," he says. "It's all the money I had that was laundered; it's clean. It's not a lot but it will get you started. Just go away, Melody. Just leave."

I fall into him and dig my nails into his clothing. "No! Jonathan, no! I can't."

"Go somewhere you've never been before. Move to a town where I would never guess you would go, in case I weaken and try to find you."

My weeping has turned to hysterics. "Jonathan, please! I'm begging you!"

"Never call me or my family again. Never call the feds or the

marshals again. Never use any of your aliases again. Do you understand?"

I bury my head in his sweater and he holds my body to keep
me from dropping to the ground. "*Yes.*"

He holds me and kisses the top of my head. "This is the last
time you will ever have to run, Melody. I promise."

And then a thought hits me like a locomotive—and my crying
instantly stops. I pull back and look him in the eye. "You knew,
didn't you. You knew that I might not be free to make the decision
to leave if we'd made love."

It's as if the tears leap from my eyes to his. "I didn't want it
to cloud your judgment. I just wanted what was best for you
in case the worst happened." He shrugs a little. "And the worst
happened."

I squeeze him tightly and he says to me, "You'll never be ripped
from a lover's arms ever again. This will be the last time."

I kiss him and I can feel people staring. There are two types of
kisses at terminals: hellos and good-byes. This one is passionate;
it's good-bye—forever.

When our lips finally part, I stand on my toes and whisper
in his ear, "You were my first, Jonathan. You will always be my
first."

He smiles and takes a deep breath and lets it out slowly. He
pulls away and holds my hands and starts to step backward and
says, "No matter what happens to us, this was all worth it." Our
hands part and he paces farther back, toward the door. "*It was all
worth it.*"

My chin wrinkles and my face aches from crying and I cannot
move as I watch him walk out the door.

As I make my way deeper into the terminal, I keep turning
around to see Jonathan sitting in his car, head on the steering
wheel, sobbing. I watch him every second that I can, and I cherish
them all.

Finally, he starts the car and slowly drives away. He is no longer in a hurry.

It takes all of my energy to focus on the moment. I have no idea what Jonathan has in mind, but he seems determined and confident that his plan will work. Now I need to do my part.

For the tenth time in my life, I have nothing—and have been given no chance to take anything with me: not the green sweater that Jonathan gave to me when we first met, not my text on string theory, not even clean underwear. I am nameless and faceless. I have no identification, no purpose, no destination.

I am nobody.

Jonathan was right; people may be worried about planes and trains being hijacked or rigged with bombs, but no one cares about the bus industry. I pay in cash and no one even looks at my face; I'm just the last fare of a long day for an hourly worker. No one checks my bag or asks me to be scanned.

There is one bus left, and with two minutes to spare I take my eighty-dollar ticket to Columbus, Ohio, and from there I will move on again. And again. I may never stop moving. I have nowhere to arrive.

$$x = |-9| + |-4|$$

It takes a long time to cross the United States, especially in a Greyhound. It might be faster to ride an actual greyhound. I've been on the road for four days, and stayed in three squalid motels with *comfort* and *quality* in the names, and each time they lied.

Instead of buying one ticket to a final destination, I simply allowed Greyhound to take me to wherever my ticket read, and when I got there, I bought a ticket for whatever bus was soonest to leave that terminal. I let fate determine my destination, as long as the direction was roughly west; I want to be as far from New York as I can get without needing a passport or other identification.

And as the bus pulls into the final terminal, having gone as far west as possible, I am the only person on the bus and it's two in the morning and when it finally comes to a stop, I sit and wait for someone to ask me to leave. They are gracious but, after all, the destination is usually the point.

I step off the bus and the wet, warm air of San Diego weighs heavy on me and the skyline looms above, a beautiful steel and concrete mixing bowl of anonymity, a place for me to plunge.

I've spent four days and nights thinking of Jonathan; the first two were tear-filled hours of loss and the second two were thought filled, waiting for some sign of what to do next, where to go, how to live.

I don't have a name.

I don't know what to do.

The only thing I know for certain is that I must begin to heal. Just like every time my life was re-created, I had to begin restoring the foundered part of my being: the lost relationships, the familiarity of a neighborhood, the sense of the person I might have been. There is an algebraic term for the technique for distributing two binomials, called the FOIL method. It stands for *first, outer; inner, last.* And that is exactly how I have learned to repair myself time after time: from the outside in.

I walk a few blocks from the bus station and find a decrepit twenty-four-hour diner. I pause at the window and gaze at the patrons, making sure the place is full of docile folks and not a place for drunken partyers to go after the bars close. It looks safe; I go in.

The counter has ten stools and four are taken, with a stool between each person. I sit at the end, in much the same way I sat at the bar in West Virginia a few days ago—except that I have a bag full of cash sitting on my lap.

The heavyset, post-retirement-age waitress behind the counter comes to me and passes a halfhearted smile and says, "What can I get you, honey?"

I speak for the first time today. "Coffee," I say in a rasp. I point behind her and add, "Slice of cherry pie."

I get the other half of her smile and she walks away.

I put my elbows up on the counter and rest my face in my hands and sigh.

My ears become more aware with my eyes closed. I hear the waitress and short-order cook chatting in front of me, the clinks of utensils and coffee cups on saucers, the whispery conversations, the distant newscaster on the television in the corner of the restaurant.

I can feel my body drifting and I shift forward as I nearly fall asleep. The din of the restaurant is soothing—the clinks, the whispers, all like parents trying not to wake the baby.

Everyone, everything, is as faint and gentle as a kiss on the cheek, a secure and welcoming urban nest.

Chatter.

Clink.

Whisper.

Then, just as I'm about to fall asleep, someone murmurs my name: *Melody Grace McCartney*.

Out of the depth of my fading awareness, I pull my hands from my face and open my eyes. I look around the diner.

Then I hear it again. *Melody Grace McCartney*.

A smile comes to my face as my eyes dart around the room randomly and I say, "Jonathan!"

"You got *that* right," the waitress says as she pours my coffee. "What an asshole *that* guy is. He deserves everything that's coming to him." She slides the pie my way and walks a few steps closer to the television. "What a waste."

I rub my eyes and look at the television and I see myself; along with the newscaster and the ticker at the bottom of the screen, CNN has a picture of me in the corner—from when I was six years old.

I stumble off my seat and run to the end of the counter so I can hear every word, but now the chatter and the clinks and the whispers are impeding my understanding of what is happening.

My eyes open wide as my picture disappears, replaced by an image of Jonathan, unshaven and disheveled, in handcuffs.

Just as I am about to tell everyone to shut up, the screen changes and I'm staring at a commercial for a Toyota Camry.

I am motionless. I am not breathing.

I walk back to the end of the counter and grab my bag of cash off the stool and clutch it to my chest. The waitress catches my eye.

"Something wrong, honey?"

I clear my throat. "I've just . . . I've just been on the road for a few days and I'm not sure, um . . ."

"What is it?"

"What, um . . . do you know what that was all about?"

She points over her shoulder. "What, you mean the Johnny Bravo business?"

"It's *Bovaro*, Rita," the cook says.

I swallow and nod.

"Boy," Rita says, "you must've been traveling on a mule because it's the only thing the news people want to cover," she says. "I'm tired of hearing about it."

My hands start to tremble; I rest them under my thighs. "Can you . . . tell me what happened?"

She leans on the counter. "Johnny Bovaro apparently found out where the government was hiding a witness, that McCartney girl, and murdered her. She was in Witness Protection for almost her whole life, like twenty years or something, and this asshole, Bovaro, kills her because her *parents* testified against his dad. The Mafia is nothing but a bunch of assholes."

"*Rita!*" the cook screams.

She rolls her eyes and waves him off.

Now my legs are shaking too.

"Anyway," she continues, "he kills her, slices her into pieces, and dumps her into the East River or the Hudson or both."

I swallow and almost choke on my saliva. I try to act casual. "How'd they find this out?"

"He turned himself in. Even brought her bloodied sundress with him."

I wipe the tears before they run down my face. "Allergies," I say.

"She was his first murder—*supposedly*—and he couldn't handle the guilt, or some crap like that. But if he hasn't lost his mind already, he will soon."

"Huh?"

"I mean *literally*."

"I don't follow."

"He's hooked up with the Justice Department and he's giving them every shred of knowledge he has on his family's operation. He's taking them all down."

An older gentleman seated three stools away from me keeps his eyes locked on his newspaper and adds, "He doesn't stand a chance. He'll be dead in a week."

"Good," Rita says, "an eye for an eye, Carl."

"The guy's a hero, if you ask me," Carl says. "He flipped on the bad guys. One less group of thugs in New York."

"He's a loser."

"He's a hero."

"He's a *loser*."

I look up and let the tears roll down my face and whisper, "He's a hero."

Carl and Rita stop their arguing.

Rita leans forward again, hands me a napkin. "What's wrong, honey? Why are you crying?"

I smile a little and say, "It's a very sad story."

She cocks her head and studies me, but says nothing.

"They ever find her body?" I ask.

Carl says, "They gave it a shot but the tides have been rough. Her body parts are probably in Lower New York Bay by now. They're never gonna find her."

I want to call Sean. I want to hold his face tightly. I want him to hear me when I say, "You see, Sean? Jonathan Bovaro was indeed my hero after all. You know *nothing*."

Jonathan gave me something the Justice Department and the U.S. Marshals and the Bovaro family could never deliver: He gave me my life back.

I reach in my bag and pull out a twenty and drop it on the counter and prepare to leave.

Rita smiles. "You, uh, new to the area? Just wondering if we'll see you again."

I shrug. "Yeah, I'm new to the area. I might be back."

She takes the twenty from the counter and asks, "What's your name?"

I walk to the door and stare at the empty street. Just before I leave, I turn and smile and say, "I haven't decided yet."

$$f(x) = 2\sin{(x - 1)}$$

I EVENTUALLY BECAME FELICIA EMERSON, NOT BECAUSE I HAD some longing for Scottish roots, but because the San Diego State University student I blackmailed outside his favorite college hangout had the name available on his template of fake IDs. At first I convinced him I was a federal agent and that he'd been nabbed helping a few freshmen gain entrance to the bar. Later, I gently extorted a host of documents out of him: driver's license, birth certificate, even a Social Security card that he reissued to me by way of a dead teenager in Alabama, all through the miracles of computers—and their vulnerability of being hacked—and high-quality printers. The kid was amazing. He even had the California seals to make the documents official.

He would have served some serious jail time.

But his real concern was how he would—or would not—be able to get into law school with a felony on his record.

He created my documents gratis and I disappeared from his life.

I moved to Los Angeles a month later, in July, where I tested into UCLA's adult education program and managed to shave off two years of school—and almost every undergraduate math course they offer.

I am now a twenty-seven-year-old college junior.

Felicia Emerson has a host of student loans, a small one-bedroom apartment near the campus, a stack of textbooks, a laptop computer, and a deep-seated, though not entirely understood, hatred for USC.

I feel at home here: the carefree nature of the students, the slow pace of academia, the gorgeous and consistent weather. I plan on staying in college until I finish my Ph.D. and, God willing, become a professor. Every day, as my unshackled existence unfolds, I get a greater understanding of the woman I am becoming—and oddly, of the girl I used to be. Without facing some certain future, my past could have no bearing.

It has been nearly five months since Jonathan returned my life to me, and every night I fall asleep thinking of him—though, rest assured, I *fall asleep*—and sleep well. I watched him in the news every day for months and saved every image I could find of him on the Internet. He was and is brave, still standing against his family and, most miraculously, still living.

You see, he entered WITSEC.

I think of him fondly each day, imagining him cooking someone's eggs at a greasy spoon in the Midwest or delivering mail in northern Wisconsin or managing a warehouse in Tennessee.

And though I will never see him again, these truths tell part of his story: The marshals protect him but they hate him; Jonathan rarely sleeps because he never knows when someone will find him; he will accidentally expose his true identity or someone will recognize him and he will be moved on to another place, another city, another state; he will be miserable every single day.

He can't say he wasn't warned.

And I hope he'll think of me the way I think of him. Men, and even some of these frat boys, have tried to meet me, to understand me, to (at a minimum) lust after me. I let them down easy, hand them some excuse that builds their sense of self because the truth would be difficult to grasp: that I am in love and no other body or mind or soul could disconnect the fetter linking me to Jonathan. Any other pair of lips would become his, any hand on my skin would become his, any word would be converted to his style and intonation. And, in the darkest, most sensual moment of the night, I would raise my mouth to the stranger's ears and whisper softly, "Jonathan, I love you. Only you can make me feel this way."

Perhaps I did fall in love with Jonathan because he set me free. But I believe we all fall in love for some esoteric and simple reason: the first time a man comes to your rescue, the way he holds you when you kiss, his smile that haunts you and has you endlessly daydreaming. I'm not sure the reason you fall is as important as the fact that you have indeed fallen. At least that's what I tell myself when I fantasize about a life I will never have with a man I will never fully know.

Oddly, it is Sean who is on my mind at this moment, as I scan the hundred wedding bands in the glass case below me.

"That one," I say to the jeweler.

He adjusts the felt ring case, removes a thin gold wedding band encased with tiny diamonds and swirls etched into the edges.

"That was handcrafted by one of our artists here."

I smile. "How much is it?"

"Two thousand, fifty."

I slide it over my knuckle and it's snug. I hold out my hand and analyze the ring in the light. It is brilliant and full of life. It's perfect.

"I'll take it."

The jeweler stares at me for a moment. "You understand it's a woman's wedding band?"

I do not look at him. "Of course."

"It's just very unusual for a lady to buy one for herself."

I open my checkbook. "I'm not buying it. At least not with my money." I can't think of a better way to spend what remains of that nine grand.

He takes my check, studies it. "May I ask why you want a wedding band if you're not married?"

I look at the jeweler and think of Sean and smile a little. "Well, no matter what, there will only ever be one Mr. Emerson. My heart is his, will always be his, and I'm going to wear this ring to remember him and . . . partly to send the message to other men that I'm not available." I hated Sean when he uttered those words, but now I fully understand them. "That sounds sort of arrogant, doesn't it?"

The jeweler grins and shakes his head. "It sounds real. I don't get that much anymore."

I leave the store and walk out into the cool afternoon and start the long journey back to campus, where I have a class in American Justice; I am the teacher's pet.

As I walk along the city streets, I watch the blasts of light shimmering from my ring and I twist it around my finger and I think of Jonathan. The clear and distinct memories are fading a bit, the exact words we said, the specific images. He is becoming larger in my mind but shifting more out of focus.

Every day I want to find him, to hunt him down the way he hunted me year after year as I grew older. But we could not and will not ever find each other. He will never know my name and I will never know his. I can't even send him a cryptic message the way the marshals used to contact distant relatives for witnesses. Our lives are separated, broken at the center and drifting aimlessly, a certain impossibility of reconnection.

Every day I want Jonathan to know that he is inside me, that he is my first, that he will be my only.

My hope, my prayer, is that he will know this truth:

He gave me my freedom; I give him my faith and fidelity.

Forever.

About the Author

DAVID CRISTOFANO has earned degrees in government and politics, and computer science from the University of Maryland at College Park and has worked for different branches of the federal government for over a decade. His short works have been published by *Like Water Burning* and *McSweeney's*. He currently works in the Washington, D.C., area, where he lives with his wife, son, and daughter. *The Girl She Used to Be* is his first novel. You can contact him through his website at www.davidcristofano.com

Reading Group Guide

Discussion Questions

(1) From the first sentence of the story, the narrator asks you to take part in the action. Why do you suppose David Cristofano decided to tell this story in the first person from the point of view of a woman? Who would have more at stake in witness protection, a man, woman, or child?

(2) Early in the novel, Melody appears conflicted in having feelings for both Sean and Jonathan. What is driving her need for affection? When does she realize she has made a decision? What solidifies this decision?

(3) At various points in the novel, the reader is given a glimpse into the previous six identities Melody has had. Which identity serves as a turning point? What event occurred that changed the trajectory of her life?

(4) The roles of good and evil are repeatedly swapped in Melody's life. Do both sides—the Feds and the Mafia—possess both good and evil, or are they really polar opposites of each other? How does Melody influence your view of each side?

(5) Though romantically inexperienced, Melody longs to be *noticed* by both Sean and Jonathan, trying different ways to capture their

eyes. In what ways has she felt invisible to men her whole life? How has she overcompensated?

(6) Due to her constant relocation, lack of parental guidance, and inability to form lasting relationships, Melody has the body of a woman but the emotional and experiential psyche of a girl. How is this dangerous? What additional problems does this pose for her, given the life she must lead? How does it influence her interaction with all the men in her life?

(7) Melody's initial interplay with every authority figure—Farquar, Sean, Donovan, Sanchez—is semi-hostile. What makes Melody react this way? How does Jonathan's influence help her to respond differently by the time she meets his family?

(8) Melody and Sean share a few conversations that expose the failings of WITSEC for both the protectors and the protected. From each of their points of view, how is the system not working? How does it work as intended? How is WITSEC more or less vital to the Justice Department today?

(9) Jonathan tries to distinguish himself from his Mafia ties in several ways. How has he successfully achieved this? In what ways is he a typical mafioso?

(10) Melody is scarred by the explicit violence she witnesses at age six. Repeatedly, she attempts to rid Jonathan of his reactionary viciousness to seemingly topical problems, though later in the story, she finds security in his violent behavior. What changes her mind? Would you react the same way? Why or why not?

(11) Throughout the entire novel, the importance of identity is explored. How is the life Melody has led different from that of a

foster child? Of a prisoner? Of an individual living under communist rule? How are they the same?

(12) How do the tangible things in Melody's story—the food, clothes, cars, hotels—reflect her happiness, security, and satisfaction? Are these things metaphorical or incidental? Would her story be different if things were reversed? Why or why not?

(13) Being in WITSEC for twenty years has had a negative impact on Melody. In what ways has it made her stronger?

(14) What is the significance of the chapter titles? How do they differ? What is the special significance of the final chapter's title?

ON WRITING (ABOUT A GIRL)

When I first started designing the framework for this novel, I had every intention of writing from a man's point of view (the working title was *Nowhere Man*), not just for the obvious reason, but because it seemed the conflict among the three focal points—the witness, the government, and the Mafia—would be more congruous.

But as the story took shape and the pages accumulated, the man-as-witness seemed to be bothered less about his circumstances than I'd intended. Men, stereotypically speaking, would be less likely to mind some of the inevitable consequences of life on the run: isolation, change, the potential for violence. And they'd be more likely to try and manipulate the system to their advantage. The issue crystallized: A woman in witness protection would have far more at stake; the loss of friendships, the instability, and the compression of self-expression would cut far deeper, especially when introduced in childhood. So, with several chapters completed, I knew I must start anew—this time from the point of view of a woman. Further, I knew it had to be written in first person, to emphasize her urgency and longing. With that, Melody Grace McCartney was born.

Easier said than done.

The immediate challenge was understanding the underlying thoughts, motivations, and needs of a woman, then how they would be diminished (or enhanced) by an identity-stripped lifetime in witness protection. I was blessed by being armed with one crucial tool: a very close, nineteen-year relationship with my wife. Having met when we were twenty-one, we've experienced the gross of life-altering events, grown through them, and grown to understand each other better with each iteration. I could, to some degree, run each of Melody's scenarios through the aggregate of my experiences with my wife, and anticipate how she might respond. Though distinctly disparate in personality, those thoughts and words and emotions helped define and form Melody.

The next level—what I would define as the romantic element—was predictably daunting. Told in first person, the story demanded the details of Melody's intimate experiences. A great deal of time was spent on her actions and desires, like what she would crave in a kiss or the way her hand might traverse the shape of a man's body. Those were brow-pinching moments.

In the end, the challenge equated to the enjoyment of producing the novel. The exercise of writing *The Girl She Used to Be* not only helped me to grow as a writer, but as a man, husband, and father, and ultimately became a catalyst to my better understanding—and genuinely appreciating—the differences between men and women.

OVERCOMING THE IDENTITY CRISIS

I have always been drawn to books and movies that deal with the concept of identity. Certainly, there have been countless excellent stories of individuals finding themselves, but what has grown to capture my attention are those accounts concerning the polar opposite; think of all the areas that have been covered, all the places that a person can get lost: amnesia, multiple personality disorders, drug addiction, brainwashing, Alzheimer's. There likely exists an endless list of possibilities for the disruption or disintegration of one's personality. It's kind of hard to believe so many of us manage to hold it together.

Then I got thinking: What if a person, with all of her wits about her, was not permitted to have an identity? It may seem like an unlikely scenario, but this occurs every day in the United States (and abroad) through the growing list of witnesses and victims who have entered the Federal Witness Protection Program.

In life—especially in a democratic society such as ours—we are told we can be whatever we want to be. Work hard and you will succeed. You're only as limited as your imagination. Eat well, exercise, get good grades; the world will be your oyster. In witness protection, however, your choices are few. You have control over virtually nothing. It makes the darkest days of Soviet communism look like a libertarian society. Live here. Work here. Friends? Probably not worth making, since you could potentially put them in danger, and the acquaintances from your past need to remain there indefinitely—friends, family, and otherwise. It leaves little to the imagination, and even less to the motivation of getting out of bed in the morning.

So, then I got thinking (again): What if a person thrown into this life was thrown in as a child? Imagine a scared little girl being tossed about from place to place, shoved through a government bureaucracy, and shot out the other side in the form and style of a contrived image generated by someone on the GS schedule. Childhood and adolescence are confusing enough; we've certainly all faced our own identity crises. But without our significant choices and goals, who are we exactly? Our successes and failures shape us as much as our hopes and dreams. And suddenly there she is: adulthood. Armed with a pseudo-independence and a vague sense of maturity, she has learned less about who she is as who the government has told her she is. This woman is now a one-dimensional twentysomething institutionalized by self-imposed bars of protection; she can see the world outside even if she is unsure of her place in it.

So, then I got thinking (a third and final time): How would she escape? How could she escape? What would have to occur to make her world eventually adjust to the point where it would have naturally evolved over the course of two decades?

The Federal Witness Protection Program is one of the most essential, if not ingenious, government programs to have ever existed, and it's made an impact on the Justice Department that no one could have foreseen. Protecting a witness to the degree of making him or her disappear is an astounding event. I suppose I just wanted to ask—and answer—this question: What happens to these people once they disappear?